Point of Contact

by

Richard Ayre

Burning Chair Limited, Trading As Burning Chair Publishing
61 Bridge Street, Kington HR5 3DJ
www.burningchairpublishing.com

By Richard Ayre
Edited by Simon Finnie and Peter Oxley
Cover by Burning Chair Publishing

First published by Richard Ayre, 2016
Second edition published by Burning Chair Publishing, 2021

ISBN: 978-1-912946-17-4

Other Books by Richard Ayre

A Life Eternal

The Prophecy Trilogy:
    Minstrel's Bargain
    Minstrel's Renaissance
    Minstrel's Requiem

Nightmares and Daydreams

A Hatful of Shadows

Stories featured in the following anthologies:
    Bad Neighborhood
    Shadows and Teeth
    It Came From The Garage!

Dedication

For Cath. For everything.

Paris, 1966

The boy stared with wide, horrified eyes at the shape slowly manifesting from the shadows of the dark room. It had been just a vague outline at first, and then details began to form. Shapes flickered out from the sides and defined themselves as arms. Twin dark tendrils descended to the floor: legs supporting the black entity. The waist took form, the chest, the darkness broiling rapidly upwards to form something that looked like a head.

He was terrified, his heart beating madly in his chest and urine spurting from him in hard, hot bursts. He was trying to look away. He was trying so hard, but he couldn't. He couldn't move. He wanted to scream, to shout for Mama and Papa, but only short, staccato grunts emerged: 'Ugh, Ugh, Ugh.'

His parents couldn't hear him anyway. They were dead. But the boy was only four; in his terror he forgot he was now an orphan.

The shape, fully formed now, stepped towards his bed. The other boys in the dormitory were fast asleep: knowing nothing, hearing nothing.

Closer the shape thing came, closer, towards the light of the tiny night lamp that shone on the drawers beside his bed.

The shaking boy uttered his craven terror again: 'Ugh, Ugh, Ugh.' The shape stepped forward one last time. Its arms reached towards the boy. Its head emerged into the light.

The boy eventually formed a scream as the shape bent down towards him and he saw its face. He screamed and screamed and screamed.

Chapter One

Mary Embleton struggled slowly up the steep hill as she had done a thousand times before. She wheezed and sweated, her bent body sweltering in the warm July air as the shopping bags cut into her hands.

Seventy-eight and still struggling up that bloody hill every day. It shouldn't be that way! Why didn't Ted have a car like everyone else? Why couldn't he at least spare some extra money for a bus or a taxi? She was too old for that hill. Her body couldn't take it anymore. It wasn't fair.

And what did Ted do about it? Nothing! His working life had entailed a variety of jobs, most of it as a handyman, and he had no pension. Mary and Ted existed on what the state provided: which was precious little. All Ted would do when she got back home was ask, 'Did you get my fags love?' And like a fool she would smile and pass them over, instead of throwing them in his bloody face for making her live like this.

She sighed as her little house came into view and as always, when she got closer, the thoughts about her husband mellowed.

It hadn't always been like this. In fact at one time Mary had been the envy of her friends in the street. Ted had been a catch; six foot tall with broad shoulders and a shock of unruly brown hair. And those eyes! She still remembered clearly the first time he had looked at her at the dance hall. His eyes were the brightest blue, and the crinkles around them when he smiled had immediately set her heart fluttering. They had danced together all night and married only a year later, the happiest year of Mary's life. The disappointments, however, started soon after.

When they found out that Ted could not have children, Mary thought she would never recover from the regret. They both watched and smiled as their friends' children were born and grew. They sent cards on birthdays and babysat once in a while but the hole, especially in Mary's heart—the *ache*—never went away. However, they eventually rallied and decided that it didn't matter. They were young, they were in love and their future was wide open. Unfortunately it was also going to be long and hard and bleak.

The drinking had started soon after the doctor told them Ted was infertile. Saturday nights with the lads to begin with, but quickly becoming an everyday occurrence. Any money they did manage to save was swiftly consumed at the pub, and the previously handsome man had quickly disintegrated into a bloated and broken-veined clown.

Oh yes, he was funny. Always had a joke to tell, a witty story that would have his fellow drinkers roaring with laughter. They thought he was great. He was their hero. Not only because of his jokes but because he could always be relied on to stand them another beer, even though he was the poorest of the lot of them. On more than one occasion she'd had to go to the pub and drag him out before he spent the entire week's budget, much to the amusement of his good-for-nothing pals.

She had thought of leaving him on more than one occasion, but never seriously. He was never violent—he was a witty and sentimental drunk—but Mary hated her life. She had hated her life for the last fifty years and there was nothing she could do about it. Nowadays it seemed like everyone was getting divorced at the first cross word spoken; marriage didn't mean the same now as it had in her day. But no. You didn't leave your husband. She had said her vows at the altar and had meant every word. For better or for worse. It was just a shame the "worse" had lasted her entire life.

With a shake of her head she came to a stop at the back gate of her house. She entered the small yard and put down her shopping with a sigh, fumbling in her purse for the key. She opened the door.

It was the smell that hit her first. An electric smell of oily burning, along with a sweet, cloying undertone. Had he put something under the grill and then fallen asleep? It wouldn't be the first time.

But as Mary entered her house she discovered that this was not the answer to the smell. The back door opened straight into the kitchen and she could see the grill was off.

She stepped into the tiny kitchen, leaving the back door open and the shopping outside in the yard. She could feel her heart beating heavily in her chest. It felt like a small beast was running around in her chest cavity, so irregular was the rhythm. Almost unnoticed in her anxiety, a dull ache was starting to pulse down her left arm.

The door into the living room was slightly ajar.

'Ted,' she called. No answer.

'What have you been doing in here?' Nothing.

Mary licked her suddenly dry lips.

There was something wrong. There was something very wrong. The stillness of the house seemed to mock her as she made her way towards the door of the sitting room. The beast in her chest began to kick with increasing tempo, making her cough.

She slowly opened the door and entered.

Nothing. The room was empty.

Mary turned back into the kitchen. The downstairs bathroom door stared at her.

'Ted,' she called out again, her heartbeat making her voice shake. She could barely breathe now. Her heart began to beat madly.

She stood in front of the closed bathroom door. She didn't want to enter. She didn't want to see what had happened to her husband, because she knew by now something *had* happened to him. But she had to know. She had no choice. Her hand pushed the unlocked door open.

The smell was very strong; it made her clasp a hand to her mouth, her widening eyes staring around the room.

All over the floor was a scattered pile of what looked like grey, gritty dust. As Mary's eyes moved disbelievingly over the utterly incomprehensible scene before her, the little beast inside her chest clasped her heart and started to shake it violently.

Through her dimming vision, Mary suddenly realised that the pile on the floor was not dust. Not dust at all. And, when she looked closer, she saw something lying half buried under the mess. Something red and blue. Kneeling on trembling legs, she reached out a hand and brushed at the pile. It was warm. Her brushing hand unveiled a tartan slipper, faded and holed. She would have recognised it anywhere. It was Ted's. And inside the slipper was a foot.

And that foot was all that remained of her husband. The rest of him had been incinerated. Turned into ashes and cinders.

As she stared in horror at the remains of her husband smeared into the palm of her hand, Mary had a split second to wonder what had caused this, and why a fire so intense had not seemed to have burned anything else in the room. But the split second was all she got.

Because the beast inside her chest grinned maliciously, grabbed her heart with both its hands, and squeezed it until it burst.

Chapter Two

The phone call clawed Ian Fenwick out of the nightmare. The usual nightmare.

He picked up the phone, taking note of the time. 4am. Four a-bloody-m! He sat, panting for a moment, and then switched on the bedside lamp and picked the phone up. On the other end of the line was Bill Curtis.

'Morning, Ian,' said Bill. 'I haven't woke you have I?'

Fenwick was silent for a second in disbelief.

'Of course you've bloody woke me,' he replied, although he said this mildly enough. Bill was his partner and friend and he hoped there was nothing too wrong for him to have called at this time in the morning.

'I know it's early, Ian, but I really need you to look at something for me.'

'Ah, come on, Bill,' moaned Fenwick, real annoyance in his voice now that he realised Bill was all right. 'I'm on vacation for Christ's sake. I only started my holidays yesterday.'

'I know, I know,' answered Bill quickly, and Fenwick could almost see him flapping his hand in his characteristic "calm down" gesture. 'But I really need you for this. I need you to investigate something.'

'Bill, I haven't had any time off for six months. What's so important you can't get one of the other lads onto it? Why ring me at stupid o'clock in the morning?'

'This is something that you have, err, specific knowledge about,' said Bill. 'I wouldn't ring if I didn't think it was important. The police want you. They asked for you personally, I've just come off the phone from them. I told them you were on holiday, but they were really quite insistent.'

A suspicion was growing in Fenwick's head. 'What "specific" knowledge do I have that no one else does?'

'There's been an incident. A fire…'

'You don't say,' broke in Fenwick, sarcastically. 'What with me being a fire investigator and everything.' His voice was becoming slightly hoarse. He could already guess what was coming. His northern accent was becoming more pronounced, a sure sign he was getting agitated.

'It was a house fire,' continued Bill, as if he hadn't heard him. Fenwick shook his head in disbelief again as the other man carried on talking. 'The local brigade were suspicious and called in the police. What they found there caused them to look up someone who might know a bit about things like this.' He paused, as if waiting for Fenwick to interrupt. When he didn't, he continued. 'They obviously came across you. Let's face it, a quick Google search is going to throw your name up fairly quickly isn't it.'

Fenwick lay back on his bed. He closed his eyes for a second and a sigh escaped his lips. From his mobile, a scratching noise informed him that Bill was talking again. He put the phone back to his ear.

'They found human remains,' Bill was saying. 'But there was something very weird about these remains. Their words, not mine.'

Fenwick remained silent, his thoughts turning to the past.

'The police want you to get up there,' Bill continued. 'See if you can help them come up with any ideas.'

'Get up where?' asked Fenwick, returning to the conversation.

'Newcastle.'

'I'm not going to bloody Newcastle!'

'Ian,' said Bill. 'You are.'

So now Fenwick sat in his Audi, driving back to the city he had not seen in ten years.

The car was a bit of an extravagance, but so what. It was the first new car he'd ever bought, and it beat the hell out of the company-owned Astra he had driven for the last couple of years. He'd picked up the gleaming black monster only the day before, thinking that his two-week holiday would be a good opportunity to put a few miles on it. He hadn't realised he would be putting the miles on by taking another job.

As co-owner of FireSafe Systems, Fenwick could now afford the car. The profits from the company also paid for his house and the Ducati Diavel he sometimes messed about on at the weekends. It had been a hard slog but he and Bill had believed in the products FireSafe sold, and in the last six years they had turned it from a small private company into an international PLC. The company dealt with everything connected to fire safety and protection, from flaming chip pans to burning buildings. FireSafe had various patented products designed to help people with the hazards of fire. Fenwick's job now mainly consisted of visiting all sorts of different premises, not just private homes, but also factories, warehouses and office blocks. He ensured that safety standards came up to British requirements and, if possible, he persuaded the owners to buy some of FireSafe's various fire prevention gadgets that were designed and manufactured by Bill's mysterious boffins who lived in the bowels of the company headquarters.

Fenwick still thought of himself as a firefighter, his job for over seventeen years, but he now sometimes sarcastically referred to himself as a salesman. He had discovered, however, that he was actually quite good at selling, and his experience and ability to sniff out new contracts had certainly helped the company expand to its present position. By far his best sale had been in persuading the government to take on the contract the company put forward for every office and workplace belonging to the Civil Service. That in itself paid for the car, the bike and the house.

Yes, his life was good. He earned decent money and his job was one he mostly enjoyed. It hadn't always been like that.

Fenwick shook his head and pushed the thought aside. He had a job to do. No point wallowing in the past. He switched on the radio and settled down for the long journey. As he drove, he went over what the police had told Bill.

Apparently, the wife of the man who had died, Embleton, had been out shopping, her husband seemingly not going out much in recent years. On her arrival home she had discovered the remains of her husband in one of the rooms, burned to cinders, only a foot remaining intact. Neighbours had heard the screams and rushed in to find Mrs Embleton slumped beside what remained of her husband, more dead than alive herself after a heart attack. She had survived so far though and was now in Intensive Care in one of the city's hospitals.

The last four of Fenwick's years with the fire service had been in investigation, and in the past he and FireSafe had helped out with numerous inquiries from various fire brigades, offering his advice and extensive knowledge. Although it did not pay much, both he and Bill knew that the connections made were very good for the company's profile. All of these investigations had so far been in the London area, and this was the first time he had been asked to look at something outside the capital, but Bill had persuaded him that these new connections might prove helpful in the future. Fenwick found himself agreeing, even though he was loathe to revisit the city of his youth. For one particular reason. He had told Bill, however, that when the investigation was over, he was definitely having a holiday. For *three* weeks.

After several stops for coffee, and with a terminally numb backside, he eventually reached Newcastle. The traffic in the city centre was abominable. Even Fenwick, who used to know the city and was a past master at driving through London's packed streets, conceded that the road system was a pretty useless setup. His temper was brittle by the time his Sat Nav informed him he'd arrived at his destination. The police station he was looking for was set slightly away from the city centre, on Forth Banks.

It was obviously an old building, perhaps warehouses once, but it had been cleaned up and modernised with a glass-and-steel extension. Typically there was nowhere to park, but Fenwick found a space in a restaurant car park across the road. He climbed out of the car and rubbed his throbbing back, noting sourly that his confinement in the vehicle had set it off again. He limped across the road, his thigh aching too, the slight lift he wore in one shoe to even out the length of his legs taking time to get itself organised. He entered the building and found himself in an airy room with a row of blue plastic seats to his right and a reception desk to his left. It looked more like the lobby of a motorway motel than a police station.

He identified himself to the young girl in civilian clothes on duty at the reception desk, and she ran an index finger down a list of names on her computer screen. She told him that a DI Parker would be here soon and led him into a nearby office.

'The DI won't be long, Mr Fenwick. Would you like a coffee or something?'

'Yeah, a coffee would be lovely,' replied Fenwick.

She smiled and left. It was very quiet in the office. Fenwick rubbed his thigh, feeling the old ragged scars underneath his suit trousers. He moved across to the window and stared out at the street opposite. The day was bright and warm outside. The sky was a cheery blue, studded with slow moving white clouds. A mini vortex of crisp packets and fag ends whirled around silently just under the windowsill.

He had just sat down when a burly man entered the room, a file under his arm and a young woman at his heels. He stood up again.

'Afternoon, Mr Fenwick,' said the man. 'I'm Detective Inspector Joe Parker, and this is Detective Sergeant Goddard.' He held out a hand and Fenwick shook it and then the young woman's, eyeing them both up.

Parker looked to be somewhere in his mid to late fifties. He was short and broad, with a thatch of gingery grey hair. His eyes were grey too and they looked out from a face that seemed wearied by its time in the world, long, curving lines wrapped around them. An old scar ran from the middle of his lower lip to just above his chin.

Goddard was an entirely different kettle of fish. Fenwick guessed she was somewhere in her mid-thirties. She wore a black trouser suit and flat shoes. Her hair was blonde—natural Fenwick guessed, but maybe with highlights—and she had an open, honest face with the most startlingly green eyes he had ever seen. She was quite tall, about five foot nine, and slender. The combination of her mostly makeup-free face and the smile she gave him when he shook her hand gave Fenwick a little jolt in his stomach, something he hadn't felt for a long time. He smiled back at her.

Parker dumped the file on the desk just as the young girl returned with Fenwick's coffee.

'Two more please, Jenny,' he said, and she disappeared again, looking disgruntled.

'You made good time,' Parker said.

Fenwick smiled. 'I've just bought a new car.'

Parker didn't reply but simply opened the file, and Fenwick pulled a face. *Suit yourself,* he thought. He caught Goddard looking and saw a half smile playing around her lips. He really could look into those eyes for a very long time.

Parker looked up and smiled benignly. 'An unusual affair, Mr Fenwick, I think you'll agree. A very unusual affair.'

He stared at him for a moment longer and, when Fenwick didn't respond, he suddenly clapped his hands together and rubbed them vigorously. He slipped on a pair of half-moon spectacles and instantly took on the air of a genial country vicar. He scanned the items inside the file briefly then turned it around and pushed it across to Fenwick.

'I know Mr Curtis has given you what information he has. But I think, if you're going to be able to assist us in this investigation, then you need to see these for yourself.'

Fenwick nodded and picked through the file.

There were several colour photographs and he looked at these first. The first one showed a general scene of the room where the foot had been found, and immediately Fenwick frowned. He put that one down for the moment and gazed at the second photo. This was a close up of the foot, showing where the fire had seemingly stopped consuming the body. The third photo was of the remains of Ted Embleton: a roughly human-shaped pile of dusty ash.

'Now then,' said Parker, 'we're seeing the house this afternoon. But before that, I've heard that Mrs Embleton has been taken off the critical list, so I thought we'd see her first. She may be able to tell us something we don't already know, although I doubt it. Anyway, after that I…'

He trailed off as Fenwick raised a hand. 'Is Mrs Embleton at the same hospital as the remains of her husband?'

Parker blinked. 'Pardon me?'

'If it's all the same to you, I'd like to see what's left of the body first.'

Parker sighed and leaned back in the chair, its plastic and metal frame creaking and cracking. He eyed Fenwick for a second or two.

'Listen,' he said, forcing a tone of civility into his voice that Fenwick was sure he didn't feel. 'We called you in—or should I say, *Detective Sergeant Goddard* called you in—to see if you could help us find out what happened in that house. But I am the detective in charge of this case. You are a civilian who may, or may not'—here he gave Goddard a disparaging glance that she chose to ignore—'be able to help. And I emphasise the word *help* here. It is my investigation and my investigations run in a particular way. Now if you'll just remember that, we'll get on, if you'll pardon the pun, like a house on fire. Okay? There's no need to see the corpse yet; and corpse is stretching the point, it's mostly nothing but ashes. We can always see it later if I think it's warranted…'

Once again he trailed off as Fenwick shook his head.

'Inspector,' he said, refusing to be intimidated. The long car journey and Parker's attitude was making him grouchy. 'I was asked to come back here to the armpit of the world to see if I can help in finding out what happened to that man and how he died, and perhaps come up with a logical explanation as to the cause of it. Believe me, I have no wish to go rummaging around a corpse for clues, but after seeing this photo,' he held up the shot of the foot, 'on this occasion I think it's essential that I do so. I want to help. If *I* can't do *my* investigation, then there's not much point in me being here.'

Parker looked ready to argue the point, but it was Goddard who spoke for the first time.

'What have you seen in the photo?' she asked.

Fenwick turned to her. 'A couple of things. There's something very odd about the way it looks. My *speciality* I suppose, and the reason you got me here I'm assuming, is my knowledge of what has come to be called "spontaneous human combustion". I've had as much experience with this supposed phenomena as anyone. And this,' he tapped the photo in front of him, 'doesn't look right. I need to see the remains with my own eyes.'

'What's wrong with it?' asked Goddard, leaning forward to stare at the photo. Fenwick got a brief trace of the perfume she was wearing. She was still leaning forward when she looked up for an answer, her face only inches from his. They stared at each other for just a fraction too long. Then she gave a nervous little smile and sat back, tucking a lock of stray hair behind her ear.

'Do you mind if we just go and have a look?' asked Fenwick, still talking to her and not Parker. 'I may be able to give you a few more answers once I've seen it.'

Parker then spoke again, seemingly unaware of the little interaction having just been played out in front of him.

'Fair enough,' he said. 'We'll play it your way. For just now.'

Fenwick was left with no doubt how long 'for just now' would be. Parker didn't like him, that was for sure, and it seemed his being there was all down to the attractive woman sitting opposite. But Parker was in charge of the case and Fenwick would have to co-operate with him. He was buggered if he was going to be slowed down by him, though. There was something about that photograph and the others in the file, something that sparked an interest in a subject he'd thought he had finished with years ago. He was getting excited by this project and *that* had not happened in a *very* long time.

'To answer your original question, the remains are at the same hospital as Mrs Embleton,' continued Parker. 'So maybe we can both get on with our jobs there.'

With that, he got up. 'Shall we go?'

*

The morgue was situated in the basement of the hospital, discreetly hidden from the general public by a steep flight of stairs and heavy fire doors. A porter asked them to wait by the doors before sauntering off to find the doctor in charge. The three of them stood in the corridor, not talking; like strangers in a lift.

Eventually a doctor appeared at the end of the corridor. A tall, lean and fit-looking man in his fifties, he had jet black hair with distinguished grey streaks at the temple and wore a tieless shirt with an ID badge hooked onto the pocket. He presented an authoritative and handsome figure and, glancing at Goddard, Fenwick could see her appraising the doctor and liking what she saw. He felt an odd sense of jealousy as he caught the look between them and frowned at this feeling, wondering what had brought it on.

'Good afternoon,' the doctor said, his voice slightly accented. 'What can I do for you?'

'Dr Ross?' asked Parker.

The doctor nodded. 'Yes, James Ross.' He shook hands with Parker.

'I'm DI Parker, this is DS Goddard and Ian Fenwick. We spoke on the phone yesterday.'

'Ah, yes. The Embleton death.' Definitely an accent, thought Fenwick, but it was so subtle he couldn't make out where it might have originated from.

'It's quite remarkable,' Ross went on. 'I've never seen anything like it.'

'Remarkable, is not the word I would use,' said Parker. He tipped his head at Fenwick. 'Mr Fenwick here is co-owner of

FireSafe, we've called him in to see if he can help with our little problem, i.e., why a man was burned to death in his bathroom. Isn't that right Mr Fenwick.'

He seemed to be in a good mood so Fenwick nodded, just to keep him bobbing along, but before he could answer he was interrupted by Ross.

'I don't know why he was burned to death, but I can tell you that, whatever happened, it was very quick. His flesh and even his bones were reduced to ashes. His veins and arteries were consumed. His body didn't even have a chance to be boiled in its own fluids, usually the case in flash fires.'

There was silence for a second as this information was taken in and then Parker opened his mouth to speak, only to be cut off by Fenwick who got in first. 'Is it possible to see the body?'

Fenwick was aware of Parker's darkening face glaring at his profile, like a kid deprived of the best lines in the school play. He groaned inwardly; this wasn't starting off too well.

The doctor nodded. 'Yes, of course: what's left of it. Follow me please.' He turned and headed off back down the corridor, and Fenwick and Parker turned at the same time, unintentionally finding themselves facing each other. Fenwick kept his face carefully blank whilst Parker directed a glower at him which was then turned on Goddard as the DS purposely stood herself between them.

'Come on, boss,' she said and set off down the corridor. Parker followed her and Fenwick shook his head before setting off in their wake.

The remains of Ted Embleton lay scattered in a big metallic bowl in the room the pathologist led them into, with the remaining foot encased in a polythene bag on a bench beside it.

'What's this?' asked Fenwick, indicating to the machine.

'If you think of it as a large magnet it will be easier for you,' said Ross. 'We're trying to find any objects alien to the body.'

'Any luck?'

The pathologist smiled. 'Not yet: only fibres from the bathroom mat. Nothing that shouldn't be there.' He moved towards the bench where the foot lay and made to open the polythene bag, but stopped as Fenwick shook his head and then peered closely at it.

'Have you got the remains of his clothes, the hem of his trousers?' he asked, but it was Parker who frowned and answered.

'The only clothes he had on was the slipper,' he said. 'He wasn't wearing the other one; that was found in the bathroom, too. Apart from that one slipper, it seems he was naked.'

Fenwick nodded once more. 'And that's why I thought there was something wrong with the photo,' he said. 'Because that's impossible.' His gaze wandered back to the bowl of ashes, his face troubled.

'Impossible,' he repeated.

Chapter Three

She was running again. They had found her once more and, if
they caught her, they would kill her. It would not be the first
time they had killed.

How many weeks had it been? Or was it months now? She
could barely remember. She was sleeping rough in the countryside,
for they were weaker there than in the cities. That made sense
obviously, for they were fewer in rural areas. She washed in streams
and rivers, begged or stole for food, stowed away on trains and
buses or hitched a lift to the next small town or village. But they
always eventually discovered her whereabouts. It occurred to
her that their numbers must be increasing, spreading across the
country like a black, malignant cancer. They were always just
behind her, always the dark shadow over her shoulder, drawing
nearer and nearer. And one day they would catch up with her and
she would die.

She did have one advantage of course. She knew when they
were getting close. They had taught her too well how to do this.
Along with the all the *other* things they had taught her.

But she couldn't go on forever. Soon they would catch her
unawares because she was exhausted by the chase. She simply could
not continue. It was too tiring. If something did not change soon
it would be too late. They knew she was weakening, for in the last
few days their searching had become even more frantic; sensing her
hopelessness they were intensifying their pursuit.

She needed help. Desperately needed help. But who could she
turn to? Who could protect her? Who would even listen to her?

No one. She continued along the path at the side of golden wheat fields, her thoughts desperate and her eyes ignoring the beauty of the scenery.

Tears of self-pity and grief blurred her vision to such a degree that it wasn't until she had stopped to wipe them away that she realised she was at the end of the gently rolling fields and in front of her, seemingly springing out of the surrounding countryside, a city suddenly sprawled.

She was back where she had started from, the place she had been running from and which now drew her back because she sensed that someone down there in that city could perhaps help her.

She stared at the urban landscape, her thin body buffeted by the small wind, warm as it was. But she didn't feel the wind, for the sight of the city had given her strength and, setting her chin, the back of a grimy hand wiping away the residue of tears, she started walking towards Newcastle.

*

Anna Pont leaned heavily on the kitchen worktop as she waited for the kettle to boil. She peered through the window at the backyard, still in daylight even though it was after 9pm. She suppressed a shudder as she waved to John, and her husband waved back. He closed the gate behind him and she watched as he walked down the back lane, his haversack bouncing dejectedly from his shoulder. For the thousandth time Anna cursed the financial situation that forced them to live like this. John hated working shifts, hated to be away from her during the long, dark nights, but it was the only way he could make enough money for them to survive. The dayshift pay was not enough to cover the rent of the house, never mind leaving anything left for utility bills and food, so they really had no choice.

So much for austerity, she though bitterly. The government forced a man to go to work every night while his wife sat shaking with fear, unable to do anything except wait for his return, jumping at every sound, every shadow.

It had not always been like this. Anna had a job once: a secretary with a local building firm. The money hadn't been brilliant, but it had helped to keep them living comfortably. Life had been hard, but good. She and John had laughed together, loved together. They had just been starting out on their married lives. Everything seemed to be falling into place. Until that night when Anna's life was ripped apart.

She had been working late in the office, the April tax deadline always a busy time for her. It was dark when she finally turned off her computer and left the building. It was only a ten-minute walk from the office to her house and she set off briskly, wondering what they would have for their tea. She had rounded the last corner, the corner that led to the small house they lived in: a nicer area than the one they could afford now. Or so it had seemed.

She cursed under her breath when she saw that the streetlamps had failed to come on again. She and other neighbours had complained to the council often enough but to no avail. They would be fixed for a while and then, after a few days, they would be off again. It wouldn't have been so bad, but the small housing estate of new builds lay on the outskirts of fields and Anna had often seen shadowy figures roaming round the bushes and trees from her bedroom window. Probably just youngsters out drinking, but worrying all the same. The thought of walking down the dark street set her pulse racing and caused a tiny tremor to run down her spine.

She scolded herself for her timidity. No one was going to hurt her. This was a *nice* neighbourhood: the saleswoman had said so when they had signed for the house. There was no one there that she could see so she had wrapped her coat tighter around her slim frame and set off quickly down the street.

She had only gone a few yards when she stopped and turned, peering into the darkness of the copse of trees next to her. Had something moved? She listened but there was nothing else, and so she moved on once more. It could have been anything. There were lots of small animals living in the fields and woods; she had even seen the occasional urban fox trotting around out there. Nevertheless, she quickened her pace.

As she hurried along the dark, deserted street she became aware of a figure up ahead, leaning nonchalantly against a tree. A cigarette bobbed in the darkness, glowing bright and then fading as the smoke was drawn into the lungs and expelled. To reach her house she would have to pass the figure she now saw was a man, and the thought sent a jet of ice through her system. She didn't know why, but there was something menacing about the shadowy figure, even though—or perhaps *because*—he was standing so still.

Pull yourself together, Anna admonished herself. *He's probably just waiting for someone, his girlfriend maybe. Just walk past him and keep walking.*

She carried on, her heels clicking a tattoo on the pavement. She was opposite him when he said, 'Got the time?'

Anna caught her breath and peered at him in the murk, trying to discern features in the darkness, but all she got was a vague impression of dark stubble and pale, deathly pale skin. Was he a drug addict? He certainly looked haggard as far as she could make out. The thought that he might be a user persuaded her to give him what he wanted and then get away as quickly as she could. She pulled at the sleeve of her coat to look at her watch, her heart beating wildly, and then the man suddenly reached out and grasped her arm. Anna stared at him, wretched with fear, a scream caught in her throat.

The man smiled, showing dirty, discoloured teeth. His fetid breath washed over her as he said, 'Doesn't matter. I know exactly what time it is.'

The next few minutes of Anna Pont's life were still very blurred in her brain. The man placed a stinking hand around her mouth and dragged her, kicking and struggling into the copse of trees, throwing her down with such force that later, at the hospital, they discovered she had two broken ribs. The pain blasted through her body and, before she could try to draw in a breath to attempt a scream, he had unfastened his trousers and was kneeling over her. One hand grasped her throat, cutting off her breath, and the other ripped at her skirt and tights. She felt his fingers enter her, and with a grunt of disgust and horror she struck out and punched him hard in the face. She managed to hit him again and continued to fight until her vision erupted into white sparks as his clenched fist cracked her hard on the jaw. Anna was knocked almost unconscious by the blow, and when he punched her again she sank into a sort of coma-like state, her recollection from that point on fragmented. Her only real memory was of the man expelling his lust quickly and painfully into her. As he did so, she noticed the streetlamps, only yards away switching on and casting a halo around his shaggy head. As she stared at the lights over his grunting head, she realised she could see the bedroom window of her own house. It was literally seconds away.

When he was finished, the man quickly stood and pulled up his trousers. Without a backwards glance at her, he disappeared into the woods. He left Anna half-naked on the ground, beaten and brutalised, her swollen eyes blank and staring and her mind unable to accept what had just happened.

It had taken months of talking and counselling before Anna even began to come to terms with her ordeal. Months of nightmares, of waking in the night screaming, that shaggy head above her in her dreams and the stinking breath wafting into her face. Months of lashing out at her husband who was trying to comfort her. Months of hell.

But slowly, she began to recover. She would not be defeated by this. It would *not* define who she was. Her triumph would be the continuance of her life.

She wanted to return to work, to prove to everyone how strong she was, but John wouldn't even entertain the thought. He refused point blank to even listen whenever she mentioned it. He hadn't wanted to work nights either, didn't want to leave her alone, but they really had no choice. They moved away from their 'nice' neighbourhood and rented the house in which they now lived to save money. So, because he did not want her to work, he had to leave her at night to sit by herself, stiffening at every noise, fearful of every shadow. It was a never-ending carousel of loneliness and despair and fear.

The police had caught the man who raped her. He was well-known to them, an addict just released from prison for drug related offences. Anna was advised to be tested for HIV because of this revelation and waiting for the results had brought the whole horrific ordeal back. As had the trial. Thankfully, she got the all-clear. At least she had that. He was still in prison. She hoped he would die in there.

She turned away from the window and her memories and pulled down the blinds, closing the coming night from herself. She poured a cup of tea, absently taking off her glasses and wiping them on the hem of her cardigan as steam misted the lenses. Then, after spooning in some sugar and taking a packet of digestives from the cupboard, she wandered into the sitting room and sat down on the sofa.

She watched the TV absently for a while, trying to take an interest in what was on but still haunted by her memories. It was always when John was away that they returned. Always when she was alone.

As she sat there, she slowly became aware of a strange sensation washing over her. It was a feeling of heat that began to pound through her body. It was so strange that she put down her tea and the remote, staring at the back of her hands which had suddenly erupted with sweat. She could see it beading on her skin. Sweat had also started to pulse from her forehead, and her heart was beating loudly in her ears. The throbbing rapidly moved deeper into her head, banging to such an extent that she had to place her trembling fingers against her slick temples, attempting to block it out. She blinked as sweat ran into her eyes.

She looked down into her lap and was amazed and terrified to see sweat stains spreading on her thin leggings. She ran a shaking hand across her soaking brow and wiped it on her tee shirt, watching as stains spread there too.

The last thought in Anna Pont's life was that she was having a seizure. That was the word she thought of. Seizure.

The thought was amputated as her body suddenly erupted in a violent, bluish white flash of light, the searing heat bathing the sitting room in electric violet for a millionth of a second. It rebounded from the TV screen and amplified, expanding in an instant until it consumed her body and vanished as suddenly as it had appeared.

When that immense, impossible light winked out, the only thing that remained of Anna Pont was memories.

*

Fenwick slept fitfully that night, the remains of Ted Embleton having upset him in a way he had thought was no longer possible. It had been such a long time ago. Such a bloody long time.

Well, maybe not. What was a decade? The years seemed to gallop by and sometimes he could not quite believe it had *been* ten years.

Seeing Embleton had brought back memories that he had thought time and hard work had erased. The memories he fought so hard to permanently forget. It was the smell of the corpse. That strange stench which had haunted him for months after Rachel died. Fenwick was used to death, and death by fire especially, but there was an odour about the remains in the morgue that bothered him. When Ross had opened the bag containing the foot he'd been instantly transported back to that awful night. That night when he'd discovered what had become of Rachel. But that smell, so subtly different to the many other bodies he had recovered from fires, troubled him. He couldn't put his finger on what was so different about Embleton's death. It was the *exact* same smell that had haunted his nights since his wife's death.

He had been the consummate professional at the morgue—

prodding, probing, investigating—but as soon as he'd checked into his hotel room he had collapsed on the bed, mentally drained.

Maybe it was too much, the past still too fresh in his mind. He remembered the feverish intensity he had thrown himself into after Rachel died. His manic determination to find out everything he could about the phenomenon known as Spontaneous Human Combustion. It had eventually culminated with the publication of his book and the general consensus of his expertise on the subject. And it was, of course, the reason why the police had asked for him personally after Embleton's death.

His body thrashed and flailed on the bed as he dreamed. He remembered the telephone call from his brother-in-law, the nightmare drive through the quiet streets of Durham, the scene in the little cul-de-sac where he lived. The ambulances, fire engines and police cars standing on and around his drive, their blue lights flashing frantically, brilliantly, uselessly. The curtains of his neighbours' windows twitching as they stared out at the scene. And he remembered the remains of his wife lying shrouded in the sitting room, once so full of life but now gone. Just gone.

His dream then played out another memory. From before? From after? In the dream he didn't really know. He was in the flames, the heat. He was with Kev, always with Kev in those days. They were crouching low and the breathing apparatus was hot and sticky over his mouth and nose, metallic tasting oxygen pumping through his system.

He remembered the awful, grinding crash, Kev disappearing as half the floor they stood on collapsed. He stared down as Kev hung there, one hand grasping the iron support girder that had saved him from falling down to the burning level below. He also remembered hesitating, staring into Kev's face, the other man's eyes wide through his BA mask as he saw Fenwick pause. The fear that he would not be helped.

But Fenwick reached down and pulled Kev up onto the precarious safety of the floor and Kev grasped and then slumped heavily onto another girder attached to the wall. They stared at each other. Kev looked like he was about to speak. What was he going to say? But then the whole section of fractured floor on which Fenwick crouched splintered with a rending crash. And he was falling, falling. Kev, still sitting on the girder with his legs now dangling above the fractured floor was disappearing rapidly above him, shouting his name, watching impotently as Fenwick vanished into the flames below. He bounced from one hulking mass of machinery to another in the burning warehouse before smashing to the floor like a rag doll, the pain in his leg colossal, all-consuming.

The memories taunted him, bathing him in sweat, not letting him go. Hospital rooms and doctors shaking their heads at him as he lay on a bed. These faces merging with Rachel's. Kev and him at a barbeque in the garden of his house in the golden glow of high summer, drinking beer and laughing, with Rachel smiling at them both. Making love to Rachel on a winter's night, snow billowing outside the window. Kev lying on the floor, his nose bleeding and one hand held up in supplication. The visions grew then exploded softly and blew away, leaving one solitary scene: his wife's face, tear streaked, pleading, begging. 'Don't leave, Ian, please don't leave, it won't happen again, I promise. Just please don't leave.'

Then a well-known feeling crept over him, a tide rising inside him, the guilt growing stronger and expanding until his mind could no longer accept it and it was rejected, letting him fall eventually into a deep and thankfully dreamless sleep.

He was woken by his phone shrilling loudly in his ear, an incessant screaming that craved attention. Looking at his watch he saw it was just coming up for 10am. He had slept late.

He reached for the phone, his eyes puffy and stinging from where he had wept in his sleep. A drum seemed to be banging in his head. He felt like he'd been up all night drinking.

'Hello,' he wheezed into the phone. 'Ian Fenwick here.'

'Fenwick,' came the reply. It was Parker, sounding harassed and irritated. At some point in the night he had apparently decided to drop the 'Mister' at the beginning of Fenwick's name.

'We've got another one,' the DI continued. 'Same M.O., only there's nothing left of this one, not a fucking thing. All we've got is a pile of ashes sitting on a couch.'

For a second, Fenwick was too stunned to answer.

'Did you hear me?' roared Parker, the phone distorting and crackling with the ferocity of the outburst.

'Yes,' said Fenwick quickly. He reached for a pen and notebook. 'Tell me where to go.'

*

There was a lot of activity in the back street of the housing estate in Fenham as he arrived. There was a group of spectators staring, most of them young and a lot of them were still dressed in pyjamas or ridiculous animal print onesies. They gaped with the wide-eyed intensity and interest that only the social media generation can understand. Facebook would be crackling with activity soon, the Tweets legion.

Fenwick had had to park a fair distance away and he walked past the fire engines and ambulances and police cars, marked and unmarked. He groaned inwardly when he saw a TV news crew standing beside the taped-off house, the forensic teams wandering around its back yard in their head-to-toe white suits. A woman reporter was arguing with a fed-up looking copper who guarded the scene.

He saw Fenwick approaching and held up his hand to stop him while he addressed the reporter. 'I've told you, no. That's final.' Then he turned to Fenwick. 'You can't come in either, you can see it's taped off.'

The copper's eyes widened as he turned to see the reporter trying to sneak under the tape and he bawled at her, 'Look, just sod off will you! For fuck's sake!'

Parker was standing in the back yard and he turned as he heard the raised voices. When he saw Fenwick he came over.

'It's okay, he can come in,' he said to the constable.

The tape was obligingly lifted for Fenwick and he ducked under, joining Parker on the other side and leaving the raised voices of the continuing argument behind him.

Almost without realising it, Fenwick found himself scanning faces, looking for Goddard. He suddenly realised that he *wanted* to see her, and he shook his head slightly at the thought, wondering what was getting into him. He had only known her for five minutes for God's sake. But even so he gave a little grunt of satisfaction when he saw the DS standing in the doorway of the house.

'When did it happen?' he asked as he and Parker stopped beside Goddard.

'Sometime between nine last night and nine this morning,' replied the DS. 'We only know that because the woman's husband was on night shift and didn't get back till that time today.'

'He found her then?'

She nodded.

'Christ, the poor bastard.' Fenwick rubbed his rough chin. 'Where is he now?'

'At the station,' said Parker. 'We've got him there with his mother.'

Fenwick nodded. 'Anything been moved?'

'No.'

'Are we allowed in?'

'Just got the all-clear from forensics. I've already been in. Not much to see to be honest. Bloody awful smell though.'

Fenwick nodded again but said nothing, the dreams of the night before still fresh in his mind. 'Let's have a look then, eh?'

The room was small as rooms go. Small but nice. Nice carpet, nice wallpaper, nice paintwork. The only thing that wasn't nice was the pile of clothes and the untidy heap of dirty grey ashes that were scattered on the settee and the floor in front of it.

Fenwick could see what had happened. Or what *looked* like had happened for, although the TV was switched off, the clothes lay in such a way as to suggest that the woman had been watching it when she died. There was even a mug of cold tea and a half-eaten packet of biscuits lying on the floor. And he could see that the ashes were *inside* the clothing as well as on the settee and floor. Some were even floating in the cup of tea.

Fenwick gazed at the scene in a kind of trance. He turned to Parker.

'There's no way this could be a set-up, is there?'

Parker blew out his cheeks and shook his head. 'As far as we can make out this is the remains of Anna Pont. We've got no evidence of anybody taking the piss. Although what we've also got is no idea what happened to her.'

Fenwick shook his head too. He stared at the clothes and ashes in front of him, noting that the clothes did not even seem to be singed and that the settee was unmarked.

'This isn't right,' he murmured, but only Goddard, standing next to him, heard him. She gave him a curious glance.

He roused himself and took a deep breath, and it was only then that he fully registered that smell. Parker was right. It *was* bloody awful, and it brought his nightmare rushing back with a vividness that actually made him sway. It was the DS who gently took his arm and led him outside, mistaking his reaction for queasiness.

'You okay?' she asked when they had moved into the yard. She was a little surprised at his reaction. When she had met him yesterday, he'd seemed like a man who was very sure of his profession and of himself. She also knew he'd spent a lot of years as a firefighter, so he must have seen his fair share of horrors. Maybe it was something you lost after a while.

'Yeah, I'm fine,' muttered Fenwick. He sat down on the doorstep, loosening his tie and sitting with his forearms resting on his knees.

He wasn't quite sure what was wrong with him. It wasn't as if this was the first time he had encountered death. As a firefighter he had seen more than his fair share of horrors. He smiled at Goddard, apologetically. Maybe it was something that disappeared after a while.

Goddard sat down beside him, studying his profile. His hair

was dark and quite close cropped and there was a sprinkling of grey in it. She knew he was forty-six, but he actually looked a little younger. He was tall with broad shoulders, but he was by no means big. Lean would be a better word for him. His eyes were dark brown, and the overall combination was very pleasant. Not film star looks by any means. But pleasant, especially when he smiled like he had smiled at her yesterday.

At that moment, though, he just looked perplexed and a little lonely sitting on the concrete step and Goddard had to consciously stop herself from squeezing his hand or putting an arm around his shoulders. Suddenly, Fenwick looked at her and they stared at each other until Goddard forced herself to look away. Fenwick coughed, a little self-consciously.

'Thanks,' he said after a while.

'What for?'

'Just… Thanks.'

They sat for a second more, looking at each other again. Then, involuntarily, they both laughed at their serious faces.

'Do you have a first name Detective Sergeant Goddard?' he asked.

'Laura.'

He nodded. 'Nice to meet you, Laura.'

They sat facing each other again, both of them smiling slightly, until a young constable came out.

'The boss wants to see you,' he said to Fenwick.

They got up and went back inside. Parker was standing beside the unlit fireplace, his face in repose. He had a pen in his hand but his eyes stared at nothing. He looked deep in thought as he stood there, surrounded by police officers, firefighters and paramedics, all of them trying to do their jobs and all getting in each other's way.

'We've got two people dead,' he said without preamble. 'There's no connection between them except that they were both reduced to nothing but that.' He waved an arm at the grizzly mess on the settee. Then he looked up at Fenwick searchingly: a normal man, doing an abnormal job in the best way he knew how.

'What's doing it?' he asked. 'Just what the fuck is doing it?'

Chapter Four

Fenwick got down to work to try and find out 'just what the fuck' was doing it.

In the next few days, along with Parker and Goddard, he attended the autopsy of Anna Pont. The pathologist, Ross, told them that the woman had died in exactly the same way as Ted Embleton. Her body had been consumed, seemingly in an instant, by a heat so intense that it had atomised her without touching anything else in the room, not even scorching the clothes she was wearing. The "ash" was in fact hard granules, similar to what was left after a cremation, but unlike a cremation, there were no larger carbonised bone fragments. The *whole* body had been consumed by an incredible heat, seemingly without affecting anything else in the immediate area.

'Like a nuclear explosion?' Parker asked the pathologist, but it was Fenwick who replied.

'No. The epicentre of a nuclear bomb is anywhere between 50 and 150 million degrees. If that had happened there would be literally nothing left of the body, and certainly nothing left of the clothes. Not to mention the house and half the city. I think we would have known if that had happened.'

He hadn't meant to sound offhand, but Parker glared at him.

'This was something different,' continued Fenwick, oblivious to the look Parker was giving him. 'It's almost as if it wasn't fire at all. Like it was a different sort of energy.'

Parker continued to glower at him, stung by the sarcastic comment about the nuclear bomb, then he shook his head and turned away.

'I can only tell you that these remains are similar to a cremated cadaver,' said Ross after a second or two of chilly silence between the two other men, and Fenwick was sure he caught the curl of a mocking smile on the man's lips. 'But cremating a body takes time and always leaves larger bone fragments. Whatever happened to these two people happened instantly.'

Fenwick wondered about this as they made their way to the ward where Mary Embleton lay. She had been too ill to talk on the day they had viewed her husband's remains, but the doctors had said they could now interview her. What could have produced that kind of energy without affecting anything else? And why had part of Ted Embleton remained intact while Anna Pont was completely consumed? These were just two items on his long list of problems, and he was beginning to have the first inkling that this was going to take a lot longer to solve than he had first envisioned. If it was ever going to be solved.

Mary Embleton was still very ill and could tell them nothing they didn't already know. The following day they interviewed Anna Pont's husband where he was staying at his mother's house in Cramlington, and his answers brought them to a similar conclusion. There seemed to be absolutely no reason why the two people had died in the manner in which they had, and Fenwick was in exactly the same position he had been in when he had first arrived in Newcastle days ago. He started to feel depression settle on him like a lead weight.

As the trio wearily strolled out into the street after interviewing Pont, they were confronted by brilliant sunshine and a clear, blue sky. The weather only emphasised the gloominess of their faces.

Fenwick leaned against the garden gate and surveyed his companions. Goddard seemed alert as ever, although she looked a little tired. Parker, however, was wearing an expression that Fenwick had seen enough times before to recognise. The DI was beginning to give up. This was a situation in which normal police procedures just didn't seem to be working. Experts called in to help could give no answers and he was starting to think that maybe this would be one of his cases marked "unsolved". And perhaps he was happy for that to happen. Maybe he wanted to get back to some good old-fashioned knifing or burglary. Something he knew how to handle.

Fenwick would keep at it of course; he wouldn't give up that easily. But he also knew that the manpower assigned would be slowly wound down and the case would eventually be closed for lack of evidence. It would lie buried in a computer memory bank, gathering metaphorical dust until—if ever—another case resembling it ever came up. Something Fenwick really doubted.

He sighed.

'Listen,' he said. 'I'm going to go back to the hotel to have a look through the cases I've worked on in the past again, see if I can find anything useful or similar to these two deaths, although I doubt it. There's nothing you two can really do to help, so if you've got anything else on at the minute, you may as well concentrate on that. I'll let you know if anything turns up.'

Parker ran a hand through his thinning hair and slowly nodded, obviously anxious to give his time to something that could be explained, something he could be credited with.

With this resolved, Fenwick limped over to his Audi and drove back to the hotel, making himself a cup of coffee and settling down at the desk in his room with his laptop in front of him.

The laptop contained all the work he had ever researched about SHC— Spontaneous Human Combustion—and, although he'd been through most of it again in the last few days, as well as scanning the internet to try and find anything remotely similar to what had happened in Newcastle, he reasoned there may have been something he'd forgotten or hadn't seen before that might be in any way be comparable to what he had seen at Anna Pont's house.

There was nothing he hadn't noticed before however, and that didn't really surprise him. He was basically doing this now for appearances sake. He didn't expect to find anything new for he had read so much on the subject of SHC before and over the last couple of days that he could quote huge portions of the books and articles he had consumed. Especially in those long, bleak months after Rachel's death. He knew there were no recorded cases similar to the deaths of Ted Embleton and Anna Pont. Not *exactly* similar anyway.

Two hours later, with his back in agony, he closed the laptop. Nothing. It had been, as he had suspected it would be, a waste of time.

Glancing at his watch, he saw it was after 7pm. He moved across to the mini bar and selected a single malt, pouring it neat into a glass. An extra bill for the expense account.

He had just lain down on the bed with the whiskey in his hands when his phone rang. He didn't recognise the number. With a muttered 'Bloody hell,' he put down his whiskey and answered the phone.

'Hello. If you're trying to sell me compensation for an accident I've had in the last five years then you're too late. Been there, done that.'

'Mr Fenwick? It's me, Laura. DS Goddard I mean.'

For a second, Fenwick didn't know what to say.

'Hi,' he said eventually, sitting straighter up on the bed. 'Sorry about that. My attempt at humour. What's up? Has something else happened?'

There was the slightest of pauses on the other end. 'Actually, I was wondering if I could talk to you.' Another pause. 'About SHC I mean.' This last part of the sentence was hurriedly added on, as if she didn't want him to misconstrue the reason behind the phone call.

Fenwick felt a slight sense of disappointment and it was only when he realised what the feeling was that he simultaneously realised that her initial question—and the fact it was her—had raised his hopes. Of what though, he didn't know.

'Of course,' he said. 'What little I know. When do you want to do this? Tomorrow at some point?'

There was a longer pause.

'Actually, I'm downstairs in the bar now.'

Fenwick actually took his phone from his ear and stared at it, feeling ridiculously nervous all of a sudden.

'I was just passing on my way home,' explained Goddard, again in a rush. 'It's no bother if you can't, I just thought that any information on the subject would be beneficial, that's all.'

'No, no. That's fine,' said Fenwick. 'I'll be down in two minutes.'

He hung up and stood, catching sight of himself in the mirror. His shirt was crumpled and so was he. He quickly dived into his case and hauled out some jeans and a pair of dark lace-up pumps, pulling on a blue v-necked sweater too and pushing the sleeves up his arms. He practically ran into the bathroom, brushed his teeth and checked out his face. He could have done with a shave but he didn't have time so he just stood there for a second, staring at himself in the mirror, his hands resting on the lip of the small sink.

'Bloody hell,' he whispered again to his reflection. Then he grabbed his room key and made for the lift.

Goddard was sitting at the bar, still wearing the clothes she had worn that day, and nursing what looked like a lemonade. He felt slightly disappointed again that the story she had given him seemed to be true. That she was just passing by and thought she might learn a little about the supposed phenomenon of Spontaneous Human Combustion.

She stood up and waved when she saw him and he waved back, noticing the vivid green of her eyes even across the small bar area.

He walked over to her, trying not to limp too much. The soft pumps didn't have the lift in them that was fitted to his work shoes and he cursed himself silently for pulling them on. God knew what she must have thought of him waddling up to her in this manner. As he approached he could see her watching his poor gait and he cursed again. He suddenly felt stupid. He hadn't entertained any serious thoughts about the DS, thinking only that she was a very good-looking woman, but totally out of his league. He wasn't really used to meeting attractive women in bars and the impression he felt he was giving was poor.

But then he scolded himself. Why would she be bothered what he looked like anyway? She was there because of work. He held no interest for her. He was at least ten years older than her and he wasn't exactly George Clooney. He was just a salesman, with one leg shorter than the other and greying hair. She was probably married or engaged anyway. Had to be. She was far too attractive to be single. Some good-looking young buck would have snapped her up years ago. He hadn't noticed any ring on her finger, but then again he hadn't been looking.

As he stopped beside her and shook her hand formally, he felt a little better that he didn't have to put on a performance as if he were on a date. Although he didn't really know what that performance would be; it had been so long since he had actually been on a date he could barely remember how to act. Even so, he glanced surreptitiously at her finger when she sat back down on the bar stool and reached for her glass. Definitely no ring. Mind, that didn't mean anything of course.

He shook his head at his jumbled thoughts. *Bloody hell!* he thought once more, and then smiled nervously at her.

'Would you like a drink?' she asked when he sat beside her.

'No, I'll get it,' he said. 'I'll stick it on the account, save you some money. Would like anything?'

She shook her head, and he ordered a pint of lager.

'So, have you come up with any new ideas?' she asked.

'I'm getting nowhere,' he replied with a shake of his head. 'I've read all there is on the subject, so I knew that any old cases I went over again weren't going to tell me anything I didn't already know. I just hoped I'd missed something first time round, but I hadn't.'

He briefly scanned the beer mat on the bar in front of him and then cocked an eyebrow at her. 'So what do you want to know?'

'Well, anything really,' she replied. 'I know nothing about the subject so I thought that while you were here you could give me some extra information about SHC. I thought anything I can find out might assist us in the investigation.'

He nodded, feeling ridiculously disappointed once more, but then put those thoughts out of his mind.

'How long have you been a DS?' he asked her.

'Three years,' she answered with a slight smile. 'Why?'

Fenwick looked around the room and saw a small table away from the bar. 'Let's sit down there,' he said, standing up. 'These bar stools hurt my leg after a while.'

They moved across to the table and sat down, Fenwick with a small sigh of relief.

'I heard you had an accident when you were in the brigade,' she said. 'You hurt your leg then?'

He hesitated. The accident was not something he was usually comfortable talking about. The months in hospital when it was touch and go whether he would even keep his leg or whether it would have to be amputated, the months of physio, the pain, the knowledge that his career on the front line was over, the re-training as an investigator. All of these things were something he usually just kept to himself, mistakenly thinking that people would not be interested in his misery. Plus, of course, everything else that had happened to him at that point in his life. But for some reason, when Goddard—Laura, he reminded himself—asked about it, he decided that he didn't need to be as cagy as he normally was. That he wanted to tell her about it. Or at least some of it.

He nodded. 'Yeah, although there's not a lot to tell. I was in a farming machinery warehouse with…with another firefighter. We were on the first floor. The floor gave way and I fell down to the level below. Unfortunately I hit about three massive threshing machines before I hit the ground.' He smiled ruefully, then shrugged. 'That's it,' he finished.

Goddard reckoned there was a bit more to it than that. She only nodded however, thinking that it was his business. It would be nice to talk to him about it though. She believed the accident had affected him a lot more than he was making out.

Her thoughts were cut off as he said, 'So. Three years as a DS and several more as a DC I would imagine?'

She nodded, sipping her own drink.

'Have you ever come across anything like what we've seen over the last couple of days?' he continued.

Goddard shook her head. 'Never. I've read a little of your research into this stuff though. You say that SHC has been disproved as a cause of death, don't you?'

'Well, most historic cases of SHC are caused by, for want of a better phrase, the candle effect.'

When her face looked blank, he smiled. 'I'll elaborate'. She smiled back. What the hell was *wrong* with her? Why did this man affect her so much? She once again forced herself to listen to what he was saying rather than just how he was saying it.

'Think of a candle,' he said. 'It has wax on the outside, and the wick—the fuse if you like—on the inside. When you light the candle the wick burns slowly, melting the wax as it goes, right?'

Goddard nodded as his hands drew an imaginary candle in the air.

'Right,' he continued, his eagerness to explain now lighting his face with an almost childlike radiance. 'Now think of the human body as a candle, the difference being that it's inside out. The wick is now the victim's clothes, and the wax can be likened to the human fat contained within the body.'

He sipped his lager and then continued. 'In almost every case of supposed SHC, this has been found to be the cause of death.'

'How do you mean?' asked Goddard, leaning forward.

'I mean, in almost every recorded case there has been a natural source of ignition. An open fire, a gas mantle, a cooking ring. Even a good old-fashioned cigarette. The victim falls asleep or has a heart attack or something and this source of ignition catches their clothes. But instead of burning, it smoulders. Think back to the candle again, the clothes acting as a wick. The wick burns and the wax, the human fat, melts. A slow burn.'

Goddard tried to but in. 'But...'

Fenwick nodded. 'I know. Let me finish though. There's always pieces of the body left. Extremities, arms or legs, a bit like

Embleton's body. These are areas where there's less fat, and just like a candle, when the wick runs out of wax it stops burning and it stops quite quickly. Some of the pieces left almost look like they've been cut off with a knife.'

Fenwick drained his lager and asked if she wanted another drink. She shook her head, and he ordered another beer.

When he sat down, he started speaking again.

'There have been lots of theories over the years. The Victorians were very much into SHC. They believed it was a punishment from God, or that it was an imbalance in the forces within the body, the humours as the medieval quacks used to call them. They even believed that alcoholics were more inclined to die from SHC. They thought their bodies were so soaked in liquor that they caught fire *inside* the body and consumed the flesh. I don't know if you've ever read any Dickens, but in *Bleak House* Mr Crook bursts into flames and dies from his drinking habits.'

He paused again to take another sip of his beer, and Goddard copied him with her lemonade.

'There was also a theory of bacteria causing these fires. Just like when you have hay bales inexplicably bursting into flames, why not a human body? The problem with that gem though, is the reason hay bales sometimes do start to burn is all down to certain bacteria that doesn't exist in humans. This bacteria basically moves around, creating friction which can sometimes cause fires under the right circumstances. But like I said, that sort of bacteria doesn't exist in humans.'

Goddard sat straighter in her chair. 'So the clothes always burn with the body?'

'Always,' said Fenwick after a pause, almost to himself, and it seemed that his mind had suddenly shifted. It was not in the bar, it was somewhere in the recesses of his memories, somewhere that had nothing to do with his work in Newcastle.

He seemed to rouse himself and his eyes lost their faraway look.

'So,' he said eventually. 'If you take the two overruling factors in all these incidents, the candle effect and the fact that there are always extremities left, then you find that it just hasn't happened in these two cases.'

'But what about Embleton?' asked Goddard. 'His foot was left intact.'

Fenwick leant forward eagerly, nodding. 'That's the thing though. One foot. No arms, no legs, nothing. And there was nothing at all left of Anna Pont. Just ashes. And what about the clothes? Embleton was naked for Christ's sake. And he was in the bathroom. Where was the naked flame?'

'He smoked. Maybe he was having a fag in the bath?'

Fenwick sat back. 'Maybe,' he conceded, 'but the fact he was naked is a problem. Another problem is that in every case of SHC there are other signs of burning. Often, the initial reports say that nothing else in the area was affected, but this rarely turns out to be true. There are always signs of burning *under* where the body is found, and usually above it too, on the ceiling. Fires tend to burn in an upward V shape. There are also frequently deposits of fat left around the area where the body is found. On furniture, carpets etc. Any flat surface. There was nothing like that found around these two bodies.'

'So that's what you meant at the morgue when Joe Parker told you the body of Embleton was naked,' said Goddard. 'You said it was impossible.'

Fenwick nodded and slumped in the chair. 'The human body is made up of something like seventy-five percent water,' he said. 'You can't just ignite it and then douse a fire with the intensity that it reduces a corpse to ashes without it affecting something else in the house. *That's* what's impossible.'

He took another sip. 'It just doesn't make sense. Why here? Why now? Within six miles and three days, two people have died in exactly the same way. Cremated and doused in what seems like a millionth of a second. It must have been that fast for it not to have even scorched the clothes of Mrs Pont.' He shook his head once more. 'Fire is very unpredictable, I know that from experience, but this is something I've never come across before. It's a completely new way of death to me.'

Goddard looked at him, her eyes narrowing.

'Are you sure?' she asked.

He frowned. 'What do you mean?'.

Goddard seem to scrutinise him for a second longer and then she glanced pointedly at her watch and drained her drink. 'Nothing,' she said. 'Well, thank you for that information, Mr Fenwick.'

'Ian.'

She gave him a cool glance and then nodded. 'Ian,' she said. 'I'll probably see you tomorrow. Thanks for your time.'

He nodded dumbly, wondering what he had done wrong, and shook her hand again. It was small and soft in his. 'Good night then,' he said.

She smiled tightly and turned on her heel, leaving through the side door of the bar.

Fenwick sat down and finished his beer, staring at nothing. Then he limped to the lift and went up to his room, still wondering what he had done to cause the change in her attitude. Back in his room, he sat on the bed for a while and thought about his conversation with Goddard. She seemed to have been able to see right through him. Seemed to know what he was thinking. Eventually he got up and sat at the desk again. He slowly opened his laptop. He still had one more case he needed to go over. He didn't want to, but he knew he had to. He had to revisit the worst year of his life. He opened the file labelled *"Rachel Fenwick: 2008"*.

Chapter Five

She crept through the deserted street, keeping to the darkest areas; a shadow amongst the shadows, looking for somewhere to sleep. She needed a wash, too: her long dark hair was twisted and lank and her face was grimed with dirt. All the public toilets she had found were closed and the river was no good, it was far too open and public.

She eventually gave up trying to find a place to wash; maybe she could find somewhere tomorrow. What she really needed was somewhere to spend the night, to get some sleep if she could. She looked up at the clear sky. At least it was warm. She needed a back alley or something, somewhere out of the way, out of sight of prying eyes. Somewhere even out of reach of the other homeless unfortunates within the city.

She found what she was looking for about an hour later: an alleyway where the delivery entrance of a shop was deep enough to shelter her. She pulled out her stained sleeping bag and climbed inside.

She lit her last cigarette, using the empty packet as an improvised ashtray, and as she smoked her thoughts drifted. Even though she didn't want to, she thought about her parents, and she thought about Connor. Her little Connor. Why had they done that to him? He was only nine. Why had they been so cruel?

She remembered her mother's last, shrieking words to her as she had left the house. 'If you go to them Lou, don't think about coming back. Ever! You will never see your family again!'

She had been wrong about that, but Ellie hadn't seen them

again in the way she had wanted.

Connor had been standing beside his mother, his face bewildered; uncomprehending and unable to understand why his sister was leaving or where she was going. Her father had said nothing. He hadn't even come to the door. He had just sat in his armchair in the sitting room, his face hidden behind a trembling newspaper, silent apart from a few stifled sobs.

But she had gone, and her memory of that day was one of tears. Her father's hidden tears, her brother's uncomprehending tears, and her mother's terrified tears. It had been a house of tears.

They had picked her up at the bus stop and drove her to the house, the huge house. The lair. They told her again and again that everything was all right, that there was nothing to worry about. They told her that she was different from her parents, superior to them. That they hadn't wanted her to leave because they didn't, *couldn't* understand. And for a while, she had believed them.

In the months that followed they had showed her things. Things that should have been impossible. Things that *were* impossible for anyone without the abilities she and they shared. That she shared with some of them anyway. They had taught her, trained her to use her mind as an instrument. As a doctor used a scalpel to heal the sick, she would use her powers to heal the world. They would show her what she must do. It was only later that she found out what they really wanted to use her abilities for. The revelation both shocked and terrified her.

Once she had realised what they—what *he*—was intending to do with her and the others like her, she had escaped, running like a fox, running as far as possible from their grasp.

Ellie sat in the dirty shop doorway and began to cry silently, fat tears welling in her eyes and running down her cheeks. The tears made her look much younger than her seventeen years. She remembered returning to her parent's house in rural Suffolk, to beg their forgiveness, to plead with them to take her back. But it was not to be.

She had left a family home, a place where she had grown up

feeling safe and secure. A place of love. She had returned to a slaughterhouse.

Her mother was still inside the porch, as if she hadn't moved since Ellie had left. It should have been a heart-warming sight. But it wasn't.

The body was the first thing she came across when she recovered the door key from under the gnome in the garden where they always left it. Her mother had been beaten almost unrecognisable. Her bloated, fly-encrusted body lay in the darkened, blood splattered porch where it had been left to die. Her head was misshapen, flattened on one side, as if it had been stamped on again and again.

She stared at the ghastly tableau in front of her. Her mind could not really take in what her eyes were seeing. She swallowed once, twice, then the vomit was gushing from her, between and around the fingers she clamped to her mouth. Some of it splashed on her mother's corpse and she spun wildly to stop it from touching her anymore. The flies from the body settled eagerly on this fresh feast.

She stumbled backwards through the open door and, when she was back outside again, she fell to her knees on the lawn, her stomach heaving long after it had anything else to give up. She lay on the untended grass. Totally drained, totally uncomprehending, totally horrified.

How long she lay there she could not now remember. It was as if her mind purposefully kept the memories weak. As if it knew that if she remembered every detail of that awful day it would drive her mad.

She eventually staggered to her feet and went around the side of the house, wanting to go inside to see what she needed to see, but unable to step across the mutilated corpse of her mother. As if in a trance she walked to the back of the house and looked in through the patio doors.

In the sitting room was her father. He was bound by cable ties to his beloved armchair. They had ripped off his fingernails and his face showed the same beating as his mother had taken. They had even drilled into his kneecaps. She could see the crusty brown blood on his legs and the drill still lying beside his body. They had eventually stuffed his mouth with rags and pushed some of Connor's modelling clay into his nostrils, plugging them, leaving him to die from blood loss, suffocation and shock.

Ellie had run from the scene, her stomach rebelling once more but only a dry, retching sound escaping her, her insides already emptied.

She had escaped into the lovely back garden with its screening of elm trees that afforded so much privacy. And there she found Connor.

He was in the little play shed that stood at the back of the garden, in the shade where he like to sit. They had beaten him too, and the thought of what must have gone through his mind as that was happening to him caused an actual physical pain in her chest. His Down's syndrome manifested itself in a love for everyone he met. He loved to cuddle people. Even strangers got a cuddle when they came to Connor's house. What had he thought when they had started to hit him? Had he seen his parents tortured and killed? What were his last few minutes on this planet like?

As she stepped closer she saw the huge, dry gash on his wrist. They had beaten him, cut his wrist and left him to die. Alone. Or had they stayed to watch? Had they laughed at the poor, utterly hurt expression on his face as he started to fall asleep, as his blood pulsed in great arcs across the green lawn?

In the shop doorway, Ellie moaned and hugged herself, her tears now coming in huge, wracking sobs. The pain, the hurt, the loss, the *guilt* was too much for her and it was all she could do not to scream at the sky in her torment.

She had finally left. There was nothing else she could have done. Her family had been slaughtered to find out where she was. Of course, they hadn't known. They could never have known, but it seemed as if her pursuers did not care. They had decided to torture and murder them anyway. She had got as far away as she could and then made an anonymous phone call from a public phone booth, reporting the crime. At least they would give them a decent burial. Not that she could go. *They* would be there. To catch her and punish her for her crime of abandoning them.

Ellie wiped her eyes roughly with her sleeve and finished her cigarette. She could not weaken. She could not give in to the emotions. She had to keep them subjugated. She had to remain cold. This was the only way she could evade their presence. She knew the police were looking for her, either to make sure she was all right, or to perhaps charge her with the murders of her family: she wasn't sure which.

But it didn't really matter anyway, for *they* had caught up with her again. Or rather, she had stepped into their web. She could feel their presence now, their mental feelers stretching out, investigating, probing and exploring every part of the city. Every corner, every shadow. And they would not stop until they found her.

She set up her own block. They would not get her tonight. But what about tomorrow? The day after? Who could tell? After everything they had shown her, she didn't have the ability to look into the future.

She settled deeper into her sleeping bag and nodded gently off. She was still unnerved and grief stricken by the memories, but she was also exhausted. Her body craved sleep. The mental guard she had erected stood watch over her like a faithful, invisible dog; ever alert, ever vigilant.

Maybe tomorrow I'll die, she thought distractedly, but tonight I can sleep undisturbed. She gently closed her eyes.

Chapter Six

Gloucester, 1975

*Y*ou did it on purpose!'

The boy just stared back at his mother, not saying anything, not trying to explain what had happened. His dark eyes were brooding. He sat at the kitchen table not saying anything.

'How could you?' screamed his mother when he didn't answer. 'How could you be so cruel?'

The boy's father stood with them in the kitchen, but his back was to the scene. He was looking down at what lay in the sink. The windows were opened to let the smell out. Every now and then he would shake his head, he would just shake his head, staring down into the sink.

'Say something,' said the boy's mother. 'Tell me why you did it. How you could do it. Make me understand why this happened!'

The boy just kept staring at her. What could he say? That he didn't really know how it had happened? That the Visitors had told him to do it? That they needed him to do it? That they had explained it was the only way to help them? His mother would not understand. She was not like him. She and his father were ordinary. Not like the Visitors. Not like him.

His father eventually turned from the sink.

'I think you need to go away for a while, William,' he said. William's mother stared in shock at her husband but did not refute his words. She turned back to William, her eyes pained and misty. Uncomprehending. William hated her for her stupidity. Why couldn't

she understand? Why was she not like him?

'I've already spoken to the school,' his father continued. 'They know what's happened, and what's happened before. They know about you. They say they can help you.' His eyes flickered towards his wife at that point and William saw the tiny, almost imperceptible nod in his father's direction. They had given up on him. Like all his "parents" gave up on him eventually. Like everyone gave up on him. Everyone except the Visitors. They were his only friends.

'You will be going this afternoon,' said his father. 'I will drive you.'

For the first time, William spoke. His voice was flat. 'How long must I go for?'

His father turned away and was silent for a long while. William turned to his mother, but she just stood and cried silently. She turned away from William and went to stand beside her husband, slipping an arm around his waist as his shoulders shook.

After a while, his father straightened and wiped a sleeve across his eyes. He turned towards William. His eyes held nothing but confusion. Confusion and fear.

'Before you go, you will make at least one thing right. You will bury Tigger.'

With that he collected a spade from the porch and returned, handing it to William who stood now, silent again.

His father reached into the sink and William heard the crackling of the black plastic bin bag as his father lifted the dead cat, mercifully hidden by the bag, from the sink. No one in the kitchen wanted to see that corpse again. It had been burned alive. Burned beyond recognition. A charred lump of matter and charcoaled fur that his father now took out into the garden. William followed, holding the spade. His face was expressionless.

*

Fenwick phoned Curtis to let him know of the latest developments. It wouldn't take long.

He doodled absently on a piece of paper as he listened to the distant ringing on the end of the line, collecting everything he had about the two deaths in his head for his report back to his partner.

But he really didn't have much to say. How could he explain why two people had suddenly, inexplicably burst into flames and been reduced to nothing but ashes?

He shook his head. He had gone over Rachel's file again, as hard as that had been. Her case was the only one he knew about that was remotely similar to what had happened to Ted Embleton and Anna Pont, but even then there were huge differences.

Fenwick remembered again back to that night ten years ago. The body of his wife was lying beside the stove in the sitting room. Her torso was gone, completely consumed, and he had stared in uncomprehending horror at what was left of her.

Her arms and legs were spread-eagled on the floor, the charred and stiff remains of her jeans still attached to her legs. Her torso was just ashes and clumps of cinder. And her head… Christ, her head.

Fenwick swallowed hard as he fought the memories, but he couldn't help *but* remember. Re-reading Rachel's file had been one of the hardest things he had ever done, but he knew he'd had to do it.

Rachel's arms and legs were all that was remotely recognisable. In a daze he had bent down and stared at the wedding ring on her hand, the hand untouched by the inferno that had consumed her. The hand he had held in his so many times.

He suddenly sat straighter on the bed. Time to stop. He was trying to be objective, but it was bloody hard. Rachel's death had been explained. She had collapsed, or passed out—the empty wine bottles lying around the house may have explained this, again causing guilt to sweep through his body—and somehow her clothes had caught fire, causing her death. It was unusual, yes, but not unexplained. Rachel's extremities had survived, backing up the theory of the slow burn, but even then—even before he had become so knowledgeable on SHC—Fenwick had known there was something odd about it. There was no sign of fire damage beneath her body for a start, or on the ceiling, or anywhere else in the room. It looked like her body had simply burst into flames and she had died without the fire burning anything else.

Once more, Fenwick purposefully pushed the thoughts aside. But still… It was that smell. It was similar to when he was a boy, playing with his Scalextric set. The smell of a hot transformer. An electric, *metallic* smell, mixed with the sweet, sickening odour of a burned body.

And *this*, along with the absence of any other fire damage, was what made Rachel's death and the deaths of the two people in Newcastle similar. Not exactly the same, but similar. And Rachel had died in Durham, relatively close to Newcastle.

Fenwick thought back to the week before. To his conversation with Goddard at the hotel bar. She had *known* he had hidden something from her. That was why her attitude had changed slightly. In the days that followed he had hardly seen her, both of them working on different aspects of the cases, but when they had met she seemed to be more distant than she had been in the first couple of days of their acquaintance, a little cool. He wondered why he was bothered about this so much.

His attention was brought back to the present when Curtis eventually answered the phone.

'Hi, Ian, how are things "up North"?' Here he affected a terrible pastiche of a Geordie accent.

'Same as they always were,' replied Fenwick. 'Horrible. I'm ringing to give you an update on the emails I've sent.'

'Go on then.'

'There is no update.'

'You've been up there a week and you have nothing?' asked Curtis. 'No idea on the cause of the fires?'

Fenwick settled himself more comfortably on his bed, his thigh and lower back aching.

'I've never seen anything like this, Bill,' he said. 'Whatever caused these deaths is something new to me, and from what I've been researching it will be new to everyone. I simply have no idea what happened to these people.'

There was a slight crackling on the line as Bill moved position in his office.

'That's a shame,' he said, 'I thought it might be good to "crack the case", as it were. Is there any point of you staying there then?'

'Not really,' replied Fenwick, for some reason thinking again of Laura Goddard. 'I've got a report to write for the police up here then I think I'll just come home. Should be on my way by tomorrow.'

'Okay,' said Curtis, 'Well, get it wrapped up and get your arse back to where it belongs. I'll talk to you either tomorrow or the day after. See you soon.'

With that Curtis rang off and Fenwick put his phone down. He stared at his laptop for a few seconds and then sat down in front of it. Better get this report finished and given to the police. Then he could leave Newcastle. Hopefully for good.

*

Laura Goddard slipped off her shoes and curled her legs under her on the settee, pouring herself a glass of wine. She picked up the paperback she was halfway through and settled down to read. She had been at the book for months but work kept getting in the way, spoiling it for her.

She read for about ten minutes and then put the book down with an almost angry slam, taking a sip of wine. It was no good, her mind was wandering too much and she kept reading the same line over and over again. Her brain wouldn't concentrate on the text. She was thinking about the unexplained deaths of Ted Embleton and Anna Pont. About what the hell could have caused them. And about the man she had insisted be brought in to help with the investigations.

It was over a week since Anna Pont had died. A week in which she and Parker had tried to work out just what had happened in those houses, what had happened to those people. She had read as much as she could on the subject of SHC and was now coming to the same conclusion as Fenwick seemed to have come to a week ago. That whatever had happened to those people, it was not this so-called phenomenon. There were too many differences between the two deaths in Newcastle and all the other deaths caused by what Fenwick called the "slow burn" theory.

She thought back to her conversation with Fenwick in the hotel bar. And about what she had uncovered when she had really started looking into his past.

It was no wonder he had been so secretive. Goddard had found out about his wife, Rachel, about why Fenwick had become the expert he was on SHC. She had also found out more about the accident that had almost cost him his leg, coming only a few months after his wife had died. That, before the floor in that warehouse had given way, before he'd fallen to what should have been his death, he had saved the life of the other firefighter with him. She had also found out what had happened to the other man.

She shook her head. *This is stupid,* she told herself. *You're thirty-four years old, a police officer, and you're acting like a fifteen-year-old girl with a crush on her teacher.* When she had found out about Fenwick's past, when she realised how it must have affected him, she had wanted to talk to him in private, to tell him how sorry she was for his loss. To comfort him. But she reasoned that it wasn't her place to do that. And anyway, Fenwick's wife's death had been explained so it didn't have any impact on the current investigations. She'd died because of external forces, most likely a spark from the wood burning fire in her house. Her death was not like the deaths of the two people in Newcastle, although some aspects did seem similar.

So Goddard had decided to just keep her distance from him. He had obviously not got over what had happened ten years ago. He still seemed mixed up and she could do without getting involved with anything like *that* again.

Her thoughts then turned to Matt, the man she was once going to marry, trying not to make a comparison between the two men but failing miserably.

Both were about the same height and they both had the same dark hair. But that really was where the similarities ended. Whereas Matt had virtually throbbed with a suppressed, nervous energy, Fenwick had a slow, measured, almost lazy manner.

She'd met Matt when they were both coppers on the beat. They had been partnered up and of course they had shared some hairy moments. Their reliance on each other soon manifested itself in an affair that was torrid and exciting at first, turning slowly into a genuine love for each other, and then finally, in the last few months, into a rancid, drunken mess.

Matt had stayed in uniform while Goddard had progressed into CID and moved from detective constable to detective sergeant, and it was then that the cracks in the relationship started to appear. Matt couldn't really deal with the fact that she now outranked him and his comments when she got home from work rapidly moved from the sarcastic to the downright nasty. She couldn't understand where all the vitriol came from. She thought they would be together forever. She was in love. Why couldn't he be happy with the way her career was going?

Goddard sighed and took another sip of wine, staring into space. The last month or so of their relationship had been awful, culminating in her discovery of Matt's affair with another, younger PC. The discovery had almost been a relief.

She got up and moved across to the dresser in the small living room, staring at it for a while before opening a drawer and picking up the engagement ring she'd thrown at him when she had found out. As she stared at it she noticed, not for the first time, how tiny the diamond was. It seemed their love had been small even then.

She shook her head and tossed the ring back into the drawer, closing it and moving back to the settee. All that had happened four years ago, and she had moved away from south east Northumberland and into the city itself. She hadn't seen Matt since and there had been no one else in those four years. She'd been out on the odd internet date but they had been so painful, and sometimes so downright embarrassing, that she soon stopped and closed her accounts. She'd decided that if something was going to happen, it would happen in its own time.

Her thoughts returned to Fenwick. She remembered the evening they had spent together at the hotel bar and smiled. He had seemed almost shy in her presence, and she could still remember the look of embarrassment on his face when he saw her watching him limp across towards her. This shyness surprised her for, although he wasn't the world's best-looking man, he certainly wasn't unattractive. But having discovered a little more about his past the quietness seemed to make sense. She knew he lived alone but she didn't know if he was seeing anyone. She decided, however, that she wasn't going to try and find out. She could do without getting involved with any sort of damaged goods again.

She sat back down on the settee, picked up her book, and stared at it.

*

DI Joe Parker sat at his kitchen table, a cup of coffee at his elbow and various reports and files laid out in front of him. He sighed again—he had been sighing a lot in the last couple of hours—and took a sip of the now cold coffee.

He was defeated. He simply could not work out what had happened to these people. He had never come across anything like this before. He hated unsolved cases but that was where these ones were going, he was sure of it. He had very few of them to his name. He liked to think he was a good detective—which he was—but these deaths had him stumped. He didn't even know whether or not they warranted his time. Maybe they had been caused by some sort of weird natural event, the fact that they'd occurred so close together in time and geography just a coincidence.

He got up and poured the cold coffee down the sink, flicking on the kettle to make a fresh brew. Denise was asleep in bed and of course the kids had left home long ago. The house was quiet and still.

For some reason his thoughts kept going back in time, to when he was a young DS with old Steve Roe as his DI. They had investigated some weird shit together that was for sure. That stuff at the ice rink in Whitley Bay, nearly thirty years ago now; the killings, the suicides, the grinning faces of the perpetrators…

He shook his head again. That had been murder though. Regardless of why it had happened or how strange it had been, that had been murder. This stuff though, he thought, returning to the table with his fresh coffee and staring at the reports and photographs. He didn't even know what this was. It was just bizarre.

He continued to stare at the bumf in front of him, his fresh coffee going cold.

*

Fenwick finished his report and re-scanned it briefly before closing down the laptop.

He got up and stretched his back, grimacing as he did so. Sometimes his back hurt more than his leg. The difference in the lengths of his thighs caused his hips to be slightly out of level, giving him a dull ache in his lower back if he sat still for too long. Or if he stood up for too long. Or if he walked for too long. Or sometimes for no bloody reason at all. He limped barefooted around the room, trying to ease both his back and thigh and thought about the investigation. And about the young DS who had been avoiding him for the last few days.

He walked into the bathroom and turned on the shower, climbing in and giving himself a good hosing down. Then he shaved and when he was finished he stared at his reflection in the mirror for a long time, noting how time was taking its toll on him. Time and experience.

What the hell had he been entertaining? Laura Goddard was an attractive woman and when they first met she had seemed interested in him, but that had soon disappeared after their meeting in the bar. He couldn't blame her. As he stared at his face in the mirror, he really could not understand how anyone would find anything remotely interesting about it. It was just ordinary. And it was starting to look old.

He flapped a dismissive hand at his reflection and turned away. He had already packed his small case and the room was bare apart from his wash bag that he left in the bathroom for the following morning, and the laptop that he now packed away too. Then he climbed into bed. He turned off the light and stared at the darkness of the ceiling.

*

Eric McGuiness was a man alone, but never a lonely man. He lived alone, he worked alone and, when the mood took him, he drank alone. When he returned from his job as a night security guard at one of the various factory warehouses scattered around the outskirts of Newcastle, he would read the newspaper, have his breakfast—always bacon and eggs, Eric had no patience with low fat diets, as his wide girth signified—and watch some daytime TV. Then he would go to bed where he would remain until six. When he woke he would have his tea—sausage and mash—have a shower and then set off to work. He had lived his life this way for over fifteen years now, ever since that hellbitch hag of a wife had left him. He liked his life and saw no reason for it not to continue in this way until he retired. Sadly, on this assumption he was wrong.

At midnight he finished his cigarette, snapped off the radio and stepped outside the glass guardhouse that was his castle and his domain. He hitched up his trousers and set off on his rounds, thanking God, the devil, and anyone else who might be listening that it wasn't raining. It seemed the warm weather was showing no signs of disappearing just yet.

As he walked, he whistled tunelessly to himself, wondering which dog he should put his money on at the weekend. Greyhound racing was his one real passion and he thought he might be able to make a few quid if he chose carefully. Over the years he had come to know some of the trainers and they sometimes gave him a heads up on the likely winners of each race. It was almost as if between them, they already knew. Eric smiled to himself. He continued on his rounds in this way, totally oblivious to the fact that within five minutes he would be dead.

He was sweating slightly as he walked. It had been warm all day, and even though the coming of the night had cooled the air down slightly he could still feel sweat under his arms and on his back, making his shirt sticky.

Funny, he thought to himself as he peered into a dark corner, his torch cutting a swathe of light in front of him. You never know where you are with the weather these days. One minute it's freezing your balls off, the next its red hot. This sent him off on another train of thought about how the weather had changed since he was young. You could rely on it then. Cold in January, rainy in April, warm and sunny in June and July. Not like today. Global warming, that's what it was. The bloody politicians had buggered up the planet. People were shooting off atoms left right and centre, burning off the ozone layer, stripping away the atmosphere. It wouldn't have been so bad, but the stuff that got pushed up into the sky didn't do any good. All those aerosols and chemicals. All they were used for was to make young girls look even sluttier, and young lads look like girls. The time it must take for some of them to do their hair! Bloody idiots.

Eric continued on his round, still half thinking, half talking to himself. After all this time alone he could actually hold real conversations with himself and he used this skill to keep him company.

It continued to get progressively warmer until it got to the point where he had to take off his short uniform jacket. He was starting to worry about his heart now, as it was beating loudly in his chest. His father had died from a heart attack and Eric had heard it was hereditary. He knew he didn't keep himself in shape either. Was this what it was like? He certainly didn't feel right. His legs were trembling and beginning to ache too. They throbbed and weakened with every step until he found he could walk no further.

He managed to stagger to a nearby bin and sat down heavily, trying to regulate his breathing and at the same time rubbing his legs, which by now felt that all circulation had stopped. He was sweating so much that his thick shirt was plastered to his chest and back and the sweat was running freely down the inside of his arms. His crotch was burning and his eyes stung as salt ran into them, creating false tears that ran down his face and dripped from the end of his nose and chin onto his already soaking chest and lap.

Twenty yards to Eric's left, where the shadows were darkest, waited a young man called Callum Cook. He had sneaked into the yard an hour earlier, just as Eric had finished his previous round. His plan, such as it was, was to belt the ageing security guard and steal the keys that hung from his belt. One of those keys opened a side door into an office block where Callum knew a regular Aladdin's cave of office equipment lay, ready and waiting for the taking. He already had a buyer who would have them off his hands in less than two hours, and a stolen Transit van stood just around the corner to transport his haul. He could be in, out and away in ten minutes. He was very quick and very seasoned, even at his young age.

A daydream overtook him for a second. It was a familiar one of him moving away to some unknown sunny beach somewhere, with a tall beer in one hand and a dark-skinned beauty in the other. The fantasy was made up from the films he had seen rather than any experience of foreign beaches, however. Callum had never been out of Newcastle. The fact he would barely clear £500 for the equipment he was about to take did not get in the way of his fantasy.

The dream started to fracture as he saw Eric sit down on a bin opposite him and begin to rub his legs.

He stared in disbelief. *Come on you old bastard,* he thought, savagely. *Get your fucking arse over here. What the fuck's wrong with you? You having a heart attack or something?* Then a thought slipped slowly into his feral—and to be honest, not very bright—young mind. Maybe that was it. Maybe the old fucker *was* going to have a heart attack or something. He couldn't be sure for it was very dark, but the man seemed to be sweating profusely. He was certainly panting for breath, because Callum could hear him.

Yeah, that was it. He was going to have a heart attack, maybe even snuff it. A wicked little smile spread across the boy's lips and lit up his dead eyes. All he had to do was wait around for a bit then he would have as long as he needed to get the stuff onto the van. More time meant more gear. More gear meant more money. His beach dream wobbled its way back into his little brain again.

He was still thinking about the girl on his arm by the lounger when Eric suddenly erupted in a hissing, gurgling blue-white flash, the unearthly light searing across Callum's vision, bathing the whole yard in electric blue for the briefest of moments. Eric's clothes dropped limply to the bin and to the ground in front of it and a noise like someone dumping a bucket of sand on the floor sounded loud in the black darkness after the flash, as his dark, gritty remains fell to the concrete and spilled around the scene.

Callum's mouth was stretched wide, his eyes burning with the after-vision of the intense light. He had instinctively closed his eyes, but he could see the image of the security guard burned into his retinas, bent double, that intense blue-white light blasting from him.

He instantly forgot about the beach and the girl and the gear in the office, and even about the stolen van just around the corner. He forgot about everything in fact, except his desperation to run from the horrific scene he had just witnessed, and the awful, oily, metallic smell that wafted towards him on the warm breeze from the direction of where Eric McGuiness had sat a second earlier. And run he did, stumbling as his blurred vision slowly returned. Out through the hole in the fence he had cut only a little while before, out into the darkness.

Chapter Seven

Fenwick was woken up by his phone ringing, barely three hours after he went to bed. Automatically glancing at his watch he saw it was just after 3am. The earliness of the call shocked him into wakefulness.

'Hello?'

'Ian, it's me. Laura.'

Fenwick struggled upright. 'Are you okay?' he asked. 'What's wrong?'

'There's been another one,' said Goddard. 'Joe's just phoned me. A security guard at a warehouse in Byker. Apparently just like the other two.'

'You're joking,' said Fenwick. 'Are you sure it's the same?'

'As far as I know, yes,' replied the DS. 'Your hotel's on the way. Do you want me to pick you up?'

Fenwick hesitated. He had a perfectly good car parked in the hotel's underground carpark. There was no reason for her to pick him up.

'Absolutely,' he said. 'I'll be ready in five minutes.'

'I'll be there by then,' she replied, 'I'm already on my way. Oh, and by the way. This one's got a witness.'

The phone went dead and Fenwick stared at it for a second, then he jumped out of bed and quickly dressed.

She was as good as her word and was waiting outside when he got downstairs. He climbed in beside her and she took off, driving skilfully through the almost deserted streets.

She was on her hands-free when Fenwick got into the car, and was obviously talking to Parker. 'Yes, I know, I'm on my way now. Just picking Ian Fenwick up.'

'What the fuck for?' came Parker's voice through the speakers.

'Boss,' she started, but Parker interrupted her.

'He's been no fucking use so far. I need you here. I don't need him.'

'We're on speakers, boss,' she managed to get in, giving Fenwick an embarrassed glance. 'He's just heard every word you've said.'

There was a long silence on the other end as Parker took in this information. They heard a muffled 'Bollocks' then the DI continued, 'Well as you're on your way you might as well see what you can come up with. I'll talk to you both soon.' He rang off.

Goddard breathed out deeply through her nose. 'Sorry about that,' she said. 'I don't think he appreciates the work you've put into this.'

'Don't worry,' replied Fenwick with a rueful grin. 'He's right, I haven't been much use really.'

By this time they were outside the police station. They went straight into the little office that Fenwick had waited in when he had first arrived in Newcastle. Parker was already there.

'We've got the witness in one of the interview rooms,' he said. 'Uniform picked him up for being drunk and disorderly. They said he was ranting on about flashing lights and clothes falling to the ground and God knows what else.'

'Is he drunk?' asked Goddard.

'Doesn't seem to be. It's Callum Cook by the way.'

'God, that little scrote,' muttered Goddard. Fenwick raised an eyebrow.

'Local scumbag,' she explained. 'He's been in and out of trouble since he was about nine. Burglary mostly.'

Fenwick nodded. 'And he saw what happened to the security guard?' he asked Parker.

'So he says,' replied the DI. 'Come on, I was just about to go down and talk to him now before we go to the warehouse. I sent a patrol and they confirmed what Cook said. A pile of clothes and a load of ashes. Forensics are on their way there now.'

He led them from the office and along a corridor to a set of interview rooms. He opened a door and entered without knocking.

A young man was sitting at the desk upon which a tape machine stood. He had a thin, pockmarked face and wore a baseball cap perched high on the back of his head. He was wearing a white t-shirt under a check shirt several sizes too big for him. He glared at the three of them with a hatred only the terminally self-centred can achieve.

'Where's me lawyer?' he asked.

'You can't afford a lawyer,' said Parker, sitting himself down at the other side of the table from Cook. 'We'll get one sorted for you but it'll be a while. You going to talk now?'

'What's the time?' asked Cook ignoring the question. 'You can't keep me here more than twenty-four hours, you know. I've seen it on the telly. You have to release me after that.' He grinned at Parker, showing crooked, discoloured teeth.

'Or arrest you,' replied Parker, not smiling back.

Cook scoffed and turned to stare at the wall, ignoring the other people in the room for a second. He shook his head slightly as if a huge injustice had been put upon him. 'Aww, here man,' he said softly.

'It's nearly four in the morning,' Parker continued, 'and if you want to get any sleep at all tonight, you're going to have to answer some questions.'

'Who's this?' asked Cook, turning from the wall and glaring at Fenwick. 'Never seen him before.' He then turned to Goddard and grinned again lasciviously. 'I know you though.' He pursed his lips and blew a kiss at the DS, who just raised her eyebrows.

'This is Mr Fenwick,' continued Parker, ignoring the bravado. 'I want you to tell us everything you remember about what happened to that security guard.'

'It wasn't anything to do with me,' started Cook, 'I was just walking past the warehouse.' The words in the thick Geordie accent came out as 'It wasn't nowt to dee wi' me, a was just waakin' past the warehoose.'

Fenwick, getting annoyed at Cook's attitude, stepped forward and leaned across the table. The boy pulled back slightly at the look on his face.

'Why don't you just tell us everything you saw,' he said, menacingly.

Parker turned in his seat and stared up at Fenwick until the other man stepped back. The DI turned back to Cook.

'Before you do, I have to inform you that we've found the cutters used to get into the warehouse grounds plus a stolen Transit van parked outside. Both are being dusted for prints as we speak. Whose prints do you think we'll find on those, Callum?'

Cook just stared back, not smiling now.

'I didn't actually take anything you know,' he said defensively.

Goddard then spoke. 'Then you've got nothing to worry about have you. All right,' she continued when he remained silent, letting the meaning of these words filter through his bird brain. 'From the top. Everything you remember.'

Cook sat a little straighter in the plastic seat, seemingly pleased to have so much attention. He looked like he was warming up for the *Jeremy Kyle Show*. 'I got to the warehouse at about quarter past eleven,' he started. 'I wanted it to be properly dark. I got through the fence and found a place to wait.

'At about twelve I heard him coming around, muttering away to himself. He was coming straight for me, but he sat down on a bin about ten feet away. He was rubbing his legs, like they were aching or something, and he was, like, panting. He'd taken his jacket off by this time...'

'He took off his jacket?' interrupted Fenwick. 'Like he was hot?'

'Aye,' said Cook, looking peeved that he had been broken off in mid flow. Fenwick indicated for him to continue.

'Anyway, he was rubbing his legs, like I said, and then...whuff! Up he goes in this blue flash.'

'He started burning?' asked Fenwick.

'Nah, it was as if he, I dunno, like he exploded or something.

He didn't burn. I didn't see any fire. It was just a big flash of light then he…he was gone. Just his clothes left.'

Fenwick looked at Goddard and then Parker in turn, his face confused.

'It wasn't nowt to dee wi' me,' Cook reiterated into the silence.

Goddard turned back to him. 'Again,' she ordered.

It was after five in the morning when they left the police station to go to the warehouse. They were in Goddard's car and Fenwick was relegated to the back seat this time. They reached the warehouse and ducked under the taped off entrance, making their way around the forensics teams who looked like they were just about finished in the vast, empty area now. The sun was already up, and long shadows formed from the chain link fence laced delicately across the yard. It seemed another unseasonably hot day was in store for the city.

Under the directions of a constable they soon found themselves standing in front of the remains of Eric McGuiness. Fenwick was surprised to see the pathologist, Ross, there, making notes and taking samples.

'I asked Mr Ross to come down to have a look at the body, in-situ as it were,' said Parker to his companions, then he turned to the pathologist. 'Same as the others?' he asked, and Ross nodded.

'It certainly seems to be,' he replied, and again Fenwick heard that slight accent in his voice. 'Same cremated remains, clothes untouched. It looks like he just went up in a blue flash.'

Fenwick looked at him then, a slight frown on his face.

They were still standing there when Goddard's radio crackled, and she turned away slightly to answer it. When she turned back her face was alive with excitement.

'That was one of the lads in the guard's cubicle,' she said. 'The monitors are all in there. Apparently it's been caught on tape.'

Parker stared at her for a second before a slight smile emerged on his face.

'Right, well let's see what happened.' He marched off to find the guard room.

*

By nine that morning the trio had seen the CCTV footage numerous times. They were back at the station by this time and were huddled around a monitor, watching it again. The fuzzy black and white image showed Eric moving silently around the yard of the warehouse in small, jerky, time freeze movements. They watched as he sat on the bin. The next frame showed nothing but a milky screen, apparently when his body had disappeared and the frame after that showed his clothes lying on the bin and on the floor. It also showed Cook scarpering from the scene. It wasn't really very clear, and Parker had already got onto technical support to try and clean it up as best they could.

Fifteen minutes later, they were back in Parker's office, sipping coffee around the table.

'Well, what *could* have caused it?' asked Parker for the thousandth time, staring at Fenwick.

Fenwick sipped his own coffee and shook his head.

'I've told you; I don't know. Whatever happened to Eric McGuiness is beyond my comprehension. I'm an expert on fire. Whatever that was, it wasn't fire.'

'But the body was cremated,' said Goddard. She was frowning across at Fenwick. 'So "fire" is the only word we've got at the minute.'

Fenwick gazed at her for a while. He just shrugged, and Parker suddenly sat up straighter, seeming to come to a decision.

'Right, well as you've said, whatever happened to the three victims was not burning. We seem to be in agreement that, whatever it is, it's not fire related. Therefore I can't really see how your help in this matter can be justified any longer.'

He stood, Fenwick copying him mutely. Parker held out his hand. 'Thank you for your assistance,' he said. 'If we need anything else we'll be in touch.'

Fenwick nodded at the cursory dismissal. He'd had a feeling

this was coming and could not really blame the DI for wanting him out of his hair. They shook hands.

'Well,' he said, turning to Goddard now. 'I'm sorry I couldn't have been more help. I hope you find out quickly what happened to these people. Please let me know if you need anything else.'

Goddard stood too and turned to Parker. 'Don't you think Mr Fenwick should stay a little longer, boss?' she asked. 'He's the only one who has any sort of previous experience of anything remotely like this.' Her eyes flickered to Fenwick who frowned.

'What do you mean: "previous experience"?' asked Parker. He turned to Fenwick. 'I thought you said you'd never seen anything like this before?'

Fenwick was still staring at Goddard, his face darkening. 'Been digging?' he asked.

Goddard held his gaze. Parker stared at the two of them, perplexed, waiting for an answer, but it was as if he had ceased to exist in the room.

Goddard sighed. 'I researched what happened to your wife, Ian,' she said softly. 'I'm sorry but I thought there were *some* similarities between her death and the deaths we've had here. And so do you. I know it must be very painful but anything similar has to be investigated thoroughly. You do understand, don't you?'

'Wife?' asked Parker, mystified. They both ignored him.

'I understand something now,' said Fenwick, picking his suit jacket from the back of the chair he had been sitting on. 'Never trust the bloody police.' With that he opened the door of the office and was gone.

Parker turned to Goddard, whose gaze was still on the open door.

'Do you mind telling me…?' he started.

But Goddard just ignored him and followed Fenwick out of the door. Parker picked up his coffee and sipped it, staring at the wall. 'Fucking hell,' he muttered.

Goddard caught up with Fenwick just as he was about to leave the building. She grabbed his arm. 'Wait, Ian, please. I'm not trying to drag up what must be horrible memories for you, but I need every scrap of information I can get to find out what happened to these people.'

'Rachel died from burns,' said Fenwick angrily, pointedly removing her hand from his arm. 'She was burned to death. Nothing like what we've just seen in there.' He nodded to the office door where Parker now stood, leaning on the door frame and observing them with his coffee in his hand.

'But nothing else in her house was burned,' replied Goddard. 'As you said about every other supposed case of SHC, there are other things near the body that are burned. That didn't happen with Rachel, did it?'

Fenwick stared out the glass doors of the exit, as if making to leave. He suddenly sighed and rubbed his chin, shaking his head as he turned back to the DS.

'They're not the same,' he said finally. 'Believe me, if I thought there was anything that Rachel's death could tell us about these occurrences, I would have told you. I've been through her file again just to make sure, but her body was burned as I said. Her clothes were burned. There are some similarities, but not enough for anyone to go poking their noses into.' He glared at Goddard, his anger rising again.

'No fire damage elsewhere,' repeated Goddard, ignoring his resentment.

Fenwick stared at her for a long time, then nodded.

'And the smell,' he said, almost to himself.

'The smell? What do you mean?'

'I've seen a lot of burned bodies, DS Goddard,' he said, and the formality of his use of her name was not lost on her. 'But the three bodies we've come across have a smell to them that I've only come across once before. And that was with Rachel.'

Goddard stared at him. 'And you didn't think to mention this?' she asked, growing angry herself, her voice rising.

'And what would you have done with that information?' asked Fenwick sarcastically. 'Cracked the case because the fireman says the bodies smell funny? I didn't mention it because it's not important. Rachel's death was investigated thoroughly. No accelerants of any kind were discovered, if that's what you're thinking. As I have said: what happened to Rachel is *not* the same as what's happened to these other people.'

'No,' Goddard shot back at him. 'But it's similar. It's the *only* similar case we know about. And *you* should have told me.' She poked a finger at his chest. She was almost shouting now, her attitude causing Fenwick to raise his own voice.

'Why the hell should I tell *you* anything?'

'Because you need to talk to someone about it!' she screamed back at him.

Fenwick's mouth clamped shut in surprise at the passion in her voice, the same surprise that was suddenly in the green eyes of Goddard. It was as if she was as mystified by her own words as he was.

She turned when there was a cheer and applause behind her. Unbeknown to her and Fenwick a small crowd of coppers had gathered near Parker, lured out of various offices by the raised voices, and they were watching the exchange with cheery interest.

By the time she turned back to Fenwick, he was gone. She watched him through the glass doors, limping away down the street, pulling on his jacket as he went.

She turned slowly back and made for the office again through the dispersing crowd of onlookers, her face reddening. Tony Harris, another DS, smiled at her.

'Laura's got a boyfriend,' he sang mockingly.

'Oh, fuck off, Tony!' she shouted, slamming the office door behind her.

*

The young couple wandered down the street slowly, silently.

'What do you mean, you're late?' asked Reece, eventually. 'How late?'

'Three weeks,' came the despondent reply. 'Three bloody weeks.'

They walked along the bright sunlit street for a few minutes more in silence. Reece took out a cigarette and lit it with shaking hands.

'Christ, Jen. What's your mam and dad going to say?'

Jenny didn't reply and they walked on for a few more yards, turning into Northumberland Street. The bright lights of the shops on each side of the wide boulevard were ignored by both of them. Reece's mind was spinning with the news. He knew what her parents would say. They would be furious. They'd never liked him; he'd got that impression on the first day Jen had brought him home. On that first occasion, her father had taken him to one side in the kitchen while Jen was changing upstairs and had stood towering over him. He said, quietly, 'If you do anything to hurt my daughter, it will be the last thing you ever do. Do we understand each other?'

He had stared down at Reece until the boy had managed to nod, then he'd moved across to the kettle. 'Tea?' he had asked pleasantly. He was a part time bouncer at one of the local nightclubs and he was built like a tank. He would beat Reece to a bloody pulp. *Jesus Christ*, he thought.

Jenny and Reece had been seeing each other for nearly six months now, and it had been great up until that point. They went out for drinks, had a bit of a snog round the back of the local pub, nothing serious really. He had tried to get into her knickers of course, but she'd always held back, stopping him just when he was getting warmed up. He had been toying with the idea of dumping her; he was getting sick of going home from a night out with an aching in his loins and his balls as hard as marbles. Then, suddenly: bingo. One night, she had taken him back to her house, telling him her parents were out all night. She had sat him down on the couch, handed him a condom and, well. Bob's your uncle.

Just about every night since, whenever they could be alone, they'd been banging away like rabbits till the early hours. He was getting used to running for taxis, paying through the nose, sneaking into his house so he wouldn't wake his own parents.

And now this. He should have taken more precautions, should have taken more notice of what it said on the side of the packet, but fucking hell, this wasn't fair! What had he done to deserve this? Seventeen years old and about to become a father!

He glanced across at Jen's miserable face. It wasn't even as if she was that nice looking. Decent pair of tits, pretty in a plain sort of way. All right for a while, for a shot off or two. But not this. Not fucking this. *Christ, her dad is massive,* he thought again. *I'll not live to see my eighteenth.*

Jenny stopped outside a shop and gazed in the window, and Reece leaned heavily on the glass, his thoughts in turmoil. He slowly realised that the shop was a jeweller's and as he glanced at what she was staring at, his heart missed a beat. Engagement rings! She was looking at fucking engagement rings!

'Bollocks to that!' he said, and Jenny looked at him.

'What else do you expect?' she asked, and Reece was sure there was a smirk on her face.

'Get rid of it,' he told her. 'Get an abortion. Christ almighty, do what you want, but I've had it. I'm off.'

He turned to leave, but she grabbed his arm. 'Don't you run away from me! You got me into this mess, and you can fucking well get me out of it!'

'Oh aye? Well how do I know it's mine, eh?' Reece nodded to himself, grasping at anything that would get him out of this nightmare. 'It's not mine, it's somebody else's. You've been slagging it off with somebody else!'

Reece knew this was virtually impossible. They had spent nearly every minute of the last six months together. But he was young, he was desperate, and he was frightened.

Jenny raised her hand to slap him in the face, just as a tall, dishevelled man with dark hair limped past them, his face troubled.

Then Jenny erupted into an incandescent light, the flash flowing outwards and upwards. The sparks from the remains of her hand caressed the cheek of Reece. He had a split second of total horror as he watched the girl in front of him die, then his own body was engulfed by the consuming heat and light, instantly igniting in the same fashion. Their clothes and the gritty remains of their bodies settled to the ground, their ashes mixed on the grimy pavement. They died together. All three of them. The boy, the girl and their unborn child.

*

Fenwick was right beside the couple when they died. He had been limping along as fast as he could, thinking about the argument with Goddard. He had calmed down a bit by then and his mood was pensive.

She was right. He *should* have told her earlier about the similarities between Rachel's death and the three here in Newcastle. But he still believed that was all they were: similarities. The differences were bigger. As he had told the DS, Rachel's body had burned, it hadn't been disintegrated like the security guard and the other two. His research since her death had proved that. The events that had occurred in Newcastle were something he simply could not understand.

He shook his head as he walked. Nothing to do with him anyway. He wasn't needed anymore by the police. Parker had made it more than clear he didn't want him around, and that was fine with Fenwick. He was sure that some sort of logical conclusion could be brought about—what that conclusion would be he couldn't imagine—and maybe the police were better off without him. At least he had proved that it wasn't some form of SHC. At least they could strike that idea from their investigation.

Raised voices ahead made him glance up. He saw a young couple arguing outside a shop and moved to the side to go past them, his thoughts still on Goddard. He felt a little ashamed that her last memory of him would be of him acting like a child. He wished it hadn't been that way. He would have liked to have left her as a friend rather than as a fool, which he now felt he had looked like. He continued walking.

A brilliant flash of bluish white light from his left smashed into his vision as he passed the arguing couple. He instinctively ducked and flung out an arm to protect himself, thinking for an instant that a bomb had gone off. But there was no sound apart from a strange whooshing noise, and no blast hammered his body. The thought of a bomb was gone from his head almost before it had formed. He did feel a wave of heat rush over him though, and in the early morning sunlight that electric, oily smell assaulted his nostrils. He heard particles of something smattering to the ground and, when he looked again, the couple were gone. Simply gone. Their clothes lay on the ground and the now familiar grey black carbonised ashes lay scattered everywhere. He stared in horror and disbelief at the remains of the young couple, slowly straightening up as he did so.

A thin solitary scream came from across the road and was then suddenly cut off and he looked across to see a woman with a pushchair holding her hands to her mouth in shock. As Fenwick turned back and moved slowly towards the clothes on the floor, other pedestrians shuffled up too, all of them with white, immobile faces, staring at what remained of the boy and girl.

The street was almost entirely silent. Only seagulls screaming overhead could be heard.

One of the people who had approached the scene turned his shocked eyes towards Fenwick and they widened even more in horror. Fenwick stared back at the man, utterly confused.

'You might want to have a look in the mirror, mate,' the man said, his voice trembling. In a daze, Fenwick stepped across to the jewellers where a mirror reflected the awful scene back at him. He looked at his face and it was only then he realised that the ashes of the couple were scattered all over his hair and a fine, black, greasy looking residue covered the left side of his face. His ear was full and the wrinkles around his eye had cut white lines through the mess. He hastily removed his jacket and scrubbed at his face and neck frantically, managing to get the majority of the awful deposit off, but leaving sooty streaks smeared across his face. He turned back to the man and the ring of other pedestrians that now stood outside the jewellers. They were all looking at the twin pair of clothes and carbonised dust on the pavement. Everyone just stood there in the sunshine. Staring.

73

Chapter Eight

Newcastle, 1987

The party was in full swing. It had started as a barbeque at midday and it was now after eleven at night. The house where the party was taking place in was student accommodation on a street just off Chillingham Road. The house was rented by four students, and their friends were all there too. The house was full. Everyone was having a great time.

Kelly Sewell stood in the kitchen watching two male students playing "beer pong". This involved bouncing a table tennis ball on the kitchen table, aiming for the pint glasses full of beer at each end. If the ball went in the person who stood beside it had to take a drink. If it missed, the person who threw the ball had to take a drink. It was simple and effective.

Kelly watched for a while and then turned back towards the sitting room, smiling and squeezing past people as she did so. She entered the packed room and the music playing on the turntable assaulted her ears. It was Don Henley: "The Boys of Summer".

Kelly looked towards where Sean had been sitting with the other young girl before, but they were gone now, their places taken by another couple. She should have known, she supposed. She had dated Sean for a few weeks about six months ago, but it had fizzled out fairly quickly. Sean had made it clear that he did not really want any sort of stable relationship. She wondered where he and the girl had got to and made her way back through the crowds, past the beer pong players and out into the yard where the barbeque was still going, supplemented by many cans of beer and cider. She saw them immediately, kissing on a bench near the barbeque itself. She quickly averted her eyes and went and stood by herself, near the kitchen door.

She tried not to stare, but her eyes seemed to have a will of their own. Whenever she looked away she suddenly found herself staring at them again. She shook her head, a little angry at herself that it was upsetting her so much and looked away again.

'I really don't think he's worth it,' said a voice in her ear, and she turned to see who had spoken.

She found herself looking into a face that had very dark eyes. She checked him over quickly, seeing a straight, aquiline nose, strong chin and longish dark hair. He was wearing jeans and a shirt with a grandad collar. A brown moleskin waistcoat hung loosely on his lean frame. He smiled at her, and instinctively she smiled back.

'Kelly isn't it?' he asked, and she nodded, staring into those liquid brown eyes. He put his hand out to shake. 'I'm William,' he finished, and the smile became wider, a friendly grin now, showing straight, even teeth.

Kelly shook his hand. 'I'm afraid....' She started to say.

'Oh, you don't need to be afraid of me,' said William, and she laughed.

'I was going to say, I'm afraid I don't know you.'

'I'm a friend of Mark's,' said William, tilting his head towards the kitchen where the beer pong players shouted and cajoled each other.

Kelly wasn't sure who Mark was, but it didn't really matter. It was a party.

William's gaze turned to Sean and the girl again, Kelly's eyes following him.

'Are you studying at Uni?' she asked him.

He looked back at her. 'No. I work here. You are, though. You're studying History and Politics. You have one year to go and then you think you will take a gap year and travel. Italy, I think.' His smile widened. 'Yes, Italy. You want to see Rome and Florence especially.'

Kelly frowned at him. How did he know all this? Was this some sort of joke? Had he talked to her friends? But even if he had, she had never mentioned what she planned to do after university to anyone.

'That's very mysterious,' she said. 'And a very good trick. Well done.' She smiled tightly at him again, afraid that he was trying to make a fool of her and then made to move past him, but he held up an arm.

'Please, I'm sorry. I was showing off. I wanted to talk to you because you looked a little lonely standing here. I'm sorry if I upset you.'

His face was so sincere that Kelly laughed softly. 'You didn't upset me; just surprised me.' She took a sip of her cider. 'So what do you work as?' she asked.

'Being surprising,' he answered, and Kelly laughed. William suddenly turned, put down his drink and then said to her, his face earnest, 'Do what I did. Know what I do.'

'What?'

'Here,' he said, holding out his hand for her drink. She frowned at him but followed his lead. He placed her drink with his.

'Now, to do this properly, you have to hold my hands,' he said. 'But don't worry, this is an experiment. There is nothing sexual about it.' He smiled again and Kelly couldn't but help but smile back. He took her hands in his. 'Unless you want it to be sexual,' he added, grinning. 'Then that would be perfectly acceptable.' Kelly laughed aloud, delighted with this strange young man.

'Now,' said William. 'I'm going to think of what my job is, and you have to guess it, okay?'

'Okay,' said Kelly, staring into his smiling eyes.

'Right,' he said. 'I'm thinking now,'

Kelly closed her eyes and thought. Nothing came to her. She frowned and tried harder, looking for inspiration. None came.

'Banking?' she guessed.

'Try again,' he said, and she felt his hands tighten slightly around hers.

She opened her eyes, smiling.

'I'm sorry,' she began, 'nothing, I...'

She halted when she looked into his eyes again. No longer smiling, they were full of distain, full of hatred even. Shocked at the change in his demeanour she tried to pull away, but he still held her hands and gripped them even tighter.

'Monkey,' he rasped through clenched teeth, and she opened her mouth in shock. 'Stupid, hairless monkey,' Kelley stared in astonishment.

'You're worse than cattle,' he hissed. 'Unknowing, unthinking cattle.' He continued to glare at her, seemingly boiling with hatred.

Kelly tried once more to pull her hands free, but he kept them in his iron grip.

'No wonder they want you gone,' he said, his voice cold and spiteful now. 'No wonder they hate your kind so much. No wonder they want you dead.'

Kelly was badly frightened now. More than this, she was terrified. His eyes held a hatred that seemed to burn from within him. She at last managed to wrench her hands free. 'Let go of me!' she shouted as she did so.

Sean, on the bench with the other girl, heard the scream and turned as everyone else did to look at Kelly and the dark-haired man standing by her. He stood up.

'Hey,' he shouted. 'What the fuck are you playing at?'

William turned to look at him. Then his gaze fell upon Kelly once more. She took a step back from the deadness of his stare, the anger replaced now with a nothingness that seemed to seep from a soul as black as Hell.

'Oh dear,' he said flatly. 'Your friend seems to be having an accident.'

Kelly frowned at him and then wrenched her head around as a scream of terror and pain came from Sean. She stared wide eyed at him there beside the barbeque. He was completely engulfed in flames, spinning and heaving as the fire ate at his body and face. He screamed and screamed, even when those quicker witted than their cringing friends dragged him to the floor and started beating the fire out.

Kelly turned in shock back to where William had been. But he was gone. He had vanished as quickly as he had arrived.

*

Fenwick sat on one of the benches in the now taped-off section of

Northumberland Street. He hadn't put his jacket back on and it lay beside him on the bench, crumpled and dirty. It was smeared with the remains of two dead people. He was never going to wear *that* thing again. A paramedic had checked him over when the first emergency vehicles had turned up and then gave him a plastic bottle of water. With his shirt sleeves rolled up he now sat in the sun, sipping the water and watching the forensic teams go about their business in their alien costumes. The masks they wore gave them a sterile, unfeeling aura.

The last half hour had gone by in a flash. A police patrol car had turned up within minutes, along with paramedics. The TV cameras had arrived not long after with the reporter (the same one who had been arguing with the PC at Anna Pont's house), trying to talk to some of the witnesses and seemingly succeeding too. It would be all over the news tonight. Fenwick had kept out of her way and the paramedic had given him his water and then moved on to look at the other people there.

He couldn't quite believe what had happened. The memory of that blue-white flash kept playing in his head, along with the sound he'd heard when the couple had died. It was a whooshing, hissing noise and Fenwick was reminded of what Cook had said. 'Whuff…up he goes.' He shook his head and sipped his water.

Fenwick had seen death many times before. He had seen bodies burned beyond recognition. He had witnessed human beings reduced to little more than pulped stains on the tarmac after road accidents. He'd pulled bodies from house fires that were totally unmarked by flames, the victims dying instead from asphyxiation as smoke and fumes had choked off their lives. What had just happened in front of him was something he had no knowledge or understanding of.

For some reason he kept thinking of an incident he had attended early on in his career, a house he had gone into after the fire was extinguished. The station commander had sidled up to him, standing in the scorched and steam-filled sitting room. Water from the hoses dripped everywhere and the furniture was blackened and melted by the intense heat.

'You may as well see this,' his boss had said. 'You need to get used to it.'

He had led Fenwick into the kitchen, smoke-scarred but not as burned as the sitting room.

He pointed under the kitchen table that stood in the centre of the room and Fenwick crouched down to see what was there, swallowing hard as he did so.

Under the table were three bodies. A woman and two children, unmarked apart from sooty deposits around their deathly white noses and mouths where the killing smoke had extinguished their lives. The children looked to be about three and six, the mother just in her twenties. Fenwick had stared at the bodies, at the woman's arms still around her children, still trying to protect them even though they were all dead now. He had wondered what their final moments must have been like. Had they screamed? Had they known they were going to die? Or did unconsciousness overcome them before they fully realised they would not live to see another day?

Their faces came to Fenwick now as he sat in the sun's heat, which was starting to have a slightly humid feel to it. At least these two died instantly, he thought. There are worse ways to go.

He looked up from his reverie as he heard his name being called and saw a now familiar silver Ford Focus parked nearby. It hadn't been there the last time he had looked and he wondered if he was suffering slightly from shock, his memory playing tricks on him. In front of him stood Goddard, looking strained and tired. And, he thought, worried.

'I said, are you okay?'

Fenwick shook his head slightly and stood up. 'Sorry, I was miles away. Yes, I'm fine.'

He nodded slightly as if to confirm this and they stood staring at each other for a while. Parker came up alongside.

'I'm going to need a statement,' he said gruffly. 'I want to know what happened here.'

Fenwick nodded again. He was about to start when Parker took his arm and led him towards the Focus. 'Not yet, and not here.' He indicated to the TV news team who hovered nearby. 'Back at the station. As soon as I've finished.'

With that he marched off towards the macabre scene of the two deaths. Goddard sighed.

'Come on,' she said. 'I'll drive you back to the station. We need to talk.'

They were both silent as Goddard drove them back. Fenwick was lost in his own thoughts and Goddard seemed happy enough to just let him think them. They reached the station and walked into the now familiar office. They sat down at the desk.

'Do you want a coffee or something?' asked Goddard. 'Or maybe you want to get cleaned up?'

He stared at her for a second. 'Both of those things,' he said. 'Where's the toilets?'

By the time he got back to the office, his coffee had arrived and his face was clear of the human debris that had been smeared into it. Goddard watched him as he sipped the coffee, giving him a bit of time. His hair was damp where he had washed out the ashes and dust and he stared at nothing, his face blank.

'Are you okay to talk?' she eventually asked. 'If you want a bit more time that's fine, but I could really do with knowing just what you saw this morning.'

'I'm fine,' he replied. He recounted what had happened on Northumberland Street quickly and professionally.

Goddard shook her head. 'We'll have loads of footage of course,' she said, 'There are cameras all over that street. Plus all the other witnesses and their phones.' She frowned and sipped her own coffee. 'Not that they're going to be able to tell us anything. We still don't know what's causing this or even what *this* is.'

They were silent for a while again. Then Fenwick spoke.

'It's true that there was no other fire damage around Rachel's body,' he said. 'I suppose that means there are similarities with all this. I'm sorry I didn't speak up about it earlier. But there are so many differences that I honestly think how she died, and how… how *they* died, that couple, and the others I mean, that I don't believe they're connected. The only things similar are the lack of burning around Rachel's body and that smell.' He shrugged. 'But maybe that's just me. It was ten years ago, and I know the memory can play tricks on the mind. Maybe I'm just imagining that the smell was the same.'

Goddard nodded at him, as if encouraging him to go on. It seemed she was interested in what had happened to him in 2008.

'The other firefighter you were with when you had that accident,' she started, and she saw that he seemed willing to listen to her, maybe to explain what had happened to him, what had shaped the man he was. But at that moment the door to the office banged open and Parker marched in. He took in the pair of them.

'Are you all right to give an official statement?' he asked Fenwick. He asked this in the manner a parent would ask someone if they were the person who had kidnapped and murdered their children.

Fenwick sighed and put down his coffee.

'Of course,' he said. They made their way to the interview rooms.

*

By the time they had finished it was late afternoon. Fenwick stood in the street with Goddard, the sun's heat intense now. He glanced up and saw that there were fat clouds building to the west. He reckoned there would be a storm in the next few days. He spied a wastepaper bin and went over and stuffed his jacket into it, shoving his wallet and phone into his trouser pockets.

Parker had asked the questions in what Fenwick thought was a rather inquisitorial manner, as if Fenwick himself was to blame for what had happened. But he had answered them as fully as he could.

When Parker was finally finished he gruffly thanked Fenwick and said, 'Please don't leave Newcastle yet, I may want to talk to you again.'

Fenwick had simply nodded and left, Goddard following him out.

'Do you want a lift to the hotel?' she asked him, and he stared at her for a second before nodding. They got into her car and she drove him back. She parked up and they sat in silence for a while.

'I'm sorry for my unprofessional behaviour this morning,' she started, but he waved a hand in dismissal.

'Not your fault. All down to me and my attitude.'

'Yes, I know that,' she said with a smile, 'but I just thought I would say.'

He smiled back at her. She turned away from him as if she couldn't trust herself and gazed out the windscreen.

'You do need to talk to someone about it you know,' she said, still not looking at him. 'I really think you do.'

Fenwick knew she was not talking about what had happened that day. He turned his own gaze outside. 'I know,' he said eventually.

They were silent for a while longer, then he made to get out. 'Thanks for the lift,' he muttered.

'If you do want to talk, you can talk to me,' she said in a rush, looking at him now.

He paused, halfway out the car, staring at her, his face unsure. Then he seemed to come to a decision and nodded. 'I think I'd like that. Give me a call when you're free.'

He climbed out of the car and she smiled once more at him. He smiled back and then she was gone, heading back towards the station.

Fenwick took out his room key and made his way to the lift, changing his mind halfway through the lobby and making a beeline for the bar instead, where he ordered a double *Glen Morangie*. He drained it in one go and stood looking at his shaking hands. He knew they were not just shaking because of what he'd witnessed that morning. He then made his way to his room. He wanted a shower.

*

The dark blue BMW stood under a glowing streetlamp, the rest of the street deserted. They had to use public phones when they communicated and the man who got out of the BMW could not understand why they couldn't just use a mobile like ordinary people. Of course, they *weren't* ordinary people, he supposed, but all this skulduggery shit was starting to wear a bit thin. He was a burly man, dressed in jeans and leather jacket, and he had a shaved, round head and hard, unblinking gaze. He was the kind of a man you would cross the road to avoid; mindless violence seemed to ebb from his very pores.

He looked back into the car's darkened interior and received a nod from the passenger in the back seat: a slow, measured movement, hardly seen in the reflected streetlamps.

The man in the leather jacket nodded back, walked around the car and stepped into the phone box.

He pressed buttons and heard the clicking, then ringing on the end of the line. Presently, a voice spoke in his ear. It was a dark, resonant voice that sent fingers of trepidation down the burly man's spine. He believed the person he now spoke to was the only man in the world he feared.

'We've found her,' he said.

'Yes. I know,' replied that reptilian voice. 'Well, you know what to do, don't you?'

The burly man nodded as if the person on the end of the line could see him, and strangely, it seemed as if he was right because the voice continued, 'Then do it.' The phone went dead.

The man replaced the receiver and went back to the car. When he was in the passenger seat beside the driver, the man in the back seat said, 'Do we do it then?'

The man in the leather jacket could hear the eagerness in the voice. Without turning round he simply nodded.

He and the driver exchanged glances when the man in the back seat began to laugh hysterically.

*

Ellie wandered the dark streets aimlessly, pausing every so often to look absently into shop windows or to light the stolen cigarettes with the stolen lighter.

It won't be long now, she thought. Won't be long before they catch me. Might even be tonight. She simply could not keep the guard up anymore, her strength was draining by the very minute. Perhaps they would kill her quickly, save her from any pain. But even before that thought had fully crossed her mind it was discarded. No. They would hurt her, as they had hurt her family. And they would hurt her for as long as they could. Not just as a warning to the others, but because they enjoyed it.

She threw the half-smoked cigarette into the gutter, her throat too dry and her stomach too empty for her to enjoy the taste. Stopping by another shop window she gazed at her ravaged reflection in the glass. She stared at the haunted eyes, the wretched, haggard face, and she began to weep. She was utterly without hope and the gulping sobs wracking her thin, wasted body until she coughed with the exertion.

She eventually managed to calm down and wiped the tears away, leaving greasy marks on her filthy face.

Whatever had drawn her back to Newcastle, however hopeful she had at first felt that she would find help here, was gone now. She was alone. Utterly alone. No one could help her.

It was then that she became aware of the figure standing just behind her and she whipped around, fearful that they had managed to sneak up on her while she was thinking of other things. She looked into the face of a young man who was staring at her, grinning. He was obviously another one of the city's down-and-outs. He had long, dirty-looking dreadlocks and wore camouflaged trousers and a multicoloured woollen top that looked three sizes too big for him. He carried a huge, oversize canvas bag over one shoulder.

'Fancy doubling up tonight?' he asked, his grin becoming wider. 'I know a place where we can go.' His smile had a wet look to it.

Ellie sighed and shook her head at her lack of alertness. She had allowed someone to approach her without her knowing about it. That was the way to an early grave.

She stared straight into his drug befuddled eyes.

'Turn around, walk for one mile, and forget you ever saw me,' she said.

Without a moment's hesitation the boy turned and started walking away, not glancing back once.

Ellie turned back to the shop window, this time gazing at the goods on display rather than at the reflection she did not want to see. The shop sold electrical goods and, even at this late hour, one or two of the televisions played away to themselves behind their protective metal grill.

The local news was on and the screens showed a taped-off section of a street. There were ambulances and police cars in the background and a woman was talking into the camera silently. The screen then showed a wider angle of the street and also the figure of a dark-haired man sitting sipping water in the distance, his shirt sleeves rolled up, his eyes seemingly staring at nothing.

That was him! That was the person she suddenly knew—*knew*—she'd been looking for. She felt hope soar within her and the mental guard that had deserted her sprang up once more, shielding her from harm. At the same time other, more fine-tuned feelers began exploring the city, spreading invisible tendrils throughout. Hunting for the only person who could help her. It would take a while, but Ellie knew that she would find him.

Chapter Nine

Fenwick pushed open the door and was immediately swamped by a barrage of noise. Inside the police station's press room were seemingly hundreds of journalists and camera crews. Some of them were sitting but most were standing, trying to be heard over the ruckus. One or two people glanced in his direction when he came in but most of them had their attention fixed on the people sitting at a long desk at the front of the room, raised on a small stage above the sea of noise.

Whilst Fenwick had spent the previous day at the hotel, Parker and Goddard had been interviewing witnesses and reviewing CCTV and mobile phone footage. It had all come to nothing. They knew what had happened to the victims, but they didn't know what it was that had killed them. Or how. After meeting with his Chief Constable, Parker had decided to hold the press conference. They both agreed that the public needed to be officially informed of what had happened and, anyway, it was already public knowledge.

Fenwick had lain on his hotel bed the previous night and watched the news. The reports on the events on Northumberland Street were numerous, but had no answers. A palpable fear seemed to be settling across the city, made worse by the heavy, muggy atmosphere in the air. Weather forecasts were predicting thundery rain, but so far it hadn't happened. As Fenwick entered the police station, sweating as soon as he got out of his car, he glanced at the sky and noted the heavy thunderheads gathering. There was going to be almighty storm soon.

Fenwick could find no seats so stood near the front against the wall, watching as the people at the table sorted themselves out and made sure that their microphones were working.

Parker was there, as was the chief constable: a man named Wright. Next to Parker was the chief executive of Newcastle City Council, Alan Brewis, and sitting next to him was Goddard. She raised her eyebrows at Fenwick, and he raised them in return.

Brewis stood up and tapped the table with his pen until a general hush fell over the proceedings.

'Ladies and gentlemen,' he began. 'You've been called here this morning to let you know about the events that have happened around the city in the last few weeks. In those weeks, five people have been killed in what can only be described as a foul and horrible manner.'

He paused here for effect and Fenwick saw Parker close his eyes in quiet desperation at Brewis' turn of phrase. Fenwick almost felt sorry for the DI.

Once he was sure he held the attention of everyone in the room, Brewis continued.

'The deaths have occurred over a wide area of Newcastle, but they all have one thing in common. All the victims were seemingly burned to death. And burned to such a degree that their bodies were reduced to nothing but ashes.'

The babble of noise sprung up once more at these words, but Brewis held up his hands until silence fell once more.

'Please,' he said, his hands still raised in the placating gesture. 'Please, if we are to conduct this meeting in a civilised and orderly fashion then you must restrain yourselves until the main points have been covered. Then a question-and-answer session will be held and the gentlemen here,' he stopped suddenly when he spotted Goddard. 'And lady of course,' he added with a leer towards her, 'will answer any questions.'

Fenwick looked at Goddard again and she rolled her eyes slightly. Brewis seemed like the sort of man who revelled in this type of public attention. He actually looked like he was enjoying himself.

'Thank you,' he said finally, dropping his hands and placing them flat on top of the table.

'Now then, before we go any further I think I should introduce the people who are at the centre of the investigation. On my left are Chief Constable Wright, Detective Inspector Parker, and Detective Sergeant Goddard of Northumbria police. Detective Inspector Parker is the officer in charge of the investigation, and he will be answering questions that are relevant to the case. In the row of chairs in front of you is Mr James Ross, the doctor who has examined the victims. Any medical questions may be answered by him.'

Fenwick hadn't noticed Ross sitting at the front, but as the pathologist turned to be acknowledged he caught Fenwick's eye and smiled his mocking smile before turning back to the front of the room.

Brewis then smiled disparagingly and placed a hand flat on his chest. 'My name is Alan Brewis, chief executive of Newcastle City Council, although I'm sure most of you know that.' He looked around the packed room in a way that suggested they'd *better* bloody well know who he was. 'And any questions I can answer,' he continued, 'I will do my utmost to answer them.'

He smiled again, a fake self-depreciative smirk, and cleared his throat.

'Now then,' he continued, his manner business like again, 'DI Parker will give you a rundown of what we know so far before any questions can be answered. I will be on hand to help out where I can.' Parker groaned aloud at this and received a warning look from Wright. Fenwick smiled.

Parker then gave a quick summary of what they knew so far, which didn't take long. He recited the facts in a flat, monotone voice, never lifting his eyes once from the written script in front of him.

When he had finished, Brewis stood again.

'All right,' he said, 'we will try to answer any questions you have, but can I just repeat that you should act in an orderly and civilised manner. That way you will all get your personal questions answered by the individual best qualified. Thank you very much.' He sat down again.

Immediately about fifty hands shot up into the air. The chief executive pointed to a youngish man near the front and the hubbub died down.

'Detective Inspector Parker,' the young reporter started. 'Are these deaths being investigated as murder?'

Parker shook his head. 'No, not at present. Although the incidents have a lot of similarities there's nothing to suggest they're even connected. Of course, given those similarities they are being looked into as a collaborative investigation.'

More hands went up and Brewis picked out someone else. Questions and answers followed and Fenwick closed his eyes, letting the babble wash over him.

Presently, Brewis pointed to another hand in the air.

'A question for Mr Fenwick,' said the reporter, and Fenwick's eyes opened in surprise as she looked across to him.

'Who?' asked Brewis, but it was Parker who spoke to the reporter.

'I'm afraid Mr Fenwick is no longer helping us with our inquiries,' he said. 'He's been very helpful but unfortunately has not been able to add anything useful to the investigation.'

'But he witnessed the events on Northumberland Street,' continued the reporter, refusing to back down. 'He's an expert on Spontaneous Human Combustion and on the effects of fire is he not? He's also standing just over there.' She pointed to Fenwick and he shifted uncomfortably as hundreds of eyes swivelled in his direction.

Brewis looked at the seated people at the table and frowned, not really understanding what was happening. Parker, Goddard and Wright stuck their heads together and a brief, whispered conversation was held. Fenwick saw Goddard nod, Parker shake his head, and then shrug at something Wright said. It was the chief constable who then spoke.

'As DI Parker has said, Mr Fenwick was helping with inquiries at the start of the investigation, but is no longer doing so. However, as he has a lot of knowledge about, eh, about such things, then perhaps it would be right for him to answer some questions that relate to the investigation.' He glanced across to Fenwick. 'Is that all right with you Mr Fenwick?' he asked.

You haven't given me much bloody choice, thought Fenwick, but he smiled and said 'Yes, of course.'

The reporter who had asked for him turned towards him, ignoring Brewis, who had indicated for her to carry on after she had already done so. Brewis was completely lost by the direction the conference was heading.

'It's a simple question really,' continued the reporter, a middle aged but trim and attractive woman. 'Do you know why these people have been killed in this manner? Burned to ashes, I mean. And do you consider that they may be instances of spontaneous human combustion? Do you think that supernatural forces may be involved?'

Fenwick stared. The woman was obviously serious about her questions, ridiculous as they were, and had obviously done her research into him. He wondered what paper or magazine she was from.

'Outer Limits magazine,' the woman supplied as if reading his thoughts.

Bloody hell, thought Fenwick, but managed to keep his face straight.

'I'm not sure that is a simple question,' he remarked and got a ripple of quiet laughter around the room. The woman reporter just smiled benignly. She probably got this reaction a lot.

'I'll try to do my best to answer it though,' continued Fenwick. 'To the first part of your question, I'm afraid "no" is the answer. As DI Parker has already said, investigations by the police are ongoing.' In his peripheral vision he saw Parker nod, looking satisfied with the answer he had given.

'As to the second part of your question,' Fenwick went on, 'the idea of supernatural forces at work has not been considered. Spontaneous Human Combustion has been completely disproved of as: one, a cause of death, and two, a supernatural force. Every case of the phenomena has been found to have been triggered by natural causes, although there are still some people who like to cling to the idea of it being some form of paranormal event.' Here Fenwick stared at the woman pointedly, and again she just smiled back kindly at him.

'The classic cases of SHC have nothing in common with what has happened here,' he continued, 'apart from the state of the victims' bodies and, even then, the differences are quite vast. So no, Ms….?'

'Cord.'

'Ms Cord. No. I am quite certain there are no supernatural forces at work here in Newcastle.'

He leaned back against the wall, thinking she was finished, but seemingly she was not.

'Is it true that there are some similarities between what has happened here and what happened to your wife ten years ago?' she asked sweetly.

Fenwick stared at her, dumbfounded. 'What?' he asked faintly, but it was Goddard who at this point spoke.

'Whatever tragic events happened to Mr Fenwick ten years ago have nothing, I repeat, nothing, to do with this investigation,' she said angrily. 'Dredging up those events does nothing to help the inquiries today. I believe I speak for all of us here when we ask that any further questions are related directly to the investigation. No ghosts or goblins please.'

There was another ripple of laughter in the crowd and Goddard sat back and looked at Fenwick, her green eyes showing regret about the line the questioning had taken. He gave her a small smile and nodded his head slightly in thanks.

Cord sat down again, still wearing her benign smile, still staring at Fenwick.

The meeting then turned to more constructive questions: Were the victims related in any way at all? What was being done to stop it? Was it going to happen again?

That was the question everyone wanted an answer for. Was it going to happen again? None of the people at the long table seemed to have an adequate answer.

Fenwick answered more questions on the effects of fire, Parker and Goddard outlined their plans for the investigation and Ross told the excited journalists that the heat—if it was heat—that had killed the victims must have been in excess of 2,000 degrees, the average operating temperature of a cremation oven. How the clothes and other objects had not been burned, why the larger bones were also consumed, or how it had happened so suddenly was a mystery that no one at present could fathom out.

Eventually the meeting broke up with everyone disappointed with the conclusion. It seemed there were no answers.

Fenwick sat down in a vacant chair at the front as the crowd dispersed, absently rubbing his leg. Eventually the room was almost empty and he leaned back in the chair, his mind blank. He was vaguely aware of Parker and Wright talking at the front, but he ignored them and just sat, thinking nothing.

It was Wright himself who came over to him. Fenwick stood up as the chief constable arrived. He was a short, black haired man and he spoke with a rolling, Northern Irish brogue.

'After consulting with DI Parker, we've decided that we would still welcome any advice you can offer about what's been happening,' he said. 'You're the only one we have local who has any sort of in-depth knowledge about the effects of heat and fire damage, et cetera, so if you would continue to help in that capacity we would be most grateful.'

Fenwick was surprised. 'Does Parker want me to continue?' he asked, glancing at the DI who was now making his way through a side door, past Goddard who was standing at a respectful distance to let the two men talk.

Wright smiled tightly. 'DI Parker is a hell of a copper, but I am ultimately in charge of what happens around here. Joe understands that you may be useful in this investigation and is more than willing to work with you on it.'

Fenwick somehow doubted that, but he nodded and shook the hand that Wright stuck out.

'Thank you,' said the Chief Constable. 'DS Goddard will fill you in on how we want to proceed.'

Wright left, nodding at Goddard as she walked over to sit down next to him. She gave him a quick glance He looked like he hadn't shaved that morning and his eyes were strained and red rimmed. His mouth was set in a grim line. But then he smiled at her and it transformed him.

'You should do that more often,' the DS said.

'So I've been told,' he said wryly. 'So what's going to happen now?'

For a second, Goddard seemed to pause, as if she was unsure of what he meant. With the investigation, or something else?

She ignored the question for the moment.

'How are you feeling?' she asked.

'Oh, okay,' he replied, rubbing his hands over his face. 'How are you?'

She only nodded as a reply. They were silent for a while, listening to the far away chatter of someone typing on a keyboard.

She was about to explain where they were heading with the investigation, but Fenwick spoke first.

'You know about Rachel,' he said, not looking at her, his eyes on the floor, and she nodded, even though he could not see this.

'We met when I was training. I was only twenty-two, she was even younger.' He smiled slightly at the memory. 'We were married four years later. I was working in Durham and we bought a little two-bedroom house on a housing estate. We had a nice life. For me, it was great. I had Rachel at home and the brigade at work. For ten years I thought I had it all. We were thinking of having children. We talked about it a lot, but for one reason or another it just never seemed to happen.' A frown appeared on his face and Goddard placed her hand on his arm as a gesture of kindness without thinking, sensing his sadness. It seemed he wanted to talk and realised that she wanted to listen. He absently took her hand and squeezed it slightly, his thumb stroking the back of it. It seemed to both of them to be the most natural thing in the world to do.

'I found out she'd been having an affair,' he continued, 'and that it was with Kev, my best mate.' He shook his head and sat straighter in the chair, her hand falling away, leaving a strange warmth on her palm.

'It wasn't pleasant,' he continued, 'as you can imagine. I left home, stayed with my sister for a while. It was difficult. Kev and I eventually had an argument. I went round to his flat and ended up clobbering him.' Fenwick shook his head again. 'He didn't even try to fight back. He knew how much he had hurt me. The two people I loved most in my life had betrayed me.'

Fenwick took a deep breath. 'That was the night Rachel died, after I had left Kev's. I got the phone call and… Well, you know what happened to her. Obviously, I was given leave, and it was then that I started researching everything I could about Spontaneous Human Combustion. I wanted an explanation, you know? I wanted facts and figures. I wanted to know how this could happen to a person I had loved so much.' Again Goddard put out a hand and held his. He smiled thankfully at her.

'Those months are a bit of a blur,' he continued. 'I drank more than was good for me at the start, but eventually the research seemed to help combat the grief. And the guilt.'

'What did you have to feel guilty about?' she asked, perplexed.

'I felt that I'd somehow abandoned her. That if I hadn't left, she may not have died. She wanted me to stay, but I was so angry. I always told her I would protect her, and that I'd never leave her. I felt I'd failed her somehow. And of course, what happened to Kev.'

Goddard shook her head. 'She had an affair with your best friend,' she started, and Fenwick nodded.

'I know, I know that now, but grief is a funny thing, isn't it? I blamed myself, thought I had done something that had made her turn to Kev. That he gave her something I couldn't.'

He took another deep breath, but kept hold of her hand.

'I kept up the research even when I went back to work. I had nothing else to occupy me in my time off, and a couple of years later I found myself as the go to expert on SHC. But that was after the accident of course.'

He suddenly stopped and looked at her full in the face for the first time.

'I'm sorry,' he said. 'This must be really boring for you. You have loads to do. Come on, let's see if anything new has come up.'

He made to stand but Goddard gripped his hand. She shook her head. 'No way. I told you that you needed to talk, and you do. I want to help, even if it's just to listen. Work can wait for ten minutes.'

He stared at her for a second, as if he was surprised that she wanted to listen. As if he was surprised anyone would be interested in his past.

'Have you ever talked about this?' she asked. 'To anyone else I mean?'

Fenwick pursed his lips, then shrugged, thinking.

'Not really,' he replied eventually. 'Didn't really think it was anybody's business but my own.'

Fenwick was a little uncomfortable about talking about his life. He found it difficult to put into words why he lived alone, why there was no one else in his life and why there hadn't been since the death of his wife ten years ago. The truth was that, for a long time, he had just wanted to exist, to live without the worry, or the responsibility of having to think about anyone else. He just didn't want to get hurt again.

'Has there been anyone since Rachel?' she asked, wanting to make sure she was correct. Her heart started beating a little faster at the thought there might be.

She was inexplicably relieved when he answered.

'No. Not really. The odd date. I did get close to someone, but

I ended it after a few months. I didn't want to get involved again. Didn't want that.'

He was quiet again. Goddard took his hand in both of hers and laid it gently on her knee. He swivelled in his chair to look at her, his eyes confused.

'Tell me about the accident,' she said.

'You already know…' he began, but again she shook her head slowly, warning him not to back off.

He got the message. 'I was back at work,' he said. 'About four months after Rachel died. Kev had been transferred to another brigade by this time but we were shorthanded, so he was back for a few shifts. It wasn't very comfortable, but we got on with it. We were professionals. And we had been friends. We were called out to an incident, the fire at the machine warehouse and Kev and I were inside. Half the floor gave way.' He shook his head. 'It happened so fast, one minute we were standing there and the next, Kev was gone. I really thought he was gone. But he managed to grab a girder.'

Here Fenwick paused, his hand lifting from Goddard's as he straightened in his chair.

'For a second, a split second, I hesitated,' he said. He looked deep into her eyes, as if weighing up whether he could trust her with this information or not. He evidently decided he could. 'I've never told anyone this, but for a second, as I watched him hanging, I almost backed away, leaving him to whatever would happen. As payback I suppose. But of course I didn't. I was a firefighter. I didn't get into the job because I didn't want to help. And as I said, we had been friends once. I grabbed him and managed to pull him up, got him onto another girder. But then the rest of the floor collapsed, and down I went.'

Again Fenwick shook his head. 'I can't really remember what happened,' he continued eventually. 'Just disjointed images really. I remember pain, such a huge pain in my leg. I had a few other injuries but the pain in my leg is what I remember the most. I think I blacked out. The next thing I remember is lying in the back of an ambulance. I asked the paramedic what had happened but she didn't really have time to talk, she was too busy getting me patched up and ready to go to the hospital. It was only later when I found out.

'Kev saved me. Came down into that inferno and got me out. But he didn't make it. My BA was shattered and the place was full of smoke and fumes. He took his own mask off and put it on me. He managed to drag me out but he collapsed just as he got me to a door. He died later that evening in hospital from smoke inhalation. He was just a few corridors away from me.'

Fenwick swallowed hard. Goddard tightened her grip on his hands, and he sighed deeply.

'I couldn't even go to his funeral,' he said. 'My leg was so badly damaged that I needed op after op just to save it. My femur was completely shattered. Apparently it was just lying around in bits inside my leg. They were worried about blood loss and pieces of the bone blocking up arteries and all sorts. They said at first the only way to save me was to have my leg amputated, but I wouldn't let them. Every time they said it, I kept saying no. I think I still believed that I would get back to work, get back to the job I loved.' He laughed, sadly.

'Of course, that was finished. After a year of operations and traction and physio they managed to build my leg up again, with a few metal plates in there to help. But it was too far gone. The brigade was good though. They said I could retire, injury through active service, or I could retrain as a fire investigator. I went for the second option and I did that for nearly four years. Whilst I was in hospital and recovering later, I continued with my studies about SHC. It kept me occupied. By now I had become almost obsessed in finding out the truth about it. Not just for Rachel, but because now I was interested in it. I wanted to know about it. Wanted to know the truth.'

He suddenly smiled at Goddard. He felt like a load had been taken from his shoulders. He seemed relieved.

'As I was working as an investigator, I was approached by Bill

Curtis. Headhunted, I think they call it. He had ideas for starting a company. He'd heard of me and offered me something I thought I would never have and, to be honest, had never really thought about. The chance to be my own boss. We worked hard on FireSafe and we built it into what it is today. As far as SHC is concerned, I'd realised by then that it was what I've been telling you. Curious incidents, yes, but not unexplained; and certainly not supernatural as that mad bat was talking about before. I didn't really have much to do with it after that. I published some papers and even a book, but I've spent the last six years or so building up the company with Bill.'

He stood up and the closeness that had built up between them in the last few minutes begin to dissipate. He was pulling back again, retiring into his shell once more. It seemed it wasn't just his leg that had been damaged that night. It seemed he was determined never to get close to anyone again. Fenwick looked down at her.

'I've never told anyone the whole story,' he said, 'not in one go, anyway. Bill knows of course, and my family, but that was put together over the years.' He smiled. 'Thank you. You were right, it was good to get it off my chest.'

But it hasn't changed the way you are, thought Goddard sadly.

She was about to say something when there was a small, scuffing noise behind them. They both turned towards the door. There stood a small, dishevelled girl, dressed in jeans and a jacket that looked too big for her. She had a waif like appearance and her hair was lank. She was staring at Fenwick.

Goddard glanced at Fenwick then stood up and walked towards the girl, an inquisitive look on her face.

'Can I help you?' she asked. 'The meeting is over I'm afraid. You've missed it.'

The young girl shook her head: a small, jerky motion. She ignored Goddard, her gaze fixed on Fenwick.

'I hope you can help me,' she said, her voice hardly more than a whisper, so soft that Fenwick could barely hear her. He walked over and joined Goddard in front of her. 'If you can't,' she continued, 'then it will be too late for everyone.'

Fenwick frowned at her, perplexed. 'What do you mean?' He looked at Goddard for help, but she simply shook her head, her eyes on the girl. Fenwick turned back to the girl.

'What do you mean?' he repeated. 'Too late for who?'

For an answer the girl delved into her jacket pocket and pulled out a piece of crumpled paper, pressing it into Fenwick's hand. On it was written the name of what he guessed to be a pub. *The Pheasant*. He looked quizzically at her and she stared back at him with haunted eyes.

'Have another look at the footage from yesterday,' she said, still just addressing Fenwick. 'And if you want to find out what's happening then be there tonight at eight.' For the first time the girl looked at Goddard, then her eyes turned back to Fenwick. 'Alone,' she finished.

With that she turned and hurried out.

'Hang on,' called Goddard, making to go after her, but she suddenly stopped and gasped, grasping her head in her hands.

Fenwick grabbed her, concern on his face and sat her down on the nearest chair.

'What's wrong?' he asked. 'Are you okay?' Goddard's eyes were screwed up in pain and her mouth was wide in a silent scream.

'Laura, what's wrong?' repeated Fenwick, almost shouting.

As suddenly as the attack had occurred, it was seemingly gone, and Goddard slowly dropped her hands and stared at him for a second.

'God, that was awful,' she said. 'It was a pain in my head like I've never known.' She slowly shook her head as if frightened the pain might return and then looked at him in wonder. 'It's completely gone.'

She stared at Fenwick for another second then, remembering the girl, she hurried out to catch her.

She was back within half a minute. 'Gone,' she said.

They both sat back down. 'You sure you're okay?' he asked.

'I'm absolutely fine. I don't know what it was; I've never felt anything like it.'

Fenwick looked again at the piece of paper in his hand. He passed it to Goddard.

'Not the nicest of hostelries,' she said. 'This place is in the darkest depths of Walker.'

Fenwick shook his head. 'This is like the bloody Twilight Zone,' he muttered. 'Who the hell was that?'

'She's not local,' she answered. 'Sounded like a southern accent. She looked to be in a terrible state.' She looked again at the paper. 'You willing to meet her?' she asked, and Fenwick shrugged.

'Why not?'

'I'll drive you.'

'She said to go alone,' he started, but trailed off when he saw the smile on her face.

'Don't worry, she won't know I'm there,' she said.

'What about Parker?' asked Fenwick, but Goddard shook her head. 'I doubt it'll come to anything,' she replied, 'and I don't want his time wasted. No, we'll go alone.' Her smile widened as she continued to look at him. 'We can call it a date,' she said, the smile becoming a grin. Fenwick could only look back at her and wonder why the thought of that was so alluring.

Chapter Ten

After the girl had left, Fenwick and Goddard made their way back into the station. Goddard wanted to look at the footage from the CCTV of Northumberland Street again, prompted by what the girl had said.

'What do you expect to find?' asked Fenwick, and Goddard had shaken her head.

'I don't know. Nothing probably, but it can't hurt having another look can it?'

She led Fenwick into the room where they had looked at the footage of McGuinness' death, with its banks of computer screens. In the room was one of the techs to whom Parker had spoken on that day.

'Hiya,' he said. 'Did you get that footage I cleaned up?'

Goddard shook her head. 'What footage?'

'The one from the warehouse. DI Parker asked me to clean it up and I've done that. I emailed it to you both this morning. You might want to have a look at it. It's a bit weird.'

Goddard and Fenwick exchanged glances.

'Have you got it here?' asked the DS. The tech nodded, indicating to a nearby screen. They sat down in front of it and the tech started punching the keyboard. The image from the security cameras rolled again silently and Eric McGuinness once more jerked around the yard on his final journey.

'This is the frame that was whited out,' said the tech. 'I managed to play around with the details. Have a look at…this.' He stopped the playback.

Fenwick and Goddard leaned in closer. The frame showed McGuinness leaning down rubbing his legs. The tech tapped a button and the playback went on frame by frame. 'Here,' he said.

Just before the screen went white, just before Eric McGuinness died, the cleaned-up footage seemed to show two faint white lines moving towards him from opposite directions. Fenwick narrowed his gaze as he looked at the lines. They seemed to appear from nowhere and they were ethereal and pale. They were similar to the thin condensation trails left by aircraft and they converged on the figure of the security guard. The next screen was the white-out.

'Do that again,' said Goddard, and the tech obliged.

They watched the footage several times, both of them shaking their heads.

'Could this be something on the tape?' asked Fenwick. 'A fault, I mean?'

The tech shook his head. 'It could be of course, but I don't think so. I think those lines converged on him just before he died.'

Goddard leaned back in her chair, stroking her chin.

'Can you get me the footage from Northumberland Street, please,' she said and the tech obliged.

Now that they knew what they were looking for, they found it almost straight away. Two nebulous, cloudy streaks of light converged on the couple in the street just before they died. But this time they seemed to be bending. They emerged into the frames of footage and seemed to be heading together to miss the young couple, then for some reason they bent and came together right where the girl and boy were standing.

Goddard raised her head over the top of the tech and stared at Fenwick, as he stared back blankly at her. Because until they bent at the last possible moment, the lines had been heading towards the third person in the shot. And that person was Fenwick.

*

The Pheasant turned out to be a modern, brightly lit monstrosity of a pub. There was a pool table, a dart board and a bar. And that was it. The carpet was sticky under Fenwick's feet as he entered. It was situated in the middle of an intimidating housing estate, and the locals inside wore universal fake Burberry. Shaved heads and shit tattoos seemed to be the fashion of the day. Fenwick got a fair few stares as he entered but he ignored them and ordered a pint, taking it to a long padded bench to his right, with round tables and plastic chairs in front of it. He sat down and the locals huddled at the end of the bar, who had ignored him after their initial appraisal, suddenly roared with laughter and reached for their drinks. Obviously the end of a joke.

There was no other room in the pub and, after half his beer was gone, Fenwick began to think he had been conned by the young girl, for she was nowhere to be seen.

He sipped his beer and thought back to what had happened after he and Goddard had reviewed the footage.

They had found Parker and the three of them had gone through it again several times, trying to decipher what it was actually showing. They hadn't really come up with anything useful. They could see the peculiar lines of light but they didn't know what they were. Parker had decided to get the footage analysed further.

Goddard told him about the strange girl and, after a bit of persuasion, Parker had agreed that Fenwick should meet her, with Goddard waiting in the car outside. But he had insisted he was coming too. As the girl had told them to review the footage, it seemed that she might indeed have some useful information on what was going on.

Fenwick had almost finished his drink when the doors opened and the girl came in. She saw him as he stood to greet her and moved over towards him.

'Thank you for coming,' she said, but her eyes were scanning the boxes of crisps lined up behind the counter.

Fenwick took in her dirty face and the gauntness of her cheeks. 'When did you last eat?' he asked.

The girl smiled sadly, but just shrugged her shoulders in reply.

Fenwick indicated for the barman to come back over. 'Another pint, a coke, and do you serve meals?'

'Aye,' replied the barman, nodding at a menu on the bar. He turned to get the drinks, giving the girl a curious glance as he did so. Fenwick took the menu and handed it to the girl.

'Get what you fancy. You look half starved.' He paid for the drinks and the food: steak and kidney pie and chips. They sat back down at the table and ten minutes later the girl was tucking into her meal.

He watched as she ate hungrily, noting the unconscious table manners even though she was obviously starving. She was soon finished, and he ordered dessert for her.

'Thank you,' she said, 'I didn't realise how hungry I was.'

Fenwick dismissed the thanks. 'What's your name?'

'Ellie. Ellie Martins.'

'Well, Ellie Martins, what are you doing wandering the streets at this time of night? Where are you from? Why aren't you at home?'

Ellie stared into her second coke for a long time, her face suddenly looking much older than her years.

'I haven't got a home,' she said eventually. 'Not anymore. My parents are dead. They were murdered. And I killed them.'

Fenwick stared at her aghast. The girl could have been talking about last year's holiday for all the emotion in her voice.

'You killed them?' he asked uneasily, wondering what he had got himself involved with.

Ellie ran a hand through her long unkempt hair, her face tired and drawn. She licked her lips and took in a long shaking breath, as if she were steeling herself to talk freely.

'I'm going to tell you what's happened to me over the last few months and why it's affecting your investigation. I'm not asking you to believe me, only to listen to me. Humour me if you must, but just listen.'

Fenwick took a deep breath himself. He was totally mystified by this young urchin, but he couldn't shake off the feeling that whatever she had to say was of the utmost importance. Not only for what had been happening in and around Newcastle, but for the girl's own sanity. He nodded to her. 'All right,' he said.

'Let's face it,' she continued as if he hadn't spoken. 'I asked you to come alone but you have Goddard and Parker sitting in the silver Focus outside. So it's the least you can do.'

Fenwick stared at her, shaking his head slightly. 'How....?' He started, but Ellie waved a dismissive hand.

'Don't worry about it. I know they're desperate to find out what's happening. They may as well get that information from you.'

The girl drained her coke. 'About a year ago, I first came into contact with the people I'm going to talk about.' She held up a hand as Fenwick opened his mouth to ask a question. 'Please,' she said, 'Just listen and I'll answer your questions when I'm finished.'

Fenwick nodded his acquiescence and the girl continued. 'They came to me, said they'd been watching me for months, noting the powers I held, picking up on the "unconscious signals" I was sending out. They said they knew what I could do. Do you have a cigarette?'

The question was so unexpected that Fenwick just stared at her. He eventually shook his head. 'Sorry, I don't smoke,' he said.

'You used to,' she replied, and then nodded to herself. 'Of course, you haven't smoked for twelve years now, have you? New Year's Day 2006.'

Fenwick frowned at her, but she continued with her story without allowing him to interrupt again.

'I suppose I had always known I was different,' she continued. 'I could see things that other people couldn't, from as early an age as I can remember. I would find things for people. Car keys, wallets and things. It became a standard joke in my family. Lost something? Ask Ellie. She always knows where things are. And it was true. I only had to think of something that was lost and I could picture where it was.'

Ellie's eyes became faraway. 'If only it had stayed like that,' she whispered.

'Gradually, things got…more extreme. I found that, not only could I locate missing items, but, as I got older, I could move them. And I don't mean with my hands. I could actually move things by the power of thought. Telekinesis.'

Fenwick continued to stare at her, becoming disappointed. She obviously had some problems. He really should have known that this would have been a waste of time. He put down his beer pointedly, about to make his excuses and leave.

His pint glass slid slowly across the tabletop and stopped in Ellie's hand. She picked it up and drained it, closing her eyes in appreciation.

Fenwick stared, his mouth opening and closing, his brain trying to form words but failing to comply. He was literally speechless.

Ellie opened her eyes and looked at him. 'I haven't got time to waste by impressing you with parlour tricks. I need you to believe me. You are literally my only hope.'

Fenwick ducked down and looked under the table, looking for magnets or something. Nothing. All he found was hardened chewing gum. He suddenly felt annoyed. He hated tricks. Hated magicians. Always had done. It was an undeserved, groundless hatred but it was there in him all the same. Bloody charlatans, the lot of them. The girl had obviously set this up. That's why she had given him the address of the pub. To trick him for some reason. What that reason was though, he didn't know.

He straightened up. 'Do that again,' he said, but Ellie shook her head. 'Please, just listen,' she said. 'Just listen.'

Fenwick was still staring at the now empty pint glass as if expecting it to move again, but he eventually looked back at the girl and nodded.

'This skill was natural to me,' she said. 'When my mum found out she told me that it was naughty, she told me I must never do it again, to forget that I could. She was frightened, I suppose. And for years I never did, not in front of her and Dad, anyway. Connor, my brother, and I sometimes played games though. I would move things in his room and he would put them back again.' She smiled sadly. 'He loved that. But as far as the rest of the world was concerned, I was the same as everyone else. I subjugated whatever it was, kept it locked inside; didn't even think about it for most of the time.'

She paused as her dessert arrived, then took up the monologue again when the barmaid was gone, punctuating each sentence with a spoonful of ice cream.

'For a long time it worked. My powers seemed to get weaker as the years went on until eventually they were just a childhood memory. I pushed them to the back of my mind. But all that changed when I went to a friend's party. You can imagine the sort. We sat around talking about boys.' She smiled sadly again. 'We were only sixteen. Eventually the subject got around to the supernatural: ghost stories, that sort of thing. Stupidly, I told them about the things I used to be able to do: moving salt sellers, cups and what have you. They asked me to do it. Just for a laugh, they said. And eventually I gave in.

'We put a glass upside down on the kitchen table and they told me to move it. I told them it had been years, but they wouldn't listen.'

She finished her ice cream and put down her spoon. 'I moved the whole table,' she said flatly. 'Didn't just move it, but threw it against the wall, smashed it to pieces. After that, I wasn't too popular with those girls, as you can imagine. It scared them to bits. Scared me to bits as well. Because when I had tried to move the glass it was as if something else had helped me. As if an outside force had intervened. I remember moving the glass, but then something else seemed to snatch it from me and hurl everything against the wall.

Things weren't the same after that. Just about everything I looked at would shudder and shake, slide around and bump about. I was at my wits' end. And that's when they came for me, when I was at my lowest ebb. They told me they knew how I felt. How, with guidance, they could help me harness the "Gift", as they called it, to turn it into a force for good. After meeting with them for weeks at different places, they asked me to join them, to help them in their work. I ran away with them. I ran away from my family and the friends I had left. I gave up everything to be with them. In return they said they would give me a power that would change the world. At the time I thought they meant for the better.'

Once more Fenwick tried to interject, but Ellie shook her head and continued.

'It only took a few weeks of being with them to realise something of what they were planning, what *he* thought he believed he had to do. And a few more weeks to believe they were serious about it. I escaped, got away in the middle of the night. And they chased me. God, I thought I'd never get away, but eventually I put some distance between us. The things they themselves had taught me enabled me to stay in front of them. I got away. Went back to my family. To beg their forgiveness.'

Fenwick saw the look on her face and put a comforting hand on her forearm, his reeling mind disbelieving, but instinct taking over.

'They had killed my family,' Ellie went on. 'My mother, my dad and my brother. They tortured them and killed them. They wanted to find out where I was but of course they didn't know. But they killed them anyway.'

She took another quivering breath.

'After that I made my way north again. I don't know why. Instinct I suppose. They were never far behind me and I eventually ended up back here. After so many months I came back to the place where someone can help me.' Her eyes stared at Fenwick. Pleading.

Fenwick leaned back in his chair and surveyed the girl, his mind in turmoil. He wasn't sure if he was dealing with someone in genuine need of help, a dangerous maniac, or just a plain looney.

'Okay,' he said presently. 'Question time. First off, who are these people who you say are following you?'

'They're just that. Followers. Of an ideal, a plan.'

'Like a cult? Are they religious?'

'No,' she said, shaking her head. 'More…' She searched for the right word 'Ideological.'

'Do they have a leader?'

'Yes.'

'Who is he? Is it a he?'

'Yes,' said Ellie again and then shook her head. 'I don't know who he is. I met him on more than one occasion but when I try to think about what he looks like now it becomes vague, like an image in a dream. I can't really remember what he looks like.'

Fenwick rubbed his stubbled jaw. 'And you think he has something to do with the deaths that have happened here?'

'The murders. The murders that have happened here.'

Fenwick suddenly gave an apologetic half laugh. 'I'm sorry,' he said. 'But how can you expect me to believe this? I mean, why should I believe you?'

Ellie stared at him. 'Because he's responsible for murders other than these ones in Newcastle,' she said. 'He's been practising for a long time. One of his first experiments happened ten years ago. In Durham.'

Fenwick's breath caught in his throat. His eyes narrowed in sudden anger.

'How dare you,' he whispered. 'How dare you try to drag my personal history into your twisted story.' He stood up. 'We're finished here,' he said.

Ellie stood also. 'I'm sorry,' she pleaded. 'Please don't leave. I know you don't want to hear this, but you have to believe me. If you don't more people are going die. Please.'

She reached out and put her hand on his arm. Fenwick looked into her eyes and a strange feeling seemed to creep through his mind. It was a feeling that the girl was absolutely telling the truth. That what she said was real. He frowned. 'What the hell are you?' he asked, perplexed.

'I'm just a girl,' said Ellie. 'And I need help. Please help me.'

Fenwick stared at her for another second, undecided what to do.

'Did you stop Laura? DS Goddard, I mean? With this power of

yours? Was it you that caused that pain in her head this afternoon?'

Ellie nodded. 'I'm sorry I hurt her, but I needed to get away. I only wanted to talk with you, not her.'

Fenwick stared at her again. He was totally lost.

'I need another drink,' he said eventually. He went to the bar and ordered a pint and another Coke, returning and giving the girl the smaller glass. She nodded her thanks and they sat down again.

'Okay,' said Fenwick again eventually. 'Let's just suppose for a second all you've told me is true. I want to ask some more questions. And the first one is: how are they killing people in this way?'

Ellie sipped her drink as she sought the easiest way to describe what she had to say.

'Try and imagine,' she said, 'two bullets, two white hot bullets, so hot they're almost molten. And two people standing at opposite ends of a room, holding a gun each. Then imagine what would happen if they both fired at the same time, and the bullets crashed together in the middle of the room. Imagine the heat that would be generated. Now, substitute the bullets for two incredible minds, and the room for the entire length of a city. Think what would happen if these two minds were blended across miles. Think what would happen to anyone caught in the middle. At the point of contact.'

'Oh, come on,' said Fenwick. 'That's preposterous. The doctor's report stated that the heat generated was massive. How can two minds do that sort of damage?'

'He's taught them,' Ellie insisted. 'He's picked people already endowed with incredible powers and he's trained them, guided them and brought them to a peak. Made it possible for them to do something like this.'

Fenwick's mind turned for an instant back to the CCTV footage he had viewed that morning. Those two, nebulous lines of light converging on Eric McGuinness and the couple on the street.

'Then how come the clothes weren't burned, or even scorched?' he asked disbelievingly. 'And apart from that, how come the whole vicinity isn't blasted to hell and back?'

'We're talking about powers of the mind,' said Ellie. 'This isn't really a physical heat, not in the sense you understand. I think it started with that, but it's evolved over time into something else. Something much more potent. That smell I know has been haunting you. That smell is the scent of the Gift. The remnants of it linger on even after death.'

Fenwick slumped back in his chair, defeated by her unwavering belief in what she was saying.

'If all this were true, he could hold the country to ransom. He would be the most powerful man in the world. So why has he chosen Newcastle, for God's sake?'

Ellie's answer was simple. And horrifying.

'Because he lives here.'

Chapter Eleven

Newcastle, 1999

Thirteen minutes to go. Thirteen minutes until a new year, a new millennium. A new dawn.

William sat on a leather chair, only a single lamp illuminating the neat sitting room of his apartment, throwing brief respite from the darkness onto the packed books in the case in the alcove. He was sipping coffee. He no longer drank alcohol; he did not need its false stimulation.

The Visitors stood with him in the room. Silently they watched him. There were dozens of them now, and they had told him in the past that there were many, many more beyond. So many that what he had to do was worth it. William was not bothered by the morals of the task they had given him. He now looked upon other people as a dangerous, evil subspecies. They polluted the world with their smoke and their filth. With their words. And with their thoughts, their stupid, animalistic thoughts. They were so greedy. They wanted money, they wanted holidays and TVs and computers, and they all wanted to be better than each other. Which was impossible for them to do because they were all the same. All monsters, all evil. They grasped and they cheated and they copulated and they bred more stupid, stinking bacteria spreading monsters to slowly strangle the world.

They didn't deserve the planet they occupied. The Visitors had once been the masters here and the world had been wonderful. William knew this because the Visitors had often described what the planet had been like before mankind had infiltrated it. It had been green and lush and the waters of the rivers and streams had been clear and cool, not filled with germs and filth as they were now. The Visitors had lived in a world of peace and happiness and plenty. No one starved, no one went without and no one wanted or needed more than they had.

But the Visitors had died out. Humans had taken their place and had corrupted the Eden the Visitors once lived in. It was now time for them to be gone. And the wonderful thing about this was that the Visitors had told William how he could do it. How he could rid the world of the problems that mankind had brought about, and that by simply doing this, by ridding them in the way they were teaching him, would bring the Visitors back to rule once more. No more pollution, no more noise; that terrible, terrible noise in William's head from their awful thoughts gone. They had promised him peace.

William looked at the clock. Only five minutes to go. Soon, sometime in the next few years he would be completely ready to help them. They had trained him well and soon he would need to look for others like himself. Higher beings. They would work together to bring back the Visitors and at the same time save the planet. William sipped his coffee.

He turned on the TV at the allotted time. The sound of Big Ben chiming midnight brought a smile to his lips. He turned to the Visitors, their bodies flashing green and red from the fireworks on the TV. He saluted them with his coffee mug.

'It's your time,' he said, still smiling.

They smiled back at him with their appalling, grimacing smiles.

*

The dark blue BMW stood silently by the kerb. Inside, the three men were eating burgers. Steam curled from the junk food and misted up the windows.

The man in the back finished his meal and threw the rubbish out of the window onto the path, leaving it open as he lit a cigarette. He settled back into his seat.

'So where is she now?' he asked the driver, the only one of them who possessed the Gift. The driver was silent for a while, his eyes closing as he concentrated on his task.

'She's close,' he said eventually.

The car swayed slightly as the man in the back leant forward. '"She's close" isn't fucking good enough though, is it? I want to know where. Exactly.'

The burly man with the leather jacket in the front seat finished his burger and took the driver's carton from him too, throwing them out of the window to sit with the rubbish already discarded from the back seat.

'Leave it out, Blunt. Mike's doing his best.'

'*Leave it out, Mike's doing his best,*' mimicked Blunt. 'I tell you, it's not good enough. I want to find her and I want to find her now. If we don't,' he continued, 'then our lives won't be worth shit.'

Blunt was another big man, if anything even bigger than the passenger in the leather jacket. He wore jeans and a combat jacket and had many scars on his face, each one telling the story of a different bar room brawl. His close-set eyes betrayed little intelligence, but his expression was one of cruel eagerness. He was going to find that little bitch and, when he did, by God was she going to suffer. Blunt didn't really know why he wanted to hurt the girl so much, why he got so much pleasure from inflicting pain on others, only that he did. He had enjoyed it ever since he could dish it out, and that had been from an early age in his East London home. All he knew was that he wanted to hurt her, and to a creature such as Blunt, this was more than enough reason.

Fletcher, the man in the passenger seat, saw the expression on the other man's face and shuddered slightly. Why Blunt had been placed in charge of the three of them was something he could not understand. He himself should have been in control of this one. He was the better man for the job; calculating, ruthless and resilient. His years in the Paras had seen to that. But Blunt… Well, Blunt was a nutter, pure and simple. A hired thug. To obtain information from people often required torture and Fletcher had no problems carrying that torture out until the information was extracted. But

Christ, the things Blunt had done to that family, especially the little kid who obviously did not have the ability to understand the questions that were being shouted at him. That was pure sadism.

But, he told himself once more, he wasn't in charge; Blunt was. Whatever he said, went. Fletcher shrugged to himself and turned back to the man in the rear of the car.

'So what now?'

Blunt just stared at him with his pig-like eyes and said nothing. Eventually Fletcher turned his head back and stared out the windscreen. *Stupid bastard*, he allowed himself silently.

The car remained in silence for a while, broken only by the hissing of the blower Mike had turned on to clear the windscreen. Suddenly, the driver stiffened and fumbled in his coat pocket for something. With a bit of tugging the object, a city map, came free and Mike scanned it intently, his thin face frowning in concentration. With a small cry of discovery he stabbed a finger on the page.

'There,' he said excitedly. 'That's where she is.'

Blunt tore the map from his hands and stared at it for a long time, as if Mike's finger may have left a mark.

'Where?' he asked eventually.

Mike pointed to a section on the map. 'Somewhere there,' he said. 'I can sense her, I can smell something.' He sniffed, closing his eyes. 'Beer,' he said eventually.

Blunt smiled wickedly. 'The little whore's in a pub. Mike, get your foot down.'

The car roared away from the kerb and pulled into the traffic of Benfield Road, overtaking everything, rapidly getting faster until Fletcher said quietly, 'Keep the speed down, Mike. No point in getting nicked, is there?'

The last part of the sentence was directed at Blunt, who smiled, happy at the thought of what he would do to that little bitch when he got hold of her.

'No,' he said. 'No point at all.'

The car slowed to thirty and ten minutes later they were parked outside *The Pheasant*. Blunt and Fletcher made to get out until they saw that Mike hadn't moved. His face was confused, and his lips were moving silently.

'What is it?' asked Blunt impatiently. 'What's wrong with you?'

Mike was silent for a while, then he turned to the other men. 'She's not alone.'

'Who's with her?' asked Fletcher.

Mike stared at him. 'Fenwick,' he replied.

*

'He lives here?' asked Fenwick. 'Where?' He couldn't quite believe he was still listening to Ellie. He should have left ages ago, but she seemed able to impress on him that what she said was true, or at least that she believed it to be so. God knows what he would tell Goddard. And Parker. Christ, he could imagine what Parker would say.

'He has a big house, somewhere out in the country surrounding the city. I've been there, but I'm not exactly sure where it is. He makes it hard to remember.'

Fenwick stared at her again for a long time. He'd been doing this a lot as he tried to work out what the best approach was to this strange girl.

'Right,' he said finally. 'You said that you had found out what he was going to do, what his plan was, why he's killed these people. Suppose you tell me.'

'The leader directs the followers' powers,' she said. 'He channels them, so they become a force for destruction, a weapon if you like. He decides where to place them, and where the point of contact will be. He knows where the victims are at any given time, although I don't think it's a precise science. I think a lot of it is just chance. Then he murders people, pure and simple. As to why these particular people were chosen, I don't know. Maybe they were just target practice. I'm not really sure what he's planning or why he's doing it. Just that he wants to kill a lot of people.'

'Target practice,' repeated Fenwick faintly, thinking again about what she had said about his wife. 'Look, Ellie, as you know there are two coppers sitting outside. I think we need to get them involved in this now. You've obviously been through a great deal. Your family has been murdered, for God's sake. They can put you in touch with your relatives. People will be worried about you. Can't you see that?'

Ellie shook her head.

'You don't believe a word I've said, do you? If I stay with my relatives, they will be killed too, don't you see? You're the only one who can help me. You're my last chance.'

Fenwick sighed. 'Do you want another drink?' he asked and she nodded, but her eyes did not leave the tabletop.

Fenwick made his way to the bar through the growing crowd of punters and ordered the drinks, going over in his mind again what the girl had told him. It was crazy; he was mad even to entertain the idea of two people using their minds like a weapon. But the image of those nebulous, ethereal lines of light on the CCTV and that pint glass sliding along the tabletop returned to him. What the hell was *that* all about?

He paid for the drinks, turned back to the table and then stopped. Ellie was gone. He looked to the door and saw a man standing there: a big, ugly man with pig-like eyes and a cruel, unshaven, scarred face. The man licked his lips and stared back at Fenwick for a second, as if weighing up whether or not to come over and smash his face in, then he smiled wickedly, turned, and made his way out of the door.

*

Ellie was sprinting down the dark streets, heading into the rabbit warren of the housing estate in which the pub sat. Idiot! She thought. She had let her guard down, let them catch up with her, too busy on making Fenwick believe her to keep up the invisible sentinel around her presence.

She had looked up as Fenwick went to the bar, knowing she had failed to make him understand what she was trying to tell him. She had been so engrossed that she didn't notice Blunt walk into the pub until it was too late. Instantly, she had known that he was there for her, that power inside her growled like a dog at his presence. Without thinking, too terrified to rationalise, she had leapt out of her seat and run from the pub. Blunt had let her pass, not wanting to cause a scene in the crowded room, but Fletcher had been waiting outside for her, missing her by inches as she sped past and twisted desperately by him. He was behind her now though, running as fast as she was, eager to catch her. Neither of them had noticed the doors of a silver Ford Focus open and a woman and man step out, the man talking urgently into a radio.

The fear of being caught squeezed ice-cold adrenalin through her system, lending speed to her headlong flight. Her feet were pumping up and down on the pavement and, slowly, confidence began to build within her. She was young and fast. They would not catch her. She would escape, find Fenwick again, and make him believe her story.

She stole a glance behind her and, with another jolt of fear, she saw that the man chasing her was almost on her heels, running with strong, wide steps. He reached out a hand and was about to grab her elbow when Ellie suddenly jerked to a halt, twisting like a jack rabbit at the same time. The man hurtled past her, surprised at the sudden manoeuvre and too heavy to stop at such short notice.

Ellie pelted back in the opposite direction, back the way she had come, the man twenty or thirty feet behind her now, but again gaining fast.

She felt the pain of a stitch in her side, the effect of eating too much on an empty stomach allied with the sudden exercise, but she tried to ignore it. She rushed past the corner of an alleyway to her left, intent on re-entering the pub and getting Fenwick to help her, but suddenly a hand shot out from the corner, grabbed her by the lapels of her jacket and spun her around to slam painfully into the rough brickwork. The wind went from her with a great whoosh of air and she opened her eyes to stare straight into what seemed like the eyes of the devil himself.

The cruel, scarred face was only inches from her own and she smelled stale cigarette smoke and oily junk food on his breath. Banana-like lips curled back to reveal crooked yellow teeth.

'Hello, Lou,' the man said. 'We're going have some fun with you darlin'. Lots and lots of fun.' The grin became wider as he added, 'Then we're going kill you.'

Now that he was near her, Ellie suddenly knew who this man was. He was the man who had tortured and killed her family. She could almost see the events in his head as he remembered them. They were disjointed, fragmented images that flashed through her horrified brain in a millisecond.

With a shout of terror and anger, she managed to knock his hand from her lapel and her other hand, fingers bent into a claw, raked at his misshapen face, gouging long red welts from his forehead to his chin. The man screamed, automatically lurching away from the source of his pain. Ellie took a step back and then kicked him as hard as she could in the groin, putting all her strength into it.

With a wail, Blunt sank to his knees and Ellie sprang over his inert form just as Fletcher reached the scene. She pelted off down the alleyway where Blunt had waited, all coherent thought gone now, the need to escape her only propellant. Behind her, Fletcher paused beside Blunt and bent down, rolling him over and examining his face impassively.

'Never mind me!' screamed the wounded man. 'Get that fucking bitch!'

Without a word Fletcher sprinted off down the alley after Ellie. Blunt, still massaging his testicles, climbed to his feet and staggered painfully after them, his eyes full of murder.

*

Fenwick sat indecisively at the table, sipping his beer. Where had she gone? She wasn't in the toilets or she would have been back by now. And who was that bloke by the door? Why had he smiled that smile at him? Was it possible that even a part of the girl's story was true? Could that have been one of the men who had murdered her family?

The questions tumbled through his aching brain, tripping over themselves in their eagerness to be the first one answered.

If it *was* one of the murderers then it seemed to indicate that the girl herself was in great danger. Whatever was happening he knew he had to find this Ellie Martins and get Goddard and Parker from outside.

His decision made, Fenwick stood up to leave. A hand suddenly clamped down on his shoulder and he was forced back into his seat. A youngish man sat beside him and calmly looked at him. Something very strange happened to Fenwick as he looked into those eyes. He felt a warm, dead weight settle over his body and his arms suddenly dropped lifeless into his lap. His legs felt like they were made out of lead. He couldn't move them at all. He sat there, his limbs useless. He tried to move them but it was as if they were stuck. His hands lay flatly in his lap like those of a stroke victim.

Fenwick stared at the young man in bewilderment and fear. Staring was just about all he could manage.

Mike smiled back at him. 'Just sit still, Mr Fenwick. I'm sure we won't be here for long.'

Mike reached across and lifted Fenwick's beer from the table in front of him, taking a sip.

'Lovely,' he said, still smiling at Fenwick.

*

The dark brick walls rushed past her, shadows of bins and boxes pressed into the blackest parts. The rustling of old newspapers seemed to whisper at her, mocking her in her flight.

Ellie was in total panic now, running on fear only, her strength starting to give up and her breath coming in jerky sobs. She looked behind her and saw no sign of her pursuers, only the shadowy tunnel of the alley.

She continued on her way. But as she made her way deeper into the alley she gradually slowed down to a trot, then a walk and finally to a total, despairing halt. She stared at the nine-foot brick wall in front of her. The alleyway was a dead end.

With her lips quivering and tears of fear forming in her eyes, Ellie turned full circle, hoping for a way out of her nightmare. But there was nothing. She was trapped.

She heard footsteps behind her and turned slowly to see the two men approaching her.

'Please,' she whimpered, her hands in front of her in supplication. 'Please don't hurt me.' She backed into a dark corner, pressing herself into it as if the shadows would protect her. One of the men approached slowly, the other keeping back, blocking any escape.

The man stepped out of the shadows and Ellie saw the glinting red claw marks on his face, vivid in the poor light.

She was trying to summon up the Gift within her, but it wasn't working. She was no longer able to conjure up any coherent thought. She was immobile with terror. She could not even move anymore.

Blunt took the last few steps in a rush and grabbed Ellie by the throat, pressing her down onto the litter strewn ground.

'Oh, but we are going to hurt you,' he whispered hoarsely. 'We're going to hurt you a lot.'

*

'What the hell are you doing to me?' asked Fenwick, with more bravado than he felt. His head was trembling, but the rest of his body was utterly still.

'Just sit quietly,' said Mike. He didn't look like he was enjoying himself now. After the initial smile directed at Fenwick, no doubt due to relief that whatever he had done to the investigator was working, the young, thin-faced man had looked pensive and shot continuous glances at the door of the pub, as if waiting for someone to return.

'Just sit quietly,' he repeated, 'and this will be all over soon. I don't want to hurt you, but I will if you start making a fuss.'

Fenwick stared at the young man, anger overcoming him. 'Why don't you let me move and I'll show you what being hurt means.'

Mike shook his head. 'I don't think I'll do that if it's all the same to you. I deplore violence.'

After another glance towards the door, he turned back to Fenwick.

'At least you know now that what she told you was real,' he said. 'At least you know she was telling the truth.'

Jesus, he's right, thought Fenwick. Ellie's story seemed to be true. It wasn't just the ramblings of some demented girl, at least some of it seemed to be real. The fact that this young man appeared to be able to paralyse Fenwick just by thinking about it indicated that these people had some sort of incredible power. Something that was beyond the realms of others.

'What are you going to do with the girl?' he asked, trying to gain time, maybe get him to drop his guard, get him to stop using this…whatever it was, on him.

Mike turned back to him.

'I won't do anything to her Mr Fenwick. As I said, violence is not something I enjoy. But obviously, she will be taken care of.'

Fenwick nodded. He could guess what that meant. 'And what about me?' he asked. 'Surely I know too much now as well?'

Mike looked indecisive, as if he had not thought about this. He shook his head but he kept silent, his eyes not looking at Fenwick. The investigator could also guess what that meant. If something didn't happen soon, they would be getting rid of him as well. He swallowed hard. Half a second, he thought. Drop your guard for half a second, you bastard, and I'll have you.

The door of the pub opened and Mike glanced across, but it was not the man he waited for and his eyes returned to Fenwick.

It was a woman who had entered the pub. A woman with

blonde hair tied back in a loose ponytail and vivid green eyes.

Fenwick saw her and his own eyes pleaded and warned her at the same time, flicking towards Mike as the man absently sipped the beer in front of him.

Goddard walked over to the bar, heeding the look on Fenwick's face. She stood very close, listening to what the two men were saying.

'How are you doing this to me?' asked Fenwick, loudly and Mike flashed a warning look at him.

'Please don't try anything silly,' he said. 'Nobody in here is going to help you. If I wanted to, I could kill you here and now.'

'I thought you deplored violence,' said Fenwick, again loudly so Goddard could hear what was being said. 'You said that when you paralysed me.'

He was desperate for Goddard to do something, but he also realised that what he was saying must have sounded ridiculous. He could only hope she would trust him enough to act now and discuss later.

Goddard got the point. She stepped over to the pair, pulling out her ID card and showing it to Mike.

'Police,' she said. 'Could we have a word?'

Mike stared at her, dumbfounded, and fear struck. He suddenly looked very young. He swallowed hard and then his wide-eyed stare turned back to Fenwick.

'I'm sorry,' he said.

Fenwick immediately felt a tightening around his chest. His lungs seemed to freeze inside him and he found that he couldn't breathe, couldn't move. His terrified eyes turned towards Goddard, the pleading in them again.

'Ian, what's wrong?' she asked, concerned. 'What's happening?'

Fenwick couldn't speak. He was sitting in a pub, on a warm balmy night and he couldn't move and he couldn't breathe. Fear washed throughout his body. He was going to suffocate! His heart was thumping heavily, his arms and legs were like lead weights and his chest was unmoving as his lungs slowly discharged carbon dioxide into his system, poisoning his body. Killing him.

He turned his bloodshot eyes to Goddard again. He tried to talk, to tell her to stop the young man, to do something to help him, but he couldn't, his vision was greying out, white sparks were beginning to flash. He was losing consciousness.

Mike was still staring at him, seemingly concentrating totally on him now, and Goddard bent down beside Fenwick who was beginning to jerk in his seat, his eyes staring and bulbous. His face was becoming mottled.

She thought he was choking and she slapped his back once, twice, but to no avail. She turned once more to Mike and saw his pale faced gaze. His upper lip was beaded with sweat, and suddenly she knew, *knew* that he had something to do with what was happening to Fenwick. She didn't know what he was doing or how he was doing it, but this man was killing Fenwick right in front of her, and all he was doing was staring at him.

Without hesitation, Goddard delved into her jacket pocket and pulled out her pepper spray. She didn't even give the man a chance. She pointed the canister at his face and pressed the trigger.

The effect was instantaneous. Mike gagged and his hands flew to his face, coughing and choking. His nose immediately began streaming as the spray burned into his eyes and throat.

Fenwick slumped forward and then lurched back. His hands, his hands that could suddenly move, grasped the tabletop and he whooped in a huge lungful of air. It smelled of stale beer and stale bodies. There was even a hint of the pepper spray, but that air was the sweetest thing he had ever tasted. He gulped it down, filling his lungs, his eyes closing again, this time in relief and ecstasy.

Goddard briefly checked that he was now breathing and then pulled out her handcuffs, dragging the still choking Mike's arms behind him and cuffing them together. She checked that he too was okay and then turned back to Fenwick, bending down beside him.

'Ian, are you all right?'

This time he managed to nod.

'What the hell happened?' asked Goddard, but Fenwick shook his head.

'No time,' he wheezed. 'Got to find the girl. That bloke was after her. They're going to kill her.'

'Parker followed them,' said Goddard. 'We saw her sprint out and the men followed her. Parker's called in for backup.'

The sounds of a siren could be heard now and a second or two later, two uniformed police came into the pub, the crowd watching them with hostile eyes.

Goddard told them to keep an eye on the young man and to wait in case either of the two other men came back and then she and Fenwick ran outside, looking around them.

'She went this way,' she said and set off into the estate. Fenwick, still getting his breath back, limped along behind her as fast as he could.

*

Ellie doubled over with pain as Blunt swung a hooked fist into her stomach.

She collapsed to the ground and the big man took a step back and then lashed out with his booted foot, the blow crashing into the girl's chest.

She whined pitifully as he kicked her again, this time catching her thigh, hitting a nerve and causing a huge pain to swell down her leg. She tried to curl herself into a ball, offering as little a target as possible, but it did her no good. Blunt picked her bodily off the ground and threw her onto a nearby plastic bin, its contents scattering and clanging as she sprawled across its hard surface.

Fletcher, standing in the mouth of the alleyway, viewed the scene dispassionately. His only thought was that he wished Blunt wouldn't make so much out of it. He was being too loud. Why didn't he just kill the girl and they could be on their way? He shook his head as Blunt continued with his work.

He didn't hear the man behind him until it was too late. The scuff of a shoe sent him spinning round and he caught sight of a short, broad figure holding something in its hand. Then all thought disintegrated as his body was thrown to the floor and he jerked like a gaffed fish as electricity surged through his body. His eyes eventually closed as unconsciousness overtook him.

Parker eyed the unconscious man dispassionately and switched off the Taser. He stepped towards the far end of the alley.

Blunt turned from the huddled form of the young girl at the noise and surveyed the shadows carefully.

'Fletcher, what the fuck are you doing?'

Parker appeared from the darkness, pepper spray in one hand and his extendable baton in the other.

'Police,' he said. 'Step away from the girl and lie on the floor face down. Right now!'

Blunt stared. Then incredibly his lips curled into a smile, totally without fear.

'So you were here too, eh? Can't say I'm that surprised.' He stared at Parker. 'Well, well, well,' he said.

Parker looked into Blunt's eyes and saw no fear, only a deep nothingness. This man was not just a criminal. There was an insanity in those eyes that bespoke a mind which did not follow normal rules. Parker had seen eyes like those enough times to know that this man was as dangerous as a snake. He could not be given an inch.

He turned his gaze towards the girl who stared back at him, petrified.

'It's all right,' he told her. 'You're safe now. Can you walk?'

Ellie stood and tried to balance herself on shaking legs. She ached where Blunt had kicked her, but feeling was starting to return to the dead leg.

'I'm all right,' she said.

Parker nodded, his eyes darting back to the big man who still stood grinning.

'Come and stand by me, then,' said the DI. She started to move but Blunt suddenly leapt behind her, one massive arm snaking around her already bruised neck, his other hand delving into his pocket and pulling out a pistol. He ground the barrel into Ellie's temple, and the sight of the weapon sent a sudden thrill of fear down Parker's back.

Behind him, he could hear Fletcher starting to stir, but he could also hear sirens. He had minutes, if that, to diffuse this situation.

'This is not going to work,' he said to Blunt. His heart had kicked into overdrive at the sight of the handgun, but he kept his voice low and calm. 'Backup's coming. You can't get away. Give it up now and it'll go better for you later on.'

Blunt ignored the words.

'This is what's happening,' he said presently. 'Me and the bitch are going to walk back up the alley. You keep out of the way. When we get to the street I'll let her go and you let me get away. How does that sound?'

Parker could hear the sirens getting louder now, homing in on his position. Time. He still needed time.

He nodded to Blunt. 'Okay then. Let's do this.'

Blunt, still with Ellie, moved slowly around Parker who stood to one side to let him past. As Blunt got near the now kneeling form of Fletcher, he gave him a kick.

'Come on, get up, you useless twat.'

Fletcher struggled to his feet and the three of them backed slowly out of the alley.

Ellie, being dragged backwards, stared at Parker with pleading eyes. He tried to smile, but his face felt frozen. What came out looked more like a grimace and probably only frightened the girl even more.

Eventually they emerged into the street proper and stood under a glowing streetlamp.

'Right,' said Blunt. 'Drop the tools and I'll let her go.'

Parker shook his head. 'No chance. Let her go and I'll let you walk. You can trust me.'

Blunt laughed derisively. 'Oh yeah, I'm sure.'

Parker nodded. 'I mean it.'

Blunt's face abruptly changed into a desperate mask. 'I don't think this is going to work,' he said. 'I think there needs to be a change of plan. I'm afraid the girl will have to die.'

His arm tightened around Ellie's neck and she started struggling as her air supply was cut off. Fletcher pointed the gun in his other hand at Parker to ward him off as he strangled the girl.

Parker started running towards Blunt now, heedless of the gun in the man's hand. He had no option. He could only hope that if the man fired he would somehow miss, and if he reached the pair then the girl was going to have to get sprayed along with him. He didn't have a choice.

Blunt suddenly cried out and staggered forward, his grip on the girl slackening and the pistol clattering to the floor. Ellie stumbled, whooping in great lungfuls of air, but even as she did so she was running from Blunt and she crashed into Parker who grabbed her and pushed her behind him.

Parker lowered his spray as he saw Fenwick and Goddard, the DS's silhouetted body standing behind Blunt, her baton in her hand. She ran forward with the baton raised to hit him again, but Blunt was too fast. He seemed to have recovered very quickly from the blow to his head and he swept around, grabbing the DS's ankle and pulling her to the ground.

Fenwick had tackled Fletcher by this time and, although the other man was bigger and stronger than him, he was still suffering from the effects of Parker's Taser. Fenwick spun him round and belted him as hard as he could on the jaw. The big man stumbled backwards, dazed by his electrocution and the blow. Then, his face full of fury, he started towards Fenwick, murder in his eyes.

By this time Blunt had stood up and was about to deliver a crushing stamp to Goddard's face but, suddenly, he stopped, his leg raised and his gaze fixed on the DS, who rolled to one side as she saw him hesitate.

Fletcher had also stopped, staring at Fenwick but seemingly unable to move. Fenwick turned his attention to Ellie.

She stood in the light from the streetlamps, her hair hanging limply around her white face in lank tresses. Her breathing was a loud panting in the sudden silence. She looked like a witch: a grimacing, pale faced, staring witch. She glared at the two men, her face showing an indescribable hatred towards them.

Slowly, they turned towards each other. Blunt picked up the pistol and both Parker and Goddard stepped forward, raising their batons again and shouting at him to drop the weapon. But they were far too late. Blunt quickly lifted the gun and fired three shots in quick succession into Fletcher's head, which disintegrated under the onslaught. He hit the ground with a thud, already dead.

Parker and Goddard were screaming at Blunt now, telling him to lower the gun but having little chance of doing anything against his pistol with their batons and pepper spray. Only Fenwick could see what was happening.

He stared at Ellie. He could see the beads of sweat on her upper lip and the fixed gaze on her face. Fenwick had seen that same gaze only minutes before in the pub. Blunt, with shaking hands and terrified eyes, slowly turned the pistol until it was pointing in his own face.

Fenwick ran forward and grabbed Ellie by the arms, spinning her to face him. 'Enough!' he shouted at her.

At the same time, two police cars came screaming around the corner, lighting the scene with flashing blue, and Blunt suddenly blinked at the barrel of the pistol. He stared around him for a second as if in a daze, then he fired more shots towards the police cars and turned and disappeared around a corner. Two of the coppers raced after him, radioing for help.

Fenwick was still staring at Ellie, her face frightened and lonely again now, her eyes wide and staring, riveted on the dead body of Fletcher. She was beginning to shake.

Fenwick turned to Goddard.

'Are you okay?' he asked her. She nodded. He turned back to Ellie. 'It's all right,' he said.

'I'm fine too,' said Parker sarcastically. But he smiled at Fenwick when he looked at him.

Fenwick looked at the body of Fletcher. His head was destroyed and his blood and brains were splashed across the road. 'Jesus,' he said weakly.

Ellie began to cry and it seemed like the most natural thing in the world for Fenwick to hold her. He held her for a long time but the tears didn't stop.

Chapter Twelve

Blunt staggered into the brightly lit telephone box. His head was still bleeding from Goddard's blow and his face was a rancid yellow. He was breathing harshly and trembling from head to foot. He had been dodging around Newcastle for hours, making sure he had completely lost the police and keeping out of the way of the helicopter that droned around the city. He remembered coming round and staring into the huge, round circle of the barrel of the pistol, could feel his finger tightening around the trigger. His hand had seemed to have a will of its own… He shook his head to clear it of the memories.

He leaned heavily on the glass of the phone box, pressing his forehead against its coolness. Then he rang the memorised number and waited with trepidation until it was picked up.

'You failed.' It wasn't a question. It was a statement, and although the voice was calm and collected it still froze Blunt for a second.

'Yes,' he whispered.

'Come back here,' the voice said, and the line was cut off.

Blunt closed his eyes again and slumped against the glass. He had never really known what fear was. But at that instant, he was shaking with terror.

*

Fenwick, Parker and Goddard were back at the station, drinking coffee. It was now after midnight and they were all lost in their own thoughts. It had been, to put it mildly, a very strange night.

When Blunt had ran, Parker had taken control of the situation, such as it was. Goddard was telling him about the young man back at the pub when they received a call from one of the police officers charged with guarding him. He had disappeared.

The two officers had been trying to question him but, in their words, something weird happened.

'What happened?' asked Parker on his radio, mystified by the message.

'I don't know sir,' came the reply. 'It's like he just disappeared. He's gone.'

Parker angrily told them to stay where they were and put the radio away, shaking his head.

Parker and Goddard returned to the pub, where they found the officers with vacant, lost expressions on their faces. That same expression was on the faces of the rest of the punters who had been told to stay for questioning. No one seemed to know what had happened to the man in the handcuffs. The handcuffs were still there but nobody knew how or when the man had managed to escape. Eventually they had reviewed the CCTV that was thankfully installed in the pub and, to their amazement, they found out exactly what had happened.

The footage showed one of the officers talking to the man. The man said something, and the officer calmly unfastened the handcuffs and stood back. The officer who had done this stared at the footage, horrified, shaking his head silently in denial while he watched the image of himself on the video standing there, unmoving along with everyone else in the lounge, as the man exited the pub. They continued to just stand around, not talking, for about thirty seconds after the escape. Then they all seemed to come back to life and just stared at the spot where the man had been. The two coppers had then run out to look for the man, returning with lost and worried looks on their faces. After questioning everyone in the pub, the same answer was given. One moment the man was there, the next he was gone, but everyone had lost about three minutes.

For them it was as if they had jumped forward in time, the escape non-existent to them.

Fletcher's body was taken away for identification, while the BMW was removed to check over and the scene was taped off. In the meantime, locals stood around and jeered at the police, some of them shouting about 'police brutality' and calling them 'murderers'. They had no idea as to the identity of the man who had been killed. It was just an excuse to have a go at the "busies".

A few hours later they were back at the station, drinking their coffee. Ellie was sleeping on a couch in one of the offices, seemingly exhausted by the night's events.

Parker eventually looked up at Goddard and Fenwick. 'Tell me again what happened to you tonight,' he said. Fenwick once more went through the events in the pub, backed up by Goddard.

'He couldn't breathe, Joe,' she said. 'He was literally suffocating right in front of me. Whatever that man did to him, it was real. He must be some sort of hypnotist or something.' She shook her head. 'I don't know what he is, but he nearly killed Ian, and he was able to make a police officer uncuff him and let him go, as well as make a pub full of people forget they saw him do it.'

Parker shook his head. 'So are we to believe what the girl says? That the deaths we've had, the incidents tonight and the murder of that girl's family are all down to some cult? That they use some sort of psychic power to kill people?'

He stared at them until their gazes fell away.

'I don't know,' said Goddard eventually. 'It fits in with what's happened tonight. You saw that man. He killed his partner—what did you say he called him? Fletcher?—and he was going to kill himself too. And he didn't want to; you could see it in his eyes. He was terrified. And what that other one did to Ian. They do seem to have some sort of power. All the same, it takes a lot of swallowing.'

'Even if all this were true,' said Parker, 'why would they kill those two men? Why not the one in the pub? And why didn't they just burn them up if they can do that. A gun is a bit old school isn't it?'

Fenwick, who knew exactly who had forced the man with the scarred face to kill the other one, said nothing.

They sipped their coffees some more.

'Even if it were all true,' repeated Parker, 'who is this leader? What's this great plan he's been practising for?' He shook his head for the hundredth time. He seemed unable to even believe he was talking about this.

'Ellie doesn't know,' said Fenwick.

'Not much of a bloody psychic then, is she,' muttered Parker, his voice disgruntled.

Once more there was silence in the room. All three of them were lost.

Eventually, Parker stood up. 'I'm going to see if we've turned up anything on those three men,' he said. 'Shouldn't be too difficult as we've got one of their names. You two get off home.' He looked at Goddard. 'I'll let you know what we turn up. See you tomorrow.' Then he glanced at his watch. 'Later on today I mean.'

Goddard and Fenwick rose too.

'Come on,' said the DS. 'I'll take you back to the hotel.'

As they were leaving, Parker said to Fenwick. 'You did all right tonight. Maybe you should have been a copper instead of a firefighter.'

Fenwick smiled wryly, nodding his thanks at the tacit attempt at reconciliation.

'What about the girl?' he asked.

'She's in a police station. She's fine. We'll find somewhere more permanent for her tomorrow. I need to talk to her, but she needs to sleep. I think she's been through quite a bit. And I don't just mean tonight. I've read the report about her family's deaths.'

As they all left, Parker indicated to Goddard, and they stood together, Fenwick waiting out of ear shot.

'Do you know where you're going with this?' he asked her. 'And I don't mean the investigation.' He looked at Fenwick pointedly.

Goddard reddened slightly, despite herself.

'Joe,' she said, not looking him in the face.

'Nothing to do with me,' he said, looking embarrassed. 'I may be old but I'm not stupid. I've seen the looks you've been giving each other. I just think he has a lot of baggage.' He paused, not looking at her. 'I don't want you getting hurt, Laura.'

Goddard smiled and laid a hand on his arm. 'Thank you, "Dad",' she said mockingly. 'But I can look after myself.'

He smiled ruefully and nodded. 'I know you can,' he said softly. Then, in a louder voice, 'Eight o'clock tomorrow morning, Goddard.' He stomped off.

Goddard joined Fenwick. 'What was all that about?' he asked, but she just shook her head.

She drove him to the hotel and he climbed out of the car.

'I'll see you tomorrow,' he said, and she nodded.

He hesitated. 'I need a drink,' he added. 'I don't suppose you want to join me?'

The offer was there. Goddard could have taken him up on it. She wanted to. She could think of nothing she would rather do. She chewed on her bottom lip for a second before finally shaking her head.

'Not tonight, Ian. Another time?'

Fenwick smiled and nodded. 'Another time.' He closed the car door and Goddard drove away. He watched the taillights until they disappeared. Then he went straight up to his room. He didn't really want a drink at all.

*

He had set his alarm for six but he woke at five, a nightmare eventually forcing him awake.

He had been outside a big house. It had a large wooden door with a lion's head brass knocker and studded metal work. The door opened and he walked inside, and then down a long corridor. At the end of the corridor was a staircase, heading down. It was pitch black in the cellar he found himself in, and he held on to the wall to guide himself, feeling damp moss under his fingers.

There were puddles on the floor; he could feel them soaking into his shoes.

Suddenly a bright light flashed on, illuminating the cavern. The light was pointing straight at him, blinding him. He lifted a hand to try and see what was going on.

A figure moved in front of the light, but Fenwick could not see the face as it was back lit by the glare. But suddenly, the figure was surrounded by a fire that raged around him, the longish hair blowing in the dry heat. He—it was a man, he could make that much out—said something, but Fenwick could not hear what it was or could not remember when he woke up. The figure pointed to something on the floor of the cellar.

Fenwick rubbed his hands over his face as the memories of the dream plagued him.

The figure on the floor was Rachel. And lying with her was Kev. They were both naked and entwined in ecstasy, seemingly unaware of Fenwick and the other man. Fenwick watched, helpless, as they made love.

Suddenly, the two figures had burst into flames. They screamed in horror and pain as their flesh started to blister and bubble. Then the skin started to melt, to run down their faces like candle wax. Rachel turned to Fenwick with blind, melting eyes, screaming at him to help her, but Fenwick could not move. He was rooted to the spot. In his dream, all he could do was watch as his wife and friend burned.

The man whose face Fenwick could not see began to laugh. He laughed and laughed as the flesh on Rachel and Kev blackened and hardened and fell in charcoaled clumps from their carbonised skeletons. When Fenwick screamed himself awake he could still hear the laughter.

He climbed out of bed and made a cup of coffee, drinking the hot liquid gladly, the sting taking away the memories of that dream. Along with that oily, electric metallic smell that seemed to be lodged in his nostrils.

He showered and shaved, luxuriating in getting rid of days'

worth of stubble, then he dressed in jeans and sweater again, taking the lift from his work shoe and placing it into the dark trainer. At least he wouldn't limp so much today.

He went down and had a light breakfast then exited into the car park. He climbed into the Audi and sat for a second, trying to analyse the now rapidly fading dream. There was something about it that was not normal. Something not right, but he couldn't work out what it was. Rousing himself with a sigh, he eventually started the car and set off for the police station.

Goddard and Parker were already there when he went into the office that was so familiar to him now, along with Ellie who looked a lot better than she had last night. A good night's sleep and a shower seemed to have done her a world of good. Fenwick smiled at her and she smiled back.

'We know who the two men in the alley were,' said Parker without preamble, and slid some photos across to Fenwick. The photos were from charge sheets, and they showed close ups of the two men's unsmiling faces. The dead one, Fletcher, was ex-army and had been in and out of prison on a number of occasions for various nefarious activities, most of them violent. The other one, the man who had got away, was called David Blunt. His records went back years. It was a litany of thuggish behaviour from a very early age. He had progressed from drug dealing to intimidation, actual bodily harm and even suspicion of murder, although that had never been proved.

'A lovely couple,' said Parker once Fenwick had read the reports.

Fenwick nodded. 'What about the other one: the one in the pub?' he asked, but Parker shook his head.

'Nothing yet. He has no records we can find, and we haven't been able to identify him so far. Something will come up though.'

Parker then turned to Ellie.

'We really need to talk,' he told her. 'I need a formal statement about last night, and I need you to tell me everything you know about what's been going on here in the last few weeks. Are you up for that?'

Fenwick was surprised by the tenderness in Parker's voice. Maybe he had misjudged the DI.

Ellie nodded but said; 'You won't believe what I tell you though.'

'At the minute I just want everything on record,' said Parker. 'Believing or not believing can come later.'

He and Goddard took Ellie down to one of the interview rooms. Here they questioned her about the events of the previous evening. They asked her where she had been living since her family's murders, what she had been doing. They questioned her about the group of people she had joined, and about what they had been training her for. Eventually they returned and Fenwick re-joined them. The coffee came out again.

They sipped the drinks for a long, quiet time. Fenwick looked at Parker and could almost see the wheels turning, thinking about each aspect of what they knew and then discarding it, trying to come up with a logical explanation as to what they had heard. Eventually he shook his head to himself and looked at Ellie.

'You don't believe me,' she said, staring back at him. 'After everything that happened last night you still don't believe me.'

Goddard gave Ellie a pitying look.

'It's hard to swallow, Ellie,' she said kindly. 'You've been through such a lot. You've seen your family killed. Do you think that perhaps this story is a way for your mind to accept the terrible things that have happened to you? A way to try and come to terms with the awful things you've seen?'

Ellie turned to Fenwick. 'What about you?' she asked, her eyes bright with disappointed tears. 'Don't you believe me either?' There was a desperation in her voice that stung Fenwick. He felt a strange sense of obligation towards this young girl. He felt like he wanted to protect her.

'Some very strange things happened last night,' he said carefully. 'I saw a glass move across a tabletop, seemingly by itself. And when I was with that other man, I literally couldn't move. Not to mention the fact that I stopped breathing.' He grimaced reflexively at the thought of that feeling, the utter helplessness of sitting in that brightly lit room, surrounded by laughing drinkers and slowly suffocating. 'But I also think that things like hypnotism can make people *believe* that certain things are happening to them. Not necessarily that they are.'

Ellie stared at him. 'What about the way he got away?' she asked, turning the stare onto Goddard and then Parker in turn. 'How can you explain that?'

They were both silent. They didn't know how to explain that.

Ellie shook her head. 'You had better start to believe me soon,' she said. 'Or more people will die.'

They were saved from having to answer that when the door opened and Chief Constable Wright entered. He nodded at Goddard and Fenwick and gave a tight-lipped smile in the general direction of Ellie.

'Good morning,' he said, the Northern Irish brogue of his voice giving a sarcastic edge to his words. He sat down at the desk and poured himself a cup of coffee from the pot on the table.

'An interesting night,' he said, holding the slim file he had in his hand, obviously the reports from the night before. 'I'd like to go over it with you,' he continued, talking to Parker.

The DI nodded. 'Of course, sir,' he said. He glanced at Goddard and she stood up, indicating for Fenwick and Ellie to follow her. They left the two men to talk.

When they were outside the office Goddard turned to Fenwick. 'I just want to check on something,' she said. 'There's a canteen just down there.' She indicated to the corridor they stood on. 'Why don't you two get some breakfast. I'll find you later on.'

Fenwick nodded, a little mystified by her behaviour. She walked off down the corridor and he turned to the girl. 'Hungry?' he asked. She nodded, her eyes downcast and her demeanour defeated. He smiled at her. 'Come on then,' he said.

*

They found the canteen and got some breakfast. Full English for the girl, more coffee for Fenwick. They sat quietly for a while, the only sound the scraping of the cutlery on Ellie's plate. Apart from a couple of women behind the serving counter the canteen was empty. Fenwick watched Ellie as she ate.

When she was finished she pushed the plate away from her and dabbed the sides of her mouth.

Fenwick sighed. 'What happened last night?' he asked.

Ellie didn't meet his eyes. She was silent, continuing to stare at the tabletop.

'I'll tell you what I think happened,' he continued. 'I think you forced that man Blunt to kill the other guy. And I think that if I hadn't stopped you, you would have forced him to kill himself too. I think you *do* have some sort of…' he shook his head. 'Of something. You have something that means you can do incredible things. I saw that beer glass move and I also saw it was nothing to you, that you could do it any time you wanted, without even breaking a sweat. And I saw what that bloke was like in the pub when he was trying to kill me, and I truly believe that what happened to me *was* down to him. He had the same look you had on your face when Blunt shot Fletcher. I believe you murdered that man.'

Ellie looked up at these words, but there was nothing in her eyes.

'Try proving that,' she said. 'No one believes a word I've said, so I don't think I need to worry about being charged with murder.'

Fenwick leaned forward. 'Ellie, you killed a man,' he said earnestly. 'I'm not saying you'll ever be charged with it. I'm saying what you did was wrong. It was immoral.'

'Immoral?' she hissed at him. 'Those men murdered my family. Tortured and murdered them, even when they were sure they knew nothing about where I was. *They're* the murderers. The man who died was the murderer.' Her eyes went down to the table again. 'I've done the world a favour,' she said, but it was an empty protest. Fenwick could tell she was devastated with the turn of events. That she had somehow turned a corner and was lost, not knowing what to do or where to go. As if there was no way out for her.

Fenwick gazed at her for a while. He reached across and took her hand. He squeezed it until she looked at him.

'That was the first and last time you will do that,' he said. 'You have something inside you that is wonderful. But it's deadly too. You will never do anything like that again. Promise me.'

She stared at him for a long time, then nodded. 'I promise,' she said finally. She smiled a sad smile at him. 'So you do believe me?'

Fenwick pursed his lips and drew in a long breath.

'I don't know what to believe,' he said. 'Let's say I believe some of it. Is that okay for you for the minute?'

The sad smile brightened a little on Ellie's face. 'For the minute,' she repeated.

*

Parker finished his report and the two men stared at each other for a second or two. Wright sucked on his teeth and then poured himself another cup of coffee.

'So what we're looking for,' he said, spooning in some sugar, 'is a group of people, who work together across the city, setting themselves up at strategic points and then meld their minds together to kill people.' He stirred his coffee, took a sip and then put it down, his eyes turning at last to Parker. 'For fuck's sake, Joe. What the hell is wrong with you?'

Parker held up his hand in defence. 'Hey, I'm not saying I believe any of this shite. I'm simply stating what happened last night, that's all, and what the girl said in her interview.'

Wright continued to stare at his DI, shaking his head.

'Right, well I want something better than that,' he said. 'Get back on it and start doing some police work, get me facts. Tell me what happened to those people and how the trio last night were involved. And put it together in a report that makes sense, not something out of the fucking *X Files*.'

As he said this, the office door burst open and a uniformed

policeman ran headlong into the room. The two men stared at him. Behind the man, Parker glimpsed something: something electric blue. Something that spun and whirled, something that somehow seemed *alive*. The uniformed officer—Parker had time to recognise Tommy Shanks, the duty sergeant—said something, but it was as if the room was suddenly in a vacuum for no sound came out. Then suddenly, faster than Parker's eye could follow, the man's head erupted in a blue flash, the same whooshing blast shooting from the cuffs of his uniform shirt and the hems of his trousers. Parker actually saw that blinding light through the fibres of Shanks's clothes before they suddenly dropped limply to the floor of the office, the shoes and socks beneath them smoking gently.

The sound suddenly returned with a bang. Shouting, screaming, running feet. And beneath this the whooshing, gurgling flashes as more people were blasted into nothingness.

Parker and Wright sat rooted in their chairs, unable to comprehend what they had just seen.

Then Parker, rousing himself, grabbed his boss by the lapels and hauled him from the chair.

'Run!' he screamed into his face.

*

Goddard sipped yet another cup of coffee and surveyed the map she had laid out on the table in front of her.

'Ridiculous,' she said to herself, then looked up guiltily to see if anyone had heard her. She was all right, though. The only other occupants in the small restaurant were two young PCs, sitting staring at each other with the unmistakable light of true love in their eyes. The woman was wearing a wedding ring but the man wasn't.

Dirty sods, thought Goddard with a slight smile. The restaurant was situated across from the police station and a lot of its clientele were coppers who popped in for a decent bite to eat rather than sit in the canteen in the station itself, which sold edible but banal meals. The trouble was, though, that a lot of the coppers also used the restaurant for meetings with people they really shouldn't be meeting with. Goddard knew of at least half a dozen of her colleagues who had been, or were still engaged in, extra marital affairs. By the look of the couple at the other table they would have to be careful if they didn't want to be added to that list.

She dismissed the two coppers from her mind and went back to her map. This was the reason she had gone to the restaurant. She didn't want prying eyes and questions from colleagues. It was a street map of Newcastle and the surrounding area, and it had lines drawn on it in various different colours, criss-crossing its length and breadth. Those lines had been drawn by Goddard herself the night before after she had dropped off Fenwick.

After the events of the previous night and even though she told herself she didn't believe a word of the girl's story, she had been sufficiently intrigued to get out the map and mark where the victims had been killed, drawing lines to and from them, triangulated by the CCTV footage of the two deaths they had caught on camera. She had worked out the directions that those weird streaks of light had seemingly come from. Finally she had got a marker on them.

But she still thought it was nothing more than coincidence that the lines crossed through a single point to the south of Newcastle and that Anna Pont's house and the home of Ted Embleton could theoretically be on similar compass points. That morning she had looked on Google Maps and actually found a residence where the lines seemed to cross. It was a house in County Durham. Quite a large house. Thrushton Hall.

She glanced out of the window, trying to get her tired brain to work, when a frown appeared on her face. Somebody seemed to be playing silly buggers with the lights across at the station, switching them on and off on both floors. But the blue flashes were more like lightning strikes. They were bright and irregular and sometimes two or three flashes would go off together.

Goddard got up and went out into the car park of the restaurant, into the hazy, muggy, heat filled morning. And it was then that the doors of the station burst open and all hell broke loose.

Chapter Thirteen

Fenwick and Ellie ran through a nightmare world. A world of screaming women, of shouting men; a world of hissing, flashing blue light. Fire slashed diagonally across the control room they had run into, a violent blast that consumed everything it touched.

They had been in the canteen when they heard the shouting start up. They had stared at each other for the longest of moments, both of them shocked into immobility. Fenwick was about to speak when one of the women behind the serving counter screamed loudly. At the same time there was a flash of blue light and her companion, standing chatting to her only a second ago, was blasted into oblivion.

Ellie turned shocked, terrified eyes to Fenwick.

'We need to get out. Now!'

She reached across to him as he was starting to stand up. He was going to go over to the woman who had screamed, to help her maybe, but she grabbed him roughly by the arm.

'Now!' she screamed again. 'They're looking for us. They know we're here. We have to get out. We need to get away!'

She had pulled him from the canteen, Fenwick's eyes still on the woman staring back at him, helpless and terrified. They left her.

Outside the canteen they ran through the first doorway they found, finding it to be the control room. Fenwick glimpsed a police officer, obviously having just entered the room from a door opposite. The officer stood aghast in the doorway, unable to comprehend what his eyes were seeing. He suddenly gasped and grabbed his stomach, bent almost double. He seemed to be in incredible pain. His eyes bulged and then burst outwards in a blast of the unearthly light, his body engulfed by it immediately. His cap fell to the floor as there was suddenly no head left to support it.

Looking to his left, Fenwick saw a woman explode in the same way, the glowing atoms of her body touching another officer who himself erupted into the same blue flash, their clothes falling together, tangled on the floor of the room.

Within seconds, what had been an orderly and subdued office was a kaleidoscope of whirling, soaring, scorching electric blue fire that arced around the room; blinding in its incandescence, deadly in its touch.

With Ellie still on his arm, Fenwick burst through the doors opposite and into another corridor, skidding in something as he went. He quickly regained his balance and glanced down, his face forming a horrified grimace as he saw what caused him to slip. The remains of the first officer he had seen lay on the floor, still smoking gently; a long, greasy black streak stretched away from it like a tyre track where his foot had slipped in it.

Almost immediately another figure cannoned into him from the corridor and Fenwick stared down into the shocked and terrified face of Parker. His hair was in disarray and his mouth was opening and closing wordlessly.

Within seconds though, he seemed to regain some semblance of control, years of experience taking over.

'Outside!' he shouted. 'Now!'

The three of them ran down the corridor, brushing past people who were panic-stricken and terrified, eager to be away from the fiery death in the control room.

Fenwick paused at the fire exit, looking around.

'Where's Laura?' he asked the DI. 'And Wright?'

Parker shook his head. 'Wright's gone. Went up in a fucking blue flash. Don't know where Laura is.'

Fenwick turned back down the corridor, undecided. He wanted to find Goddard, to make sure she was okay, but he also wanted to get Ellie out. A terrible thought suddenly struck him. What if

Laura had been in that room? What if she had been struck by that awful light?

He turned to Parker. 'Get her out of here. Get her safe.'

Parker looked like he was going to argue, but Fenwick grabbed his arm.

'She needs you more than she needs me!' he shouted. 'Whatever the fuck is going on, she needs protection. Police protection.'

Parker just stared at him.

'They're behind this,' shouted Ellie to Fenwick. 'You know that don't you. We know too much.'

Fenwick simply nodded and gave her a little push towards Parker. 'Go!' he shouted.

Parker hesitated for one more second. Then his professional mind took over, understanding that what Fenwick had said was true. At least he hoped it was. He grabbed the girl and kicked open the fire doors, dragging her out.

Fenwick turned back towards the corridor, terrified he might see a pile of familiar clothes lying on the floor but he hadn't gone two paces before a massive explosion rocked the building. Heat and smoke billowed down the corridor, the shock of the blast knocking him to the floor. Chunks of masonry rained down around him, and he curled himself into a ball to try and prevent serious damage.

When he looked up through the dust and smoke, there were red and yellow flames belching from the end of the corridor, swiftly consuming everything in their way.

Fenwick shook his head. There was no way he could go back down that corridor. He thought it might have been a gas leak, but at that minute he didn't care. He was desperate to know what had happened to Goddard but there was no way he could make it down that corridor. It was nothing more than a crackling, fume filled tunnel and the flames were spreading fast. He had to leave. He took a last, despairing look at the burning interior, then turned back towards the fire doors at his end.

Just as he did so he heard a scream and he stared back into the smoke and heat to see a woman staggering towards him, her arms weaving blindly. She only had one shoe on.

A hissing noise suddenly came to his ears and he ducked instinctively, thinking it was that killing light and that his body would be engulfed in the strange and terrifying fire. But it was only the sprinklers kicking in, little use against the size of the fire that burned in the police station.

As fast as he could, limping badly now, he made his way towards the woman.

*

Parker and Ellie burst through into the bright, sunlit day, the fire door flapping in their wake. They skidded to a halt and Ellie looked back at the building just as the massive blast split the air. She fell to the ground as the earth seemed to shake and Parker dived on top of her, trying to shield her but mostly just knocking the breath from her body.

When she looked again flames were belching from the upper windows and broken glass was tinkling to the road around her.

She heard running footsteps and turned to see Goddard looming over her, her face pale.

'Are you both all right?' she shouted above the din of the flames and the fire alarms. 'Are you hurt?'

Ellie shook her head unsteadily, looking back again at the building. She tried to move but Parker's body pinned her. He was unconscious, a deep cut in his scalp. Something from the blast must have hit him.

'Ian's still in there,' she said to the DS. 'He was looking for you.' She managed to extricate herself from under the inert form of Parker and turned to go back into the building, but Goddard caught her arm.

'Stay here,' she ordered. 'Look after him,' she indicated to Parker. With that, Goddard sprinted towards the building.

She burst through the doors and was confronted with bedlam.

The sprinklers were soaking everything, turning the heat from the fire into a black, cloying steam. People splashed through the puddles on the floor, helping wounded colleagues. The air was thick with smoke and masonry dust and the emergency lighting added an eerie red sheen to the confusion. The screams of people still trapped upstairs seemed to echo around the whole building.

Goddard glimpsed a sergeant she knew directing people towards the fire doors. She ran over to him.

'The brigade's on its way, Ali,' she shouted.

The sergeant nodded then ducked as the plaster of the ceiling, already weakened by the blast, gave way with the weight of the water from the sprinklers upstairs. Goddard pressed herself against the wall as the plasterboards came crashing down, then shouted at the sergeant, 'Get everybody out, Ali, quick as you can.' The sergeant, already doing this, just nodded distractedly and continued with his task.

Goddard turned her attention to the billowing, smoke laden corridor, her heart beating fast in her chest. How could anyone survive that? How could Fenwick still be alive? She was panicking now. The thought of losing Fenwick before she had even begun to know him was a physical pain in her chest. It was a feeling of utter despair.

Suddenly a figure stumbled from the flames and smoke. A filthy, soot-stained figure that limped terribly, tripping over jagged rubble. The figure was half carrying, half dragging the semi-conscious figure of a woman.

Goddard ran up to him, as did Ali who took the woman from Fenwick and led her out. Fenwick and Goddard stared at each other. They just stood in the flames and the smoke and stared.

'Thank God,' Fenwick muttered as he looked at her.

Goddard was the first to rouse herself. 'Let's get out of here,' she said.

'It's them,' said Fenwick. 'It's the followers, they did this.'

Goddard stared back at him for a second. She didn't say anything, but her eyes betrayed the truth of Fenwick's words.

Another piece of the plaster ceiling gave way with a rending crash.

'Come on,' she said. 'Let's go.'

Arm in arm they picked their way through the shambles, now clear of other people, and staggered out into the street, smoke and dust billowing out with them.

Two fire engines were already on the scene, the firefighters rushing with professional haste, organising themselves quickly. An ambulance arrived, then another, and the paramedics started piling the worst affected people into them. Other wounded people sat or lay on the path and the road, waiting for their turn to be treated, their faces already taking on blank, shocked expressions.

They saw Ellie and Parker sitting on the kerb, Parker now conscious and holding a blood-soaked bandage to his temple, and they made their way towards them.

Ellie saw them and ran over. She hugged Fenwick tightly and, with a surprised look on his face, he hugged her back. 'I'm okay,' he said, smiling down at her.

'You believe me now, don't you?' she said.

Fenwick nodded. 'I believe you.'

'Well, what are we going to do about it?' asked Goddard. 'We can't prove anything. As far as anyone will work out, this was just a gas leak or something. Nothing… Nothing supernatural.'

They stared at her, realising that she was right.

'But the bodies,' said Parker weakly, still sitting on the kerb and staring up at the other people. His face was pale through the blood and soot and he shook uncontrollably. 'The bodies will be discovered. People will know they're the same as the ones we've been investigating.'

Fenwick shook his head. 'Between the blast and the water from the sprinklers there'll be nothing to say they didn't just die in a fire,' he said. 'Laura's right, we've no proof that this was anything more than a tragic accident. The bastards have covered their tracks.'

'What bodies?' asked Goddard, but they ignored her for the minute. Fenwick turned to Ellie.

'Do you know where this place is where this leader lives?' he asked, but she shook her head.

'I do,' said Goddard. 'At least, I've got an address that might be useful.'

Fenwick took a deep breath and surveyed the building. It was burning fiercely now.

'Then I think it's about time we paid him a call.' he said.

Chapter Fourteen

Newcastle, 2008

William wandered slowly through his new house. He had picked up the keys almost eight months ago and the work he'd had done was extensive. His hands gently caressed the new oak panelling of the hallway, and he smiled slightly at the touch. He walked into a room lit by a crystal chandelier in the middle of a huge ceiling rose, the ceiling high and ornate. There was more oak panelling in here, along with the huge bookshelves that ran around the room.

Each shelf was filled with leather bound tomes, a lot of them first editions. William breathed in the scent of the books along with the rich, deep odour of the wood panelling itself.

His footsteps echoed as he made his way into the sitting room, the floorboards sanded and polished to a high sheen. He sat down on one of the leather settees set either side of the large open fire and crossed his legs. He picked up the cup of tea that sat on the small table beside him.

He had so much power now. It had taken years. Years of study, years of practise, years of instruction from his strange allies. They knew what needed to be done. They had told him what needed to be done. They had explained why the destruction of one species would lead to the inevitable rise of another. A better species. A more worthy species. A species that the world deserved. That the world needed.

William sipped his tea, relishing the quietness of the big house. It was only here where his mind could relax. It was as if his new house stopped the noise of the brutish beasts outside its walls, stopped the clamour of their monstrous thoughts. He had at last found his refuge.

The Visitors had told him to buy the house, and at first he had resisted. It had cost a small fortune and, although he had a well-paid job, it had still taken a lot of persuasion to get the loan for the mortgage. But of course, persuasion was what he was good at. He had simply planted visions of wealth and avarice into the minds of the mortgage lenders. They thought they would make lots of money from his purchase. They were wrong, of course. They would not make any money. They would only die. Soon. Along with every other hairless ape that blundered around on this planet that did not belong to them. The planet that belonged instead to the Visitors.

He heard a door creak and he looked up. The Visitors stared down at him, their faces terrifying to anyone other than William. They crowded into the room. There were more and more of them now, their new existence due to William and his wonderful work. Soon there would be millions. Soon they would re-inherit the Earth.

They grimaced down at him, only William knowing that these grimaces were smiles, and although their mouths—if one could call them mouths—did not move, their thoughts slid into William's brain.

'More,' they said. 'More.'

William put down his tea. 'I'm still not strong enough,' he said. 'I can give you more, but not like you need. The energy released will still be weak. Not the energy you need.'

The Visitors just stood there in his beautiful sitting room, their grotesque bodies fading in and out of William's vision. They wavered and flickered, but they always returned.

'More,' they insisted.

William nodded. 'Of course.'

He closed his eyes and stretched out his mind, searching for the familiar feelings that made his work easier. The feelings of sadness, the feelings of despair. These were the senses his own mind could hook onto. The fools who felt these emotions were the instigators of their own demise. They had no idea how easy they made it for him. They had no idea of anything.

He felt the sensations, his mind homing in on them like a magnet. His thoughts swooped and soared across the land, finding the source of the emotions, and William revelled in them. He believed they were female. They were feelings of regret, of guilt, of despair. Another stupid beast regretting its actions but too late to rectify its mistakes.

William's face was pale now and sweating slightly. His thoughts locked onto the wailing woman. He recognised where she was, she lived not far from this place.

William's deadly thoughts, more powerful than lightning, crashed down into the weeping woman in Durham. He made her burn.

And another Visitor stepped into the sitting room.

*

Fenwick and Ellie were drinking coffee in Goddard's house. The DI herself had accompanied Parker to hospital, but she had given Fenwick her key and address and they expected her back any time. They had both showered and Fenwick had been surprised by the state of his body when he looked at himself in the bathroom mirror. He was bruised all down the left side of his ribs. He must have been hit by something in the explosion although he couldn't remember being hurt. He glanced down at the old, ragged scars that looped around his left thigh and shook his head. He was a mess. He had no other clothes with him, so he had to dress in the same ones he had worn that day; he smelled like a bonfire.

Ellie was protecting them. Or so she said. Fenwick glanced at her every now and again, but she didn't seem to be in that trance-like state she had been in when she had forced Blunt to do his terrible work. She just sat quietly and drank her coffee, her freshly washed hair wrapped in a towel, wearing Goddard's dressing gown.

'So what are we going to do?' she asked after a long while.

'Have a look at the place Laura found,' replied Fenwick. 'See what's there.' He shrugged. He didn't really know *what* they were going to do.

'Well, when are we going?'

'*We* aren't going any time,' he replied. 'Laura and I are going. You're staying here.'

'No I'm not,' said Ellie, setting down her coffee. 'I'm coming with you.'

Fenwick shook his head, but Ellie wasn't finished. 'I'm protecting you,' she continued. 'That's one reason why you need me. You'd be dead in half a minute without me. The second reason I'm going with you is that I've been to the house. I'll tell you if it's the right place as soon as we get there. And another reason.' Here she stopped as a sudden sob caught in her throat. She swallowed hard and composed herself. 'Another reason is that he killed my family. I want him stopped.'

Fenwick was about to argue, was about to ask her what exactly she meant by '*stopped*', but the sound of a key turning in the lock halted him.

Goddard entered, looking tired and drawn, still soot-smeared from the fire. Fenwick got up, grimacing at the pain in his side and his leg and went over to her. She smiled at him and, without even thinking about it, he bent down and kissed her cheek. She stared up at him for a second. Then her smile broadened.

'You okay?' he asked.

She nodded. 'Yeah. I am now,' she replied, still smiling.

Fenwick led her to the chair he had been sitting in and she sat down gratefully. 'Coffee?' he asked, but she shook her head.

'There's something a little better on the kitchen workbench. I'll have a large one.'

Fenwick entered the kitchen and saw the bottle of brandy standing there like a prize. He found a glass and poured her a large measure then, on reflection, got himself one as well. He brought them back into the lounge.

'Hope you don't mind,' he said, indicating to his own glass and she shook her head. 'Knock yourself out,' she murmured, taking a long swallow and closing her eyes.

Fenwick sat down beside Ellie and sipped his own drink. 'How was it at the hospital?' he asked.

'Bloody chaos,' she replied. 'The place is packed out. Forty-one people injured, twelve of them seriously. Fifteen people definitely dead, although the figure was rising all the time. Not everyone has been accounted for yet.'

She was quiet for a while, thinking of lost friends, then she said; 'Oh, nearly forgot. That bloke from the pub. The one who disappeared?'

Fenwick nodded.

'He turned up dead. A body was found this afternoon in a park in Gateshead. He'd been stabbed. The DI in charge recognised his face from the CCTV footage we sent out.'

Fenwick looked at Ellie, who just looked back.

'Do we know who he is?' he asked, but Goddard shook her head. 'Nobody does. No ID, no fingerprints that we can match, nobody that recognises his face. It's like he just turned up one day fully formed. We don't even have a name.'

Fenwick ran a hand through his still damp hair. 'Christ, who are these people?' he said.

Goddard shook her head. She drained her brandy. 'I'm going to have a shower, then we'll sort out what we're going to do. Have you two eaten?'

They shook their heads. 'There's mince and stuff in the fridge,' she started, but Fenwick got up.

'I'll rustle something up. You have your shower.'

He moved into the kitchen and fumbled around for a while until he found everything he needed to make a spaghetti bolognaise. He was stirring this and sipping some red wine he had found when Goddard emerged from the shower, wrapped only in a towel. He stopped stirring.

Goddard caught him staring. 'Catching flies?' she asked, smiling slightly.

Fenwick immediately averted his gaze, feeling his cheeks reddening. 'Should be ready in about half an hour,' he stuttered, drinking more wine as cover.

Goddard, still smiling, sidled up beside him, one hand clasping the towel at her chest. She stood very close to Fenwick and bent over the bubbling pan.

'Smells lovely,' she said.

Fenwick nodded dumbly, feeling her damp hair brushing his arm.

She turned to him. 'I like a man who can cook,' she said. Then she stretched up and kissed him on the lips. It was a short kiss, gone before it had really started, but it sent a wave of electricity through him.

'I'll get changed,' she whispered, and he nodded again. She went out of the kitchen and Fenwick heard her padding up the stairs. He caught sight of Ellie sitting in the lounge, regarding him through the open door with a smile on her face.

He frowned at her. She just continued to smile back.

Goddard came back downstairs dressed in shapeless jogging trousers and a sweatshirt, and they sat down to eat. When they had finished, they cleared the table and Goddard got her map out. They crowded around it.

Goddard traced the lines she had drawn on the map and pointed at various different sections.

'This is where Embleton was killed,' she said. 'And this is Anna Pont's house.' Her finger moved again. 'Eric McGuiness, the couple on Northumberland Street, and the police station.' She glanced at the other two. 'Are we really going down this route?' she asked. 'Are we saying that we believe that each of these deaths was caused by some sort of supernatural force?' She shook her head. 'There *has* to be a logical explanation to all this. What we're talking about is fantasy. It's ridiculous.'

Fenwick sighed softly. 'It is ridiculous,' he agreed. 'But I don't know anything else that can explain it at the minute. I, for one, am willing to believe that Ellie and these other people have some sort of ability that means they can move things around, even control people's thoughts and actions. How else do you explain that man escaping from the pub? A police officer let him go and everyone in there didn't see a thing. It was as if he froze time for them. And what he did to me. I don't know what it was, but I know what I felt. He was killing me, and he wasn't even touching me.'

'But using their minds to burn people?' asked Goddard. 'Can we believe that this is even remotely possible?'

'It's all the same power,' said Ellie. 'Why is it such a jump from controlling inanimate objects to controlling minds?' She turned to Fenwick. 'You saw what I did.'

Fenwick wasn't sure whether she was talking about the pint glass or what Blunt had done, but he just nodded.

'I think they're getting stronger,' said the girl. 'He's getting better.'

'How do you mean?' asked Goddard, sipping her wine.

'At the beginning, it was just him,' said Ellie. 'He practised on people; why, I don't know. But when he was by himself I think he found he could do certain things, but that he needed more power. He needed an amplifier, if you like. And I think that was when he started to recruit people like me.'

Fenwick thought for a second, then turned to Goddard. 'Remember that footage of McGuiness?' he said. The DS nodded.

'He was sweating,' continued the investigator. 'Whatever happened to him happened relatively slowly. But the couple beside me on the street, they just,' he shook his head, 'they just disappeared. No warning signs at all. And of course the attack this morning. God knows how they were killed, but they were killed instantly: no warning, no sweating. That would seem to indicate they're getting better.'

Goddard was about to answer, but Ellie interrupted him.

'You were beside them?' she asked. 'The people on the street?'

He nodded.

'What were they doing?'

'What do you mean?' he asked. 'They were just on the street.'

'Did they seem okay?'

'I think they were having an argument of some sort,' replied Fenwick. He stopped when he realised that Ellie was not listening.

'Of course,' she was saying to herself. 'That makes sense, I suppose.'

'What?' asked Goddard, frowning at the girl. This really was becoming too much for her. She wanted answers to things that seemingly had no answers.

'He was after Ian,' said Ellie, facing Goddard. 'I think he wants him dead. Maybe wants everyone involved in the investigation to die. To get you out of the way. So he can get on with what he wants to do.'

Goddard let out a long sigh and sat back in her chair, picking her wine up again, but Fenwick held up a hand to her, turning back to Ellie.

'So what's that got to do with the couple on the street?' he asked.

'I think this power they have, this ability to kill, I think it may be attracted to heightened emotional states. At least, it *used* to be. As I said, he's getting better. He's more able now to direct this power, but maybe when people's emotions are at a peak, maybe it acts as a…a better target.'

Goddard and Fenwick stared at each other, both of them remembering those nebulous, pale lines converging on Fenwick and then suddenly veering away to kill the boy and girl.

'But the people at the station,' said Fenwick. 'They weren't in any sort of "heightened emotional state"; not in the beginning, anyway.'

'I was protecting you all,' said Ellie. 'I have been since we met. I think that was an attack on anyone involved with this case. When Parker came round outside the station, he said that Wright was one of the first people to be killed. And he was right beside him when he died.'

She shook her head. 'Can I have a glass of wine?' she asked Goddard.

'How old are you?'

'Seventeen.'

'Close enough,' muttered the DS and poured her some wine, topping up her own glass at the same time.

'So you're saying that people's emotions are important?' asked Fenwick.

Ellie sipped her wine and nodded.

'As I said. I think it *was* important. But I also think that, with every person who dies, he becomes stronger. As if the powers he has get stronger with every death.'

'We know Anna Pont was raped a few years ago,' said Goddard into the silence that followed this statement. 'That would be enough to heighten anyone's emotions.' She shrugged. 'If she was thinking about it.'

'What about McGuiness?' asked Fenwick. 'Anything in his past?'

Goddard just shrugged again.

'I'm not saying the victims *have* to be like this,' said Ellie. 'Just that it may make it easier. I know for a fact that when I do things with my mind it's a very emotional feeling.'

'Oh, this is stupid,' said Goddard, pushing her chair back and standing. 'I refuse to believe in any of this. I am a police officer. I deal with facts, not make-believe. What you're talking about is impossible and I won't entertain it any longer.'

She walked into the kitchen. They heard the sound of running water and the angry clash of glasses and cutlery as she started washing up. Fenwick picked up his wine and drained it, staring at Ellie, who just stared back at him.

Fenwick eventually turned the map and looked at the coloured lines, staring at the point where they all connected, then at the print off from the Street View of Google Maps. The image showed a large, detached house in the countryside surrounding Durham. There were no other houses nearby. The house had a high wall and tall, metal gates with ivy growing up either side of it. He shook his head and poured more wine, lost as to what to do next.

Eventually Goddard came back into the sitting room, a coffee in her hand.

'I don't believe a word you've said,' she said to Ellie. 'But I do believe that some very strange things have happened today and over the last few weeks. And I know you have been through a lot.' She sipped her coffee, then continued. 'My DI is incapacitated, my chief constable is dead, and until I hear otherwise, that puts me in charge of this investigation.' She turned to Fenwick. 'I won't be able to persuade anyone else in authority that going to this house will in any way help.' She indicated to the map. 'But my decision is that I want to have a look at it. And I would appreciate it if you came with me.' She looked hard at Fenwick who just nodded.

'I'm coming too,' said Ellie, but Goddard shook her head. 'No you're not. You're staying here.'

Ellie was about to argue but Fenwick butted in.

'Laura's right,' he said. 'If what you say is true then you can protect us both just as well from here then if you were with us.' He turned back to Goddard.

'When do you want to go?' he asked, and she nodded, as if coming to a decision.

'Tomorrow.'

They organised sleeping arrangements. Fenwick was all for driving back to the hotel, but he'd had a couple of drinks and Goddard wouldn't hear of it. Her house had three bedrooms so it wasn't a problem. Ellie got the small, single room and Fenwick got the larger spare bedroom.

He got ready for bed and climbed in thankfully, exhausted but unable to sleep, his mind in a whirl. He didn't know what to believe, but he hoped that some answers might be found at that house. At Thrushton. Eventually he drifted off to sleep.

*

He was woken in the dead of the night when he felt the duvet move and someone climb in beside him. He felt Goddard's slim, naked body. He was about to say something but she put her fingers to his lips. He felt rather than saw her shake her head in the darkness and her arms went around his waist. He resisted for a second. He didn't want to feel like this again. He didn't want that responsibility. But as she pushed herself towards him and her mouth found his, he realised he didn't have any choice. He had felt like this from the moment he had first set eyes on her.

*

Outside Goddard's flat, a grey Mondeo pulled up. The man inside watched the lights go out and smiled, the grin on his scarred face looking wicked in the darkness. The leader had been right. The address was correct. He had wanted to break down the door, to beat that bastard Fenwick to a pulp, to feel his bones break under his hands. And that fucking bitch. He wanted to hurt her so badly, wanted to hear her scream for mercy as he slowly choked off her life. And then of course there was that copper. A real beauty. She would be fun.

But the leader had said no. He had said that things were too advanced now to waste time and Blunt was not so stupid as to disobey an order from *him*. He had seen with his own eyes what he could do.

But he would have his fun the following night. The leader had allowed him that because, by then, it wouldn't matter anymore. By then the world would be changing.

A flash of sheet lightning lit the road for an instant and a few seconds later distant thunder rumbled.

There was a storm coming.

Smiling again, and with a last, wistful look at the upper windows of Goddard's house, Blunt started the car and drove slowly away.

Chapter Fifteen

The next morning, Fenwick found Goddard gone from his bed. He shook his head at what had happened and then smiled.

It was as if, by making love with her, he had finally expunged his past. There was no guilt attached to what had happened, as there always had been in the past on the few occasions he'd had sex with someone. Instead of the dread and hopelessness he always felt, his night with Goddard made him feel something he had not felt for years. Hope.

He showered and dressed, still in the slightly smoky smelling clothes from the day before, and went downstairs.

Goddard was in the kitchen making coffee. Ellie was still in bed. The DS's hair was loose around her shoulders and she was wearing pyjama bottoms and a tight white vest, and he instantly noticed she wasn't wearing a bra underneath. He took in a deep breath. She handed him a coffee and smiled at him. He smiled back. Neither of them said anything.

Ellie came in, rubbing her eyes, her hair tousled. She looked at the pair of them and a little smile spread across her own face. She accepted a coffee from Goddard and murmured her thanks. She glanced at Fenwick as she walked past him and raised her eyebrows. She said nothing however and took her coffee into the dining room where she sat at the table with the map still spread out on it.

Fenwick and Goddard followed her into the room and they all sat drinking their coffee. Goddard was the first to speak.

'Right, we'll go to Thrushton this afternoon. I need to check in with the station and find out what's happening. I also want to see how Joe's doing. I'll be back in a couple of hours.'

She finished her coffee and went upstairs to shower and change. Once more Fenwick and Ellie were left alone, the two of them sitting in silence.

'What do you think he has planned?' asked Fenwick. 'What's he doing?'

Ellie shook her head. 'I don't know. I've tried a couple of times to find out, but I've got the feeling that when I do I become easier to see. That it might be dangerous for me to keep trying. But whatever it is, it's big.'

'Well, hopefully having a look at this house might help,' said Fenwick. He hesitated. 'You mentioned something in the pub about my wife,' he said carefully, not sure whether he wanted to pick at those old scabs again. Especially after what had happened between him and Laura. 'About Rachel.'

He stopped and looked at Ellie, who sighed. To Fenwick it sounded like a sigh of pity.

'I believe she was his victim,' she said. 'I think he killed her.'

Fenwick sipped his coffee, his eyes staring at the cup in front of him but not really seeing it.

'Why?' he asked finally.

Ellie shook her head.

'It's like I said. I think she was in emotional stress. And I truly think that's the only reason. He killed her to either try out his powers, or for whatever reason he believes he's doing this for. She was an easy target.'

Fenwick nodded slightly at this, thinking again back to that awful night. The grief was still there, but there was also a feeling almost of relief. If what Ellie said was true, then he was not responsible for his wife's death. That his leaving her had not been the reason why she died. The leader was. Rachel had simply been a test of some sort. He wasn't sure whether that made him feel better or worse. He said nothing more about it, however, and Ellie seemed to understand this. He finished his coffee and then washed the few cups in the sink. By the time he was finished Goddard had reappeared, dressed in jeans and a tee shirt.

'I'll be back as soon as I can,' she said to them, pulling on a short jacket, then left.

The temperature outside was boiling, the air thick and humid with no breeze. It was like being inside, so still and warm was the air. Looking up, Goddard saw green looking clouds building in the distance. The atmosphere seemed to be full of electricity. There was going to be an almighty storm soon, the heat of the last few weeks building into thunderheads that broiled to the West. She got into the Focus and drove to the station, still wondering what she had allowed herself to get involved in.

*

She was back by twelve and filled them in on the condition of Parker—okay, but still disorientated—and the station—destroyed. Operations had been moved to various other locations and the general consensus was that a gas leak had occurred. At least that was what the press were being told. Those who had seen their workmates and friends blasted into nothingness had been told to keep those details under wraps for the moment. She had told no one where she was going and, to be honest, no one had asked. In the general confusion of trying to sort out the shambles of the police station she wouldn't be missed for an hour or two.

'Don't you think we should have someone else with us?' asked Fenwick as they were preparing to leave. 'Backup or something?'

Goddard laughed softly through her nose. 'At the minute, I'm the only police help we're going to get. If we go, and try anything illegal,' here she looked at Fenwick pointedly, 'then I'm sacked, and probably nicked.' She paused. 'Were you thinking of doing anything illegal?'

Fenwick shook his head. 'Of course not. We're just going to have a look around aren't we? Maybe talk to the owner? Find out who they are? What they do for a living?'

Goddard nodded. 'But that's the problem. I don't need to ask anything about the owner, because I know who lives at that address. I looked it up this morning.'

Ellie had joined them now and she and Fenwick stared at Goddard, waiting for the information.

'It belongs to the pathologist, James Ross,' said the DS. 'Dr William James Ross.'

*

They drove in silence, the only sound the faraway whisper of the Audi's engine and the tyres rumbling over the road surface.

Fenwick glanced across at Goddard but her face was troubled, as if she were deep in thought. Eventually she seemed to rouse herself.

'He can't have anything to do with this,' she said, shaking her head. She turned to Fenwick. 'We've got this all wrong, Ian. Ross is an MBE for God's sake. He's a renowned doctor and pathologist. In the last year he's given almost twelve thousand pounds to various different charities. He has no record of ever being involved in any kind of nefarious activities. I really think the fact that those lines cross at his house is just coincidence.'

Fenwick glanced at her again before turning back to the road. 'Maybe,' he said. 'Remember when we went to the warehouse? When McGuinness was killed?'

She nodded, frowning at this turn in the conversation.

'Ross said something then,' continued Fenwick. 'I dismissed it at the time, but it could make sense now. He said that McGuinness looked like he had gone up in a blue flash.'

He glanced at her again to see if she got the message. When she continued to just look at him, he continued. 'He said *blue* flash,' he emphasised. 'At that point no one apart from Cook had seen what had happened, and he said the same thing. And at the station yesterday, that's exactly what was happening. People evaporating in a blue-white flash. How did he know? Why say blue? Why not just say a flash?'

Goddard eventually turned her head towards the windscreen again. 'It's a bit tenuous,' she said finally. 'It could have just been a figure of speech.'

'Maybe,' Fenwick conceded. 'Or maybe he's seen this sort of thing before. Maybe he knew exactly what it looked like.'

Goddard was saved from answering by the Sat Nav chiming in, telling them to take the next left.

Fenwick followed the directions, turning from the main road, and they found themselves on a twisting, turning single carriageway that climbed slowly up a hill. The trees on either side were in full leaf but they drooped limply in the heat of the afternoon. Above the trees the sky was darkening. It looked menacing and full of fury. The day outside the air-conditioned car hung endlessly.

They drove in silence for a couple of miles, both lost in their own thoughts. At one point Fenwick turned on the radio, but once the news was finished he snapped it off again. Neither of them wanted to listen to music. It was as if an invisible weight had settled on the car and was getting worse the further they travelled. The weather outside only added to the leaden feeling. It seemed to drag their spirits down to the lowest ebb, sapping their will until only blind pig-headedness kept them going. Fenwick slowed the car to a stop, looking at Goddard.

'Do you feel that?' he asked her.

She didn't answer but her face told him what he needed to know.

'About last night,' he began, but Goddard shook her head.

'Not now,' she said softly. She smiled at him. 'I want to talk about it, but later. Not now.'

Fenwick hesitated, but then nodded. He started forward down the road again, that leaden, smothering sensation still on him. It was almost a relief when they rounded a bend in the road and surveyed Thrushton for the first time.

It lay about two hundred yards back from the road. Beyond the ivy-framed, wrought iron gate, a long, gravel strewn driveway led straight up to the three wide steps that stood below the double front door. The door seemed to have a large knocker on it, but they couldn't make it out properly from where they waited. It was a big house and Fenwick guessed it must have had eight or nine bedrooms. There were two large dormer windows perched on the steep, sloping, pan-tiled roof. There was ivy on the house too, on either side of the big front door. It spread like green wings right up to the base of the first floor windows. These windows gleamed, as did the rest of the woodwork, under what looked like a very fresh coat of sparkling white paint. The brightness of the paint contrasted starkly with the rustic red of the pan tiles, as well as with the grey / green sky above. There was a lawn in front of the house, cut into two by the gravel driveway and, looking at it, Fenwick guessed it had been mowed recently. It was like a bowling green.

He glanced at his watch. It was only two in the afternoon but it was already getting dark, the broiling skies cutting off any light from the summer sun.

As they sat there, he thought for a while of what had happened to him since he had returned to his native city. Only weeks had passed, but it seemed like he had been caught up in this weirdness for far longer. First the death of Ted Embleton, a seemingly one-off incident. Then Anna Pont, then Eric McGuinness. Then that young couple who had been right by him when they burnt up, and the attack on the station yesterday. At least twenty people killed. And, of course, the fact that Rachel seemed to have been a victim of whatever was going on too. He had been, albeit unknowingly, involved in this investigation for ten years now. It seemed to him that something was building to a head, the cloying closeness of the day aiding that feeling. Fenwick couldn't shake the sensation that more was going to happen. He glanced at Goddard. He hoped he was wrong.

He stared at her profile for a while as she stared at the front of the house, wondering what they were going to do now they were here. He was aware that, between them, it was Goddard who had the most experience in anything that could even begin to be called "covert".

She turned to look at him and she nodded at the unspoken question. She didn't really know what Fenwick wanted to do and she believed he would be hard pressed to answer that himself. But she also knew that she was the police officer and that from now on she was in charge. She didn't begrudge this. Like Fenwick, she had known, ever since she had walked into that house in Blaydon where the remains of Ted Embleton lay, she had instinctively known that events were leading to something big. And now that they seemed to have arrived the only help she had with her was a man who walked with a limp and had no experience of police work.

However, as she looked into Fenwick's calm brown eyes, she decided she felt quite happy with that thought.

'For now, we'll wait,' she said.

*

Suddenly, Blunt knew something was wrong. He gently applied the brakes and guided the Mondeo onto a grass verge. He sat silently for a while, the engine throbbing gently beneath him, his ugly scarred face utterly devoid of any expression.

He reached for the ignition key and turned the engine off. The sudden silence was overwhelming. The oppression of the day outside pressed against the windows. He picked distractedly at the scabbed lines that Ellie had clawed into his face.

They were here. They had discovered the house and they were here. Must be that bitch copper and that fucker Fenwick, maybe with the girl as well. He licked his lips in anticipation of what he would do to *her* if *she* was with them.

It wasn't any psychic ability that told Blunt this, it was simply experience. A sixth sense of danger that came from a long life of living on the edge, of fighting for survival in the cruel landscape of East End pubs and drug den housing estates he had grown up in.

His old man had started his education in fear and brutality. The regular beatings he had received at his hands had taught him very early on that the world was cruel and dirty and dark. He had been sorted eventually, though. As soon as he had grown big enough he had beaten his father to a bloodied pulp and thrown him out of the house. He hadn't seen him since that day and, to be honest, had never really thought about him. He was gone and Blunt and his mother had finally been safe. Until she had died only a year later, her smoking habit sending her to an early grave in an orgy of blood and vomit.

Blunt didn't usually go in for introspection. He was not an intelligent man. His formal education, such as it was, had not lasted long. He had instead used his school days to hone his abilities. He fought with anyone and everyone, including the teachers. He simply would not give in, no matter how much they punished him, no matter how many times he had been excluded and expelled. He just did not care about himself that much. He could take pain and he could—and did—dish pain out. He was the bully in the yard who everyone kept away from, even the older lads whose backgrounds were similar to his own. He had earned respect through fear.

Once his short education was over he had progressed into the gangs of his city. He became an enforcer, a man who got the job done. A man who everyone feared would knock on their door in the middle of the night. He had plied his trade of brutality for so long now that there was no humanity left within him. It had been stripped away. He liked inflicting pain. He *enjoyed* it. Blunt truly believed it was the only thing he was good at.

Then that night had come. That night when he had overstepped the mark. His boss had told him to sort someone out. A dealer who'd had the temerity to work *their* streets. To take away *their* clients. Blunt had beaten the man to such a degree he had slipped into a coma and had later died from his injuries. Of course, at the time, Blunt hadn't known that he was the nephew of a different gangland boss. A man with much bigger and far-reaching connections than the one he had been working for. And this man wanted revenge.

His own boss had disowned him. In fact, because of the twisted sense of loyalty the gangland leaders had towards each other, he had actually been tricked and turned over. He had fought them when they came. He wasn't scared of anyone! But there had been too many of them and they had done to him what he had done to so many others. They had beaten him, tortured him, scarred him and left him for dead.

He remembered regaining consciousness as the icy waters of the Thames flooded over his body, and he shuddered at the memory. His hands and feet were bound and he was sinking, sinking, his nose and mouth filling with the filthy water and his wide eyes staring at the surface of the river moving away from him. Getting darker and darker.

The next thing he remembered was lying on the mud. Puking, shaking, freezing, paralysed with pain and shock. And he remembered the tall, dark figure standing above him, hands buried in the pockets of a long black coat. For a second he thought they had retrieved him only to finish him off, but the figure bent down beside him and those dark eyes bored into his own.

'You look like you need a job,' the figure said, and Blunt had caught a slight accent in the voice. Then the man straightened and turned away. 'If you do, follow me.' Blunt staggered to his feet, a broken arm hanging loosely, his face battered beyond all recognition, the cuts on his face washed by the river and smeared with the mud. He followed the man who led him. He followed him away from his underworld home in the south. He followed him north.

Blunt looked out of the window at the black fringe of the forest. Although it was not yet three in the afternoon, darkness had closed in. The sky was almost totally green now, shot through with grey, and the clouds bubbled and boiled upwards, cutting off the sun, cutting off the light. It was a perfect harbinger for what the leader was going to start tonight. The planet itself seemed to be holding its breath, ready to release its violence when the time was right.

He stepped out of the car, his patrol of the area forgotten now, and made his way across the road. He disappeared into the shadows of the trees, his footsteps muted by the soft, yielding forest floor and his body erupting into sweat from the heavy, humid atmosphere. He walked for about twenty minutes until he made out that he was coming to the furthest edge of the forest. He stopped and stood by a dark tree.

From there he could see Thrushton, a few lights illuminating its upper windows even at that time of day. There was a car parked just down from the main gates. A big car. Blunt narrowed his eyes and just managed to discern movement within the car and his awful smile flittered across his face again. He was right. His feral instincts had not let him down.

He delved inside his coat pocket and pulled out the handgun, loving the way it felt in his hand. Loving the power it gave him. Then, crouching low, he made his way towards the car.

*

Fenwick and Goddard sat, crunching mints inside the Audi.

'How much longer are we going to wait?' asked Fenwick finally, the unbelievable, almost overpowering oppression inside the car getting to him at last. He felt as if invisible weights were being systematically placed on his shoulders, pressing him further and further into his seat. With each passing minute it felt like they were getting heavier. With a tremendous amount of willpower he sat up, partially succeeding in shaking off the claustrophobic feeling, but it quickly returned.

'Just until something happens,' replied Goddard, still staring past him at the house. 'We have absolutely no evidence of anything going on here. The only thing we can do is just wait to see if anything turns up.'

She looked at Fenwick. 'If nothing happens in the next hour, we'll just go and knock on the door. Maybe pretend we've come to ask him if anything else has turned up about any of the bodies.' She shrugged. 'It's a bit lame but we might be able to ask him a few questions.'

Fenwick eventually nodded. They both helped themselves to more mints.

Goddard glanced at the dashboard clock. It was 3:30. She would give it until 4:30 and then go up to the house. Then they would take it from there.

She glanced outside again, this time looking at the darkening forest, just for a change of scenery. She paused, squinting her eyes, trying to pierce the gathering green gloom. Had something moved out there? She wiped a hand across the moisture that had accumulated on the passenger window and her eyes widened in shock. Not twenty yards away, a man stood, his legs spread wide, his body only a blacker part of the forest behind him. That was all the impression Goddard got, for her eyes were riveted on the pistol that the man held in both hands.

She just had time to bellow 'Get down!' before the side window shattered and the bullet embedded itself in the dashboard in front of her, spraying jagged pieces of plastic around the interior of the car.

Fenwick yelped as his face was pierced by what seemed like a thousand tiny needles, but even as he did so, his hands were scrabbling for the push button starter in an automatic response. The engine fired immediately. He stuck it into "D" and gave it a boot full of throttle, at the same time endeavouring to keep his head below the level of the windscreen.

There was another thunderous explosion and the front windscreen spiderwebbed. Goddard cried out but Fenwick didn't have time to look. He pressed his foot hard on the accelerator and the car shot forward, all four wheels spinning on the dusty road until they grabbed some traction.

Once more the man fired, this time the back windscreen taking the blast, spiderwebbing like the front, but the tough safety glass prevented any serious damage. The man fired again and again, the car rocking as the bullets tore into its body.

Fenwick glanced across at Goddard. 'Are you okay?' he shouted at her, desperation in his voice.

'Yes, I'm fine,' came the reply. 'I think I got hit with a ricochet. It's nothing serious.' She was holding the back of her neck; Fenwick, one eye still on the road, lifted her ponytail out of the way. There was a bleeding slice across the back of her neck, about an inch long, but the blood was oozing, not flowing. He closed his eyes for a second in relief.

Goddard began scrambling around, looking in her handbag, then searching around the dark interior of the car.

'What are you after?' he asked her.

'My radio,' she replied. 'We can have backup here in twenty minutes.' She craned her neck, looking all around.

'Where the fuck is it?' she shouted to herself. Then she lurched forward as Fenwick slammed on the brakes, only the anti-lock system stopping the wheels from skidding.

She looked at Fenwick, then stared through the starred windscreen, realising why he had stopped.

In front of them were trees. Nothing but trees. The road simply stopped. There was no way forward.

They stared at each other, speechless. Just then a huge flash of light lit up the entire scene, bathing the woods and the car in flashing staccato. A boom of thunder followed a second later. In the false silence after the thunder they heard fat raindrops begin to patter on the car.

'We have to turn round,' said Goddard. 'Go back the other way.'

'Are you crazy?' shouted Fenwick. There's some fucker with a gun back there!'

'I can't find my radio,' said Goddard in a remarkably calm voice. 'I don't know where it is, but it's not here. So we have to go for help.'

A thought struck her, and she suddenly scrabbled around in her bag again for her phone. No signal. She cursed and phoned 999 anyway but it was useless. It was almost as if something was jamming the signal.

'Try yours,' she said, and Fenwick did the same. Nothing.

'We have to go back,' she repeated. 'If he's still there we have to get round him. Run him down if you have to, but get past him. We've got all the evidence we need now.'

Fenwick had been looking through the rear-view mirror, half expecting to see the man with the gun appear, but the road behind looked deserted in the reflection from the taillights.

He shook his head unbelievingly. 'Christ alive,' he muttered, then he did a hasty three-point-turn and started back down the road, building up speed quickly. If they were going to do this, he wanted to do it fast.

A strange calmness seemed to overtake him. It was the same feeling he'd had when he was a firefighter. When other people were screaming and shouting and panicking, his job had been to purposely enter dangerous and potentially deadly situations, and he'd been bloody good at it. He had always remained calm. That same feeling descended upon him now and he relished it.

He realised he could hardly see through the bullet-scarred windscreen. He gave it an exploratory push and the whole thing came free from its housing, hanging loosely by a corner on Goddard's side until it was battered into fragments by the road.

Cracking his eyes against the howling gale and rain that now rushed into the speeding car, Fenwick saw a figure up ahead, standing pinned in the headlights. He must have known they would have to come back that way and he stood calmly and widened his legs, the pistol held out in front of him once more.

Fenwick suddenly recognised the man as Blunt, the man who had chased after Ellie. The man who had killed Fletcher, his own colleague. One of the men who had tortured and killed Ellie's family, including a young disabled boy. For the first time, anger welled up inside him and he floored the accelerator, the car automatically dropping a gear. It bounced forward, its engine howling, screaming as it reached the red line. But Fenwick did not let up. Blunt still stood in front of them, standing calmly, waiting for the car to get nearer.

Fifty yards to go. Blunt's face cracked into an imitation of a smile. Forty yards: he flexed his neck. Thirty yards: he took aim, sighting down the barrel on Fenwick's face. Twenty yards, ten. Blunt squeezed the trigger. The gun jammed.

Blunt stared at the gun. He couldn't believe it. He looked up and the car was just feet away from him. He dived to one side.

He was lucky. Fenwick twitched the wheel instinctively as they were upon him, unable to just murder a man in cold blood, and he chose the left. Blunt dived to the right. The car roared past him, doing at least ninety, its lights and body flashing by in a millisecond and disappearing rapidly down the lane. Blunt lay stunned for a second, his mind blank with the nearness of his own death, then slowly he stood up, watching the red taillights rapidly vanish. Another flash of lightning lit up the sky, this time forked. It crackled across the landscape, followed almost immediately by the tearing sound of thunder that was very close. The rain started pouring down.

Blunt stood in the sudden downpour, soaked immediately by its force, and pulled out another pistol, this one a revolver. The automatic had been lost when he had dived out of the way of the car but you could never be too careful. Two was always better than one. A crackling noise sounded from the two-way radio in his top pocket and he pulled it out, clicking the button to speak.

'Yes?'

'Alive, Blunt,' said that voice he feared so much. 'I want him alive'.

Blunt sighed with the unfairness of it all, not even wondering how the man on the other end of the line knew what was happening. He simply said 'Okay,' and started jogging through the rain after the car, turning into an old bridle path to the left a few hundred yards down. He knew a shortcut.

*

About two miles down the road, Fenwick slowed down, eventually rolling to a stop.

Goddard looked at him. 'What are you doing?' she asked.

'I want to see that neck of yours,' he replied, leaning over.

'We haven't got time…' she started, but he ignored her, lifting her hair again and staring at the wound. It was a cut that would probably require a stitch or two, but it still didn't look too bad. He leaned across her and opened the glove box, pulling out a first aid kit. He selected a pad and some gauze and quickly and professionally tied it round her neck, stemming the blood.

'Are you okay?' he asked her again.

She nodded. 'I'm fine,' she replied, but her face looked pale. She was looking at her phone again. Still no signal.

'I reckon we're about five miles from the nearest town,' she said. 'I think we should get there and find somewhere to get in touch with the police. Get them down here.'

Fenwick nodded and reached towards the starter. But before he could do this the driver's door was wrenched open and he found himself once more staring down the barrel of a gun. His gaze slowly travelled up the arm of the person holding the gun and eventually settled on the grinning face of a man he recognised.

Blunt smiled triumphantly in the downpour as another flash of lightning and a crash of thunder rolled across the skies. He waited until the noise had faded.

'Evening all,' he said.

Chapter Sixteen

County Durham, 2015

William stood at the head of the large table. He smiled at the twenty or so people who sat around it. They had eaten and now sat drinking coffee. There were chocolates and mints scattered around the remains of the meal.

The people at the table waited for him to speak. The conversation died down as William raised his hands.

'I want to thank you,' said William. 'I want to thank you for being who you are, for being what you are. For coming to me when I called. For heeding my plea.'

He paused to sip his own after dinner coffee, his smiling eyes surveying his people. His followers.

'You now know what we are tasked with,' he continued. 'You know what is at stake. Nothing less than the survival of the entire planet.'

William looked at each one of the people in turn, and they smiled back at him. They were happy. They were the chosen ones. They had been tasked with a mission more important than anything in history. In manmade history, anyway.

'We will be ready soon,' said William after his appraisal of his followers. 'In a few short years, we will be strong enough to begin our task. And, after that, we will live in a world of happiness and calm. A world without the bestial hosts that have ruined our heritage.'

He raised his coffee cup in a toast, and his followers stood.

'To the future,' William said.

The followers raised their own cups in a salute.

'The future,' they shouted.
The Visitors stood around the walls and smiled.

*

Blunt climbed into the backseat of the car, brushing glass from the seat as he did so.

He looked across at Goddard who was slouched across the passenger seat, seemingly unconscious.

'What's wrong with her?' he asked Fenwick.

Fenwick thought quickly. He had seen Goddard adopt this position when the door opened and assumed she was up to something. What, he didn't know, but he had to give her time.

'You shot her, you bastard,' he said. 'I was trying to help her.'

Blunt sniggered and Fenwick felt the hard, cold barrel of the revolver being pressed against the back of his neck. He immediately felt a cold sweat break out on his body, adding to the wetness pouring in through the missing windscreen.

'Watch your language, cocker,' said Blunt softly. 'You don't want to go upsetting the man with the gun, do you?' The barrel was pressed hard into Fenwick's neck. 'Now drive,' he said.

Fenwick pressed the starter. 'Where to?' he asked, his voice calmer than he felt.

'Don't play the giddy bloody goat with me, Fenwick. Up to the house. And don't forget about this here.' He jabbed the pistol forward again into his neck. 'No arsing about.'

Fenwick nodded imperceptibly and slowly turned the car, heading once more up the road, towards the house. After a couple of miles they found themselves back outside the electric gates which slowly started to open. Someone had obviously been watching and Fenwick slowed the car, waiting for the gates to open fully.

Suddenly the passenger door flew open and Goddard half leapt, half fell from the car. Fenwick was so startled by the move that he instinctively stood on the brakes, even though the car was hardly moving. Which was a good thing, for the aim Blunt was taking was spoiled as he lurched forward. The revolver went off with a huge explosion just beside Fenwick, deafening him. He leaned forward, his hand to his left ear, a terrible whining noise erupting in his head, drowning out the sound of everything else. He could see Blunt taking aim at Goddard's fleeing figure though and he jerked the car forward, again spoiling the big man's shot. This bullet actually went up through the roof and Fenwick was rewarded with the sight of Goddard disappearing into the soaking blackness of the forest.

A strong hand grabbed him by the hair and his head was jerked backwards, the pain excruciating.

Blunt ground the barrel of the revolver into the side of his head.

'Do anything like that again, and I'll kill you,' he whispered, and although Fenwick couldn't see his face, he knew he wasn't smiling now.

Blunt let go of his hair and Fenwick sagged forward, gasping for air.

'She'll get help,' he wheezed. 'This place will be crawling with coppers in less than an hour.'

Blunt chuckled. 'Yeah, maybe. But that forest can be very dangerous for strangers.' He laughed again. 'Very dangerous. What's in there might get what's left of you after he's finished with you. If they're lucky. Now drive.'

Fenwick drove, not trying anything. He hoped against hope that Goddard would get through the forest alive. He didn't know what Blunt meant by dangerous, but he didn't doubt the man was telling the truth. But Goddard was now his only chance. If she didn't make it, they were both dead, he had no doubt about that now, no doubt at all. Whatever was going on at this house, whatever "plan" this leader had, it was important enough to kill people to keep secret. He hoped again that Goddard would get away.

'Stop here,' ordered Blunt as they pulled up beside the front door of the house. Fenwick could see it clearly now, even through the pouring rain, and he stared. It was the wooden door from his dream, the one with the lion's head doorknocker. He suddenly realised that it hadn't been a dream. It hadn't been a dream at all. It had been a warning. A warning by someone who had the power to invade his subconscious thoughts. As he stared up at that house in the pouring rain, Fenwick wished he had heeded the warning.

A not-too-gentle tap from the gun told him to get out of the car and, with a wordless gesture, Blunt followed him up the steps. Fenwick stared as the door slowly opened.

*

Goddard blundered through the pitch-black forest, her footsteps squelching through the mud that was rapidly forming from the storm overhead. Lightning was flashing every minute or so now and the thunder banged and crackled rather than rumbled. The huge storm was right overhead.

She held out her arms in front of her to ward off any low branches or twigs, but even so some of them caught her face and scratched her. Her neck was aching now, and the trees seemed to loom out of the darkness to grab her clothes or strike spitefully at her eyes. The rustling through the forest as the rain filtered through was like a thousand voices whispering, as if the trees themselves were discussing how to trap her.

She ran into a small clearing, the rain heavier without the foliage above, and she stopped, spinning around, desperately trying to get her bearings. Her breath was coming in ragged gasps and she clasped a hand over her mouth as if to silence herself. She was shaking and trembling, and she recognised the symptoms for what they were. The adrenalin that had been coursing through her body from the shootings and from the wound to her neck was starting to dissipate, leaving her feeling lethargic. She wanted nothing more than to lie down on the soft forest floor and close her eyes, to be dowsed and cleansed by the rain.

Christ, what a mess. Her thoughts turned again to Fenwick. When she had seen the gunman, there had been no time to warn

Fenwick. Her only hope was to fake unconsciousness and wait for a chance to get away, praying that the investigator would understand.

He had been good, though. He had instinctively known she was up to something and had helped her deceit expertly. She hoped to God he was all right. If anything happened to him, especially now when she had left him, she would be lost. She shook her head. She could not quite come to terms with what her future might be like without him now. She had never felt this way about anyone. Not even Matt. If he died now…

Shaking her head again, she pushed thoughts of Fenwick out of her head. She needed to stay strong. She needed to get some support and get it fast. That was the only way to help him.

She knew there were villages dotted all around the area, old mining communities that had no real purpose of existence anymore, but simply struggled on because people continued to live there. She had to find one of these villages, get to a phone and get some help down here. As quickly as possible.

She set off once more, to her left this time, and a few minutes later she found herself beside the road where the man had shot at them.

She started to walk down the road, knowing it led to the dual carriageway they had used to get to Thrushton, but she stepped on something and looked down. The old Browning HI Power that the man had used against them was lying in the road, rapidly becoming a gurgling stream as the rain poured down.

Goddard picked it up and soon found why the man had not fired at them. A round was jammed in the breech. She fiddled with it for a second or two and then stopped. Had she heard something? She listened, but the sound of the rain drowned everything out. Lightning forked again and thunder made the ground shake. She ignored whatever the noise was and continued with her task, pushing her sodden hair out of her eyes and eventually flicking out the round and inspecting it in the pouring half-light.

After making sure the round was not damaged, she popped out

the remaining bullets. She had three in all and she gave them the once over. They seemed to be fine so she pushed them back into the magazine one at a time and snapped it back into the butt of the handgun. She placed the handgun in the pocket of her short, soaking jacket, the heavy bulge comforting. She started off once more down the road, towards what she hoped would be salvation.

And it was then that the undergrowth behind her erupted in a frenzy of smashing branches and the three huge dogs came bounding down the track towards her.

*

The door of the house opened. Fenwick took a step towards Blunt as the other man's eyes turned to the door, but the gun was instantly pointed at him again.

'Don't fuck with me, Fenwick,' said the big man. 'I've got more than enough reason to blow your head off right now, so if you want to live a little bit longer, do exactly what I say, and nothing else.'

Fenwick immediately stood still. There was a brightness in Blunt's small eyes that spoke of a madness beyond. Fenwick could see that this man was insane. He had to treat him like a wild animal. There could be no civilised discussion with him.

The door swung open on well-oiled hinges, revealing a brightly lit hall behind. A man was standing behind the half open door and he was as different to Blunt as it was possible to be.

He looked to be about nineteen or twenty and his frame was small and spare. Big black glasses were perched on his long nose, magnifying the eyes behind them to such a degree that he seemed to regard the two men with a look of permanent astonishment.

'Oh, it's you,' he said with evident dislike to Blunt, who glared at him in return.

'Yeah, it's me. Now get out of the fucking way, you faggot, its pouring down out here.' A flash of lightning and a clap of thunder emphasised the menace in Blunt's voice.

With a flounce, the young man moved aside and Blunt pushed

his captive into the bright interior, both of them wiping water from their faces. The young man closed the door against the storm outside and gazed at Fenwick, his eyes lingering on him.

'Well,' he said softly. 'Who's this?'

Blunt grinned, enjoying Fenwick's discomfort under that reptilian stare.

'Someone you might get to know intimately, Fox. If you're lucky.'

Fox's smile became wider. 'That might be nice,' he said. He actually licked his lips, his owlish gaze appraising the investigator.

Fenwick held the young man's gaze.

'Try it,' he said. 'I'm just in the mood for breaking someone's face.'

For a moment it looked as if the young man was going to attack him, but with a visible effort he calmed himself down.

'He's in the drawing room,' he said sulkily and then stormed off up the stairs in the centre of the room they stood in, his face mottled with petulant anger.

Fenwick turned to Blunt. 'Friend of yours?'

Blunt just shook his head, as if knowing Fenwick was trying to wind him up. He ordered Fenwick down the corridor and the investigator was once again reminded of his dream. Thankfully they stopped before they got to the door at the end of the corridor, and the stairs that Fenwick knew led down behind it.

'Wait,' muttered Blunt. With the revolver still pointing at Fenwick he stepped towards the door and raised his hand to knock. Before he could this, a voice came from the other side of the door.

'I'll see him straight away, Blunt.'

Blunt turned to Fenwick with a twisted grin. 'I fucking hate it when he does that.' He opened the door and with another glance at Fenwick, pushed him into the room before him. He slammed the door behind him.

Fenwick was alone with the leader.

*

Goddard whirled at the sudden crashing sound from the undergrowth, her heart missing a beat as another lightning flash lit up what looked like a scene from hell.

The three dogs were pelting towards her, their flanks glistening with water. Their massive paws splashed through the rivulets of water streaming down the road and their teeth were bared. They looked massive.

Goddard didn't recognise the breed. She only knew that they were big and black and brutal looking. She turned and ran in the opposite direction. She instantly knew that this was the wrong thing to do but she was helpless against her instincts. She glanced around in her headlong flight and with a jolt of fresh fear she saw that the lead dog was only ten or twelve yards behind her. She suddenly cut to her left, off the road and towards the forest, hoping to find a tree to climb, away from those massive, crushing teeth. A low growl, seemingly right behind her, spurred her on, pushing every inch of her depleted energy into her pounding feet, a whining noise coming from her lips as her chest heaved. She stole another glance behind her and saw the dog, its jaws gaping, only inches from her ankle, then a white flash erupted in her vision and pain seared through her head as she crashed headlong into a tree on the outskirts of the forest, actually bouncing backwards with the force of the collision.

She caught a disjointed image of the dog sliding under her feet, its front paws braced outwards as it tried in vain to stop itself, surprised by its quarry's actions. It crunched into the tree, a small yelp coming from its throat as its shoulder broke with the impact. It slammed to the ground but immediately tried to scramble back to its feet, not understanding why its foreleg would not work. It turned and twisted and snapped at Goddard who lay stunned on the ground behind it.

Her vision was blurred and she blinked rapidly to clear the rain that suddenly seemed to be coloured red from her eyes. She crawled away backwards from the beast, her hand scrabbling for the gun in her jacket pocket. She tugged the gun free from the lining, aiming it at the dog as it limped towards her. She fired point blank into its face just as it reached her feet.

The dog was smashed backwards as the bullet funnelled through its head and emerged from the back of its skull, decorating the tree with blood and grey brain matter. It twitched and its legs fluttered, then it lay still.

Goddard sagged, her energy completely drained. She could feel blood running down her face from a wound high up on her temple, diluted by the pouring rain, and that whole side of her face felt numb, adding to the pain already in her neck. She lay back on the soft, wet ground, watching the lightning sparkle and flash overhead.

She suddenly stiffened when she heard a small twig crack behind her, then she flung herself onto her stomach, just in time to see another dog launch itself at her prone form. She fired wildly and saw her bullet miss, then the dog was upon her, its huge jaws lunging towards her throat. She flung up her left arm and the dog bit savagely into it, just below the elbow. It shook its head violently and she felt her skin puncture and tear. She screamed with the sudden pain.

She managed to stagger to her feet, the dog still hanging from her arm, and she felt the flesh rip as she lifted it higher. She knew she had only one chance at this and, with another shout of fear and pain, she jerked her arm as high as it would go, the dog's teeth slicing deep grooves over her elbow as its head was jerked sideways with the motion. Goddard stuck the pistol in its unprotected stomach and fired.

The force of the shot flung the dog from her, but even then it would not give up. Its jaws snapped and its front legs scrabbled at the ground as it tried to get its useless back legs to work. The bullet had shattered its spine. Goddard stared in horror at the vile pantomime, watching as the scrabbling became less and less. Finally, the dog lay still, its pumping blood instantly washed away by the downpour.

She stumbled away from the two corpses and slumped against another tree, slowly sliding down until her rump touched the ground. She hung her head between her knees, her breathing coming in ragged gasps. After a while, she climbed stiffly to her feet and looked carefully around her for the other dog in that raging storm, the lightning coming with such frequency that it seemed the thunder could not keep up.

She couldn't see anything. She felt along her arm and winced when she felt the rents in her forearm, sticky blood oozing from them.

There was nothing she could do about it though, so she tried to forget it. She set off once more, her eyes constantly roving the storm lashed woodland around her. For the threat she knew still lurked there.

Chapter Seventeen

The room that Fox had described as the drawing room had an antique air to it. Dark oak panelling decorated the walls and the window shutters, closed off to the storm raging outside, were of the same colour. A floor lamp glowed in one corner of the big room, throwing insubstantial, yellow light which was helped by the log fire that burned in the grate opposite where Fenwick now stood.

In another corner sat a large leather topped writing desk, its top cluttered with yellowing photographs and a gold writing set. The pen from that set lay open on the desk along with a sheet of lavender paper engraved with the initials *W.J.R.*

A log cracked in the fireplace and Fenwick's attention was brought to it. And to the figure who sat next to it on a leather settee sipping what looked like a cup of tea. Ross smiled at him.

'Good afternoon, Mr Fenwick,' he said, his rich, slightly accented voice perfectly at home in these surroundings. 'Please, sit down.' He indicated to a twin of the settee opposite where he sat, his legs crossed comfortably.

Fenwick stood where he was for a second, using the time to study properly the man behind the façade of the doctor.

He was as tall as Fenwick, about six foot, and he was long limbed and loose jointed. He had a lithe look about him and his hands, resting now in his lap, were like a pianist's hands, strong looking and long fingered.

His hair was thick and straight and quite long, brushing the collar of his open necked shirt and it was naturally very black apart from the wisps of grey at his temples.

But it was his face that captured Fenwick's attention. It was long and lean like his body, with a very straight nose and dark brown eyes. Those eyes looked as black as night in the flickering light from the fire.

'Please,' said Ross, indicating to the settee. 'I know your leg is hurting.'

Fenwick sat down. He didn't have much choice. Ross stared at him, his head cocked to one side, as if weighing him up.

'I suppose you're wondering what has been happening,' he said eventually. 'Why those people died in the manner they have. I'm supposing Ellie has told you everything she knows.' He smiled, and it looked to Fenwick like a sad smile. A smile of regret.

'She had so much promise,' he said wistfully. 'She could have been on a par with myself, given time. When she left, it actually pushed my plans back several months. It has taken a lot to get ready for tonight.'

Again, Fenwick said nothing. Thunder cracked outside the shutters. It sounded like it was getting closer. After the rumble came a renewed hissing of rain on the windows and in the fireplace.

Ross suddenly leaned forward in his seat, his elbow on his knee and his chin resting on his knuckles. He sighed.

'What am I to do with you?' he asked, almost to himself. 'You are a good man. I knew that as soon as I met you. You really do want to help people. I find that curious. Why would you want to help others like yourself? What is the point in that?' He stared at Fenwick, waiting for an answer. He seemed genuinely confused.

'What do you mean?' asked Fenwick, breaking his silence. 'Others like myself?'

Ross frowned and shook his head.

'You know what I mean, Fenwick. People not like me.'

'Oh,' said Fenwick, feigning understanding. 'Not murdering fucking psychopaths.'

Ross tutted and sat back. 'Really,' he said to himself, as if disgusted with Fenwick's response. He stared at him again.

'I see you are just the same as the rest of the pathetic creatures who play on this planet. Unthinking and unknowing.'

He stood up and pulled a cord beside the fireplace. A minute later Blunt came into the room, smiling at Fenwick in anticipation. That look sent a shiver of ice down Fenwick's spine and he swallowed hard. He listened as Ross talked to Blunt in hushed tones, the smile on the bulkier man's face fading slightly and then becoming wider as the doctor finished talking. With another grinning glance at Fenwick, the big man turned and left the room.

Ross contemplated Fenwick again.

'It hasn't been easy, you know,' he said, standing in front of the fire and turning his attention to the flames. 'Although every creature I have dispatched has deserved its fate, it hasn't been easy. I have trained for decades. Trained to save lives, not take them.' He smiled into the flames. 'Of course, that was before they told me what humans had done. How they had taken everything that didn't belong to them. How they had ruined the very planet they squatted on.'

Fenwick stared at the profile of the standing man. What the hell was he talking about? It made no sense. Ross was as mad as Blunt. But if everything that Fenwick now believed to be true was correct, he was much more dangerous.

Ross turned to him again, and Fenwick looked deep into those black, soulless eyes.

'It is my mission,' said Ross finally, and it really seemed to Fenwick that he was trying to put a point across. As if he were trying to persuade Fenwick that he really had no choice. The doctor sat down again and spoke earnestly to Fenwick.

'All of my life, I have had the Gift,' he said. 'And it is a gift, even though it can cause great harm.'

Fenwick nodded slightly. *Keep talking, you mad bastard,* he thought. *Keep talking until help gets here and they drag you off to the looney bin.*

'My parents died because of it,' continued Ross, seemingly intent on making Fenwick understand something. What that something was though, was lost on the investigator.

'I didn't mean to kill them,' continued Ross. 'I was only four at the time. My father was a doctor too, you know. An English doctor. My mother was French. We lived near Paris, although I can barely remember that part of my life. It was before the Visitors.'

Fenwick continued to stare at him. Visitors? The man was talking nonsense.

'Anyway. They died in a fire,' continued Ross, his eyes focussed on the burning logs in the fireplace again, seemingly lost in the past.

'I was taken to an orphanage and it was there that the first Visitor came to me. They had recognised the Gift, you see. Had homed in on it like a beacon.'

He turned once more and looked at Fenwick. 'It was my parents' deaths, you see. Their deaths had been caused by me, even though I hadn't meant it to happen. It opened the door. And a Visitor came through.'

Fenwick was trying to look like he understood what Ross was talking about and nodded again, encouraging him to continue. He had to play for time. He had to believe that Goddard would be able to get help. But he was listening to the rantings of a mad man. What Ross was saying made no sense at all. He licked his dry lips.

'I'm afraid that first Visitor did nothing except terrify me,' said Ross with a sad smile. 'I was only small. I didn't understand at the time. But as I grew, as I was passed from foster parent to foster parent, as more things died, more Visitors came. And they were able to explain what needed to be done. *Why* it needed to be done'. He turned to Fenwick again. 'And how I could do it.'

He sat down on the settee opposite Fenwick once more, who continued to just stare at him. He was totally mystified about where this monologue was going.

'The Gift helped in other ways too,' continued Ross. 'I was sent to a…*special* school. A school that took in people with certain problems. But I fooled them all. I made my teachers write glowing reports for me, made them give me top marks in everything I did and it wasn't hard to be enrolled into Oxford, the college of my choice. The school really believed that they had changed me. That they had found and cured whatever it was they thought was wrong with me. I remember, later on, that the head teacher of that school burned to death in a house fire. It was all very sad.' He laughed softly. 'Anyway, at University I read medicine and concentrated on pathology. I was fascinated by the physiology of humans. I wanted to know if there were physical differences between them and me.

Needless to say, I gained a reputation as being one of the finest students they had ever taught. All because of the Gift. I put those thoughts into the professors' heads you see, just as I had at school. I made them believe I was their greatest prodigy.'

Ross paused and once more gazed into the fire and Fenwick took the opportunity to talk again, his interest unwillingly aroused by this man who so casually admitted that he was no genius, but instead a man with an incredible power. Who had used that power not to help others, but simply to further his career.

'So you're nothing but a conman,' he said, still hoping for the advantage of time.

'A conman?' repeated Ross, amusement showing on his face. 'Let me tell you something, Fenwick. Even when I was at that school I could see the way the world was going. Morals disappearing, perversion rife, wars in every corner of the globe. Poverty, unrest and want. The world was a cesspit inhabited by sewer rats and it still is. Idiots on all continents have stockpiled enough nuclear weaponry to destroy the Earth a hundred times over. Fools today are blowing up themselves and others in the name of a god that other fools have promised them condones it. It's only a matter of time before someone pushes the button. The Visitors showed me that there was another future the world could have. A different, better future. And they told me how I could help them make that future happen.

'I will try to make this easy for you to understand,' he continued. 'The Gift is the gift of fire, of heat. Like Prometheus, I slowly began to understand its power. Unlike Prometheus of course, I did not give the secret to the humans. I kept it for myself. And later, for the others like me.'

'Like Ellie?' asked Fenwick. He couldn't help but listen to the other man. He didn't really know where this story was going, but he was finding himself engrossed in it. And in the doctor himself. Here was a man who could seemingly kill just with the power of his mind. On a whim. Or for a reason. Fenwick wanted to know what that reason was.

Ross nodded eagerly. 'Yes, Like Ellie. Like Fox, whom you met earlier.'

'And like that man in the pub who tried to kill me?'

Ross stared at him for a second, then his eyes showed what looked like regret. He gazed at the floor for a while.

'Yes, like Michael. It was a shame I had to get rid of him, but he had become recognised by the police. He was no longer any use to me.'

'You killed him?' asked Fenwick. 'You stabbed him in that park?'

Ross frowned, as if such a thing was beneath him.

'Of course not. I had someone much more adept at that sort of thing than I.'

'You mean Blunt,' said Fenwick. It was a statement, not a question.

Ross did not answer, but gave a long sigh instead. He leaned back in his settee, crossing one leg over the other.

'I have the Gift. The Visitors need the Gift to set them free. The more humans who die, the more of the Visitors can cross over. The more Visitors who cross over, the stronger the Gift becomes. It is an ever-increasing circle of life.'

Fenwick stared at him, shaking his head.

'Or of death,' he said.

Ross scoffed. 'Human deaths. What is that to me? Or to the Visitors? They told me.' He wagged a finger at Fenwick, as if what he was saying was irrefutable proof of his beliefs. 'They explained everything. Humans polluted the world the Visitors lived in. Took it from them. They *raped* it and changed it into what it is today. A habitat fit only for their kind!'

Ross was seemingly becoming enraged as he spoke these words. He stood up and paced the room, as if he could not contain his anger.

'Every human that dies is one less human this planet has to suffer. One less flea. One less scorpion.' He stopped in his pacing and stood in front of Fenwick, staring down at him, breathing hard. He looked as if he was furious and barely able to keep his anger in check.

'When this is done,' he continued, 'the world will be restored to what it once was. It will be restored to perfection.'

Fenwick stared at him, open mouthed. This was—if possible— worse than he had originally thought. The man in front of him was a maniac. He was an absolute maniac. But he was a maniac with incredible powers. A maniac who was seemingly bent on killing as many people as he could. He licked his lips again. They felt very dry.

'Let me get this straight,' he said, still playing for as much time as he could. 'You're saying that there is a group of—what? People? Beings?—that you call the Visitors. They want the Earth and, to get it, you have to use this gift of yours to kill people.'

'Not people,' said Ross, seeming to calm down a little. 'Humans.'

Fenwick frowned.

'You're human,' he said.

'I am beyond human,' said the doctor, and a strange smile flickered over his face. 'I and my followers are the next step. We are what the Visitors have been waiting for. For aeons. We, and the Visitors, are the meek who shall inherit the Earth.'

Fenwick shook his head, unable to keep up the pretence anymore.

'You're a fucking lunatic. That's what you are.'

Ross was very quiet for a long time, staring at Fenwick. Then he took a deep breath, nodding to himself as if this was to be expected. He turned back to the settee and sat down, one leg crossing the other again in what seemed like a customary position.

'I should have known better,' he said. 'Explaining this to the likes of you is like trying to explain quantum physics to a germ cell.'

He suddenly frowned at Fenwick, totally at ease now. His moods seemed mercurial. He looked down at the foot that was crossed over his knee and closed one eye, lining it up with something in his line of vision. Then he gazed curiously at Fenwick, his head cocked to one side again.

'I don't think I've ever met any other human like you, Fenwick,' he said. 'You interest me, and you also…frighten me. That's what my senses are telling me. That I should fear you. Now why should that be when I have you completely at my mercy?'

'Perhaps I'm the one who's going to stop you doing whatever it is you think you're going to do,' said Fenwick.

Ross frowned again and a flicker of something played over his face, a dark shadow of uncertainty that dulled the fire in his black eyes, just for a moment.

'Perhaps,' he said, quietly. 'I can't see into the future. Not yet, anyway.'

Then he suddenly smiled, his arrogance reappearing.

'And perhaps not. Perhaps—and I really do think this is the most likely outcome—perhaps you will just die tonight. You may even be the first of your kind to go. Your demise may be the turning point that will start the world on a new setting. A new era. One without your kind. Only mine. And the visitors of course.'

Ross continued to stare at Fenwick. 'I've tried to kill you twice now,' he said. 'But in a way I'm pleased you're still here. I'm pleased I failed.'

He glanced at his watch. 'Only a few hours to go, Fenwick,' he said. 'A few hours until the world will begin its inevitable change towards harmony. I almost wish you could be around to see the outcome. But then, if you were, we wouldn't have done our jobs properly, would we?'

Fenwick suddenly understood what Ross was implying. He

suddenly burst out laughing.

'Hang on,' he said to the confused looking Ross. 'Hang on. Let me get this straight. Are you saying that, tonight, you are going to kill millions of people? That you're going to kill *all* the people in the world so you and your make-believe friends can live in peace and harmony? Like some sort of Bond villain?' He stared at Ross as if waiting for the other man to reply. 'Have you even *seen* a Bond film?' He asked. 'Do you know what happens to the villains?' He laughed again.

Ross waited until he was finished, his face impassive.

'*Bond* is make-believe, Fenwick. The Visitors and I are not.'

'So what about Blunt?' asked Fenwick, changing tack, trying to find a chink in the other man's armour. 'He's far from what I would call a "higher being". Where does he fit in?'

Ross nodded slowly. 'You're right, of course. I have found that I have a need for what you might call "enforcers". The only people who could be used were people without morals. Rapists, murderers. People who would do anything for the right price. Ironically, the very type of humans who have turned the world into what it is today.'

Ross laughed softly, almost to himself.

'After tonight, Blunt and the others like him I have recruited will no longer be needed. I can't have monsters remaining in our new world.'

Fenwick was speechless. This man was talking about killing people who had done his bidding as if he was talking about ridding his house of mice.

'The one thing I needed of course, was secrecy,' continued Ross, ignoring Fenwick's stunned expression. 'No one could know what I was intending to do until I was ready. I'm afraid I was a little overzealous with my practise sessions with my followers. I didn't think it through completely. I didn't realise the police would enlist someone like you to help them.'

Ross gazed at Fenwick again, the stare suddenly reptilian. 'It's strange, don't you think, that one of the first people I disposed of, one of the first humans to be destroyed so the Visitors could gather in numbers, would be related to the man who now sits before me. I suppose you could call me the man who made you what you are today. What was her name? Rachel, wasn't it?' He shrugged, smiling at the look on Fenwick's face. 'Fate I suppose.'

Fenwick lunged across the room, his anger sudden and overwhelming. He had every intention of beating this bastard into the ground, but as soon as he tried to move, he once again found himself gripped in that terrible paralysis that had held in the pub. Except this time Ross seemed to accomplish the feat seemingly without even thinking about it. He even glanced at his watch again. Fenwick strained against the force that held him immobile but to no avail. He screamed in his anger and his hatred.

Ross shook his head in disgust at him. He stood and pulled the cord.

The door opened and Blunt appeared again.

The doctor glanced at Fenwick again, his dark eyes unfathomable. 'I told Blunt earlier to send some of his friends to deal with Ellie.' He looked at Blunt quizzically and the other man nodded. 'I believe she's concentrating so much on you that she'll have little power left to deal with them.' He watched Fenwick struggle ineffectually against the invisible restraints that held him. Then he addressed Blunt once more.

'Take him downstairs.'

Fenwick struggled. He tried to fight, but he couldn't move a muscle. Blunt strode over to him, picked him up and carried him off like a sack of coal.

Chapter Eighteen

Goddard staggered out of the confines of the forest and leaned heavily on a nearby tree. Her chest was heaving and her left arm hung limply by her side. It felt numb, but every second or two a lance of pain would shoot through it, causing her to grimace. It also felt tight under her jacket, as if it was pressing against the inside of the torn sleeve.

She surveyed the grey Mondeo standing abandoned in the pouring rain, wiping water from her eyes. Lightning flashed again and thunder boomed over the top of her, lighting up the scene like a strobe light in a night club.

She glanced to her left and right, satisfying herself that the third dog was not there, lurking in the soaked undergrowth, then she walked over to the car, and without even hesitating she hefted the empty pistol she still carried and hammered it into the side window. The glass was tougher than she had expected, or perhaps she was a lot weaker than she thought she was, but after several more attempts at battering and hammering, the window smashed inwards. It was only when she put her hand inside to open the door that she realised it hadn't been locked.

She slumped into the driver's seat and lay back for a few seconds, her head spinning and her body swimming in a sea of pain. She had lost some blood, but not enough to make her feel like this. It was the events of the night that were clouding her vision, making her dizzy. Fearing she would pass out if she stayed in that position any longer, she straightened up. She had to continue. Had to find some help.

Willing herself to move she leaned forward. Had the driver left the key in the ignition? No. She looked in the glove box. Nothing. She flipped the passenger sun visor. A car key fell onto the passenger seat.

She stared at it for a second in disbelief. It was the first stroke of luck she'd had all day. She'd thought she would have had to try and hotwire the vehicle, but the owner had made it easy. She breathed a silent prayer of thanks, then stuck the key into the ignition and switched the engine on.

Just as she did this, lightning flashed again and to her right she caught sight of the third dog leaping towards the open window through the air, its jaws seeming to stretch to an impossible size in her disoriented mind. Without even thinking about it and, ignoring the pain in her arm, the DS stuck the car into first and floored it. The car shot forward and the dog bounced off the rear passenger window, but Goddard's foot slipped from the clutch in her panic and the car stalled. The dog dropped to the ground, but immediately got back to its feet, shaking itself. Its face turned towards Goddard. She looked back at it in the side mirror. In that flashing downpour it appeared seriously pissed off with her manoeuvre.

She wasted no time. She started the car again, stuck it into reverse, swung the wheel sharply and simply ran the dog down, wincing as she felt the bumps of the animal being flattened into the soft ground.

'Fuck you,' she muttered, her heart beating wildly in her chest. She stuck the car into first again and drove swiftly away and it was a few miles before she realised she was driving without lights. The windscreen wipers doubled their pace before she found the right switch and the trees on either side of the road were suddenly illuminated.

Once more, her vision swam. She stuck her head through the smashed window to let the rain revive her, but rapidly brought it back in again. She couldn't see where she was going like that in the downpour. She wasn't thinking straight. She had to force herself to keep her eyes open, the temptation to close them was almost overpowering. To simply sleep, to never have to move again. To let her battered body and mind just rest. Her vision greyed out and her head slumped forward.

She woke again with a start as the wheel flicked through her fingers, the car's front wheels brushing the soft verge. The Mondeo swerved several times before she got it back under control again.

She had to stay awake! She forced her eyes as wide as she could, concentrating only on driving the car in a straight line.

She drove in this fashion for what seemed like hours, only realising she was back on the dual carriageway when she had been on it for a few miles. She looked into the rear-view mirror and a stranger stared back at her.

Her face all down one side was grazed and swollen, with scratches that must have come from branches adding their own zigzag patterns to the party. Her bottom lip was swollen. Somewhere high up on her temple was a cut. She knew this not only because she could feel it throbbing, but because a single, thin line of blood was sliding down her cheek and discolouring her wet hair. Her left eye was half closed and looked red and angry. It would be as black as midnight in a few days. The back of her neck throbbed under the soaking pad that Fenwick had put on her. Goddard frowned and turned away, not particularly enamoured with her new looks.

She glanced down at her injured arm and was not surprised to see that the sleeve of her jacket was ripped to shreds. She didn't want to see what the arm underneath was like, so she didn't look. Instead she returned her red-eyed gaze to the road ahead and kept her mind on the impossible task of driving.

It wasn't until blue lights started flashing into her eyes from the mirror that she realised she had been driving in the fast lane at about forty miles an hour. It was lucky that the night was so stormy. It meant few people were out and about.

She pulled into the emergency lane and slowed to a stop, switching off the ignition. The sudden silence, albeit with the pounding of the rain on the roof hurt her ears. She lay her throbbing head back in the seat and she must have immediately passed out, for the next thing she knew, a copper was shining his torch in her face. It was as black as night now in that storm, even though it was barely 5pm.

The police patrolman, rain streaming from his waterproof jacket, eyed the broken window silently for a second. Then he noticed the automatic on the passenger seat beside the driver. He immediately pulled out his CS gas and pointed it Goddard, even though she didn't look like she was able to put up much of a fight. His partner opened the passenger door and took the pistol, also holding his pepper spray.

Goddard moved and both coppers shouted at her to keep still.

'It's okay,' she managed to say. 'I'm police; it's okay.'

'ID,' barked the first copper, and Goddard thought, *That's what I'm trying to show you, you idiot,* but she couldn't form the words properly. Instead, she simply pulled open her jacket weakly and the patrolman pulled out her CID card.

He put the canister away and indicated for his partner to do the same.

'Are you pissed?' he asked. 'What the hell's happened to you?'

Goddard tried to explain. She tried to tell the copper what had happened at Thrushton, but her eyes were so heavy. Her lips tried to form the words, but her eyelids drooped, her head following rapidly, and she slipped into unconsciousness.

*

Blunt carried Fenwick down to the cellar. It was the same cellar as in his dream, which didn't really surprise him. He had expected it to be cold, but it wasn't. Instead it was warm and humid, like a greenhouse. At the bottom of the stairs Blunt dropped him unceremoniously and he whacked his head painfully on the floor, unable to put out his arms to break his fall. Blunt pulled out his pistol and Fenwick once more found himself staring down a gun barrel. Feeling returned to his arms and legs; he could move again.

Blunt indicated for him to get up and he did so. His clothes, which had started to dry out by Ross's fire, were wet again from the puddles on the floor. He massaged his arm, which was tingling with the aftereffects of whatever Ross had done to him.

There was a click as Blunt turned on the lights, and the cellar was suddenly illuminated with powerful arc lamps, their brilliant light chasing the shadows to all but the furthest corners. Fenwick blinked a couple of times until his eyes adjusted to the light, and then stared around him, surprised by the size of the cellar.

It extended before him a good hundred feet and the ceiling was high, about ten feet, its surface smooth concrete where Fenwick and his captor stood, but turning into roughhewn stone after about fifteen yards. Fenwick slowly realised that the cellar had been extended at some point in the past and the stone was where it had been tunnelled into the very ground on which the house stood. He couldn't help but wonder why.

Set into the side of the cavernous cellar were three prison-like doors, thick metal gates set solidly into the surrounding stonework, a small grill in the middle of each one.

Blunt pushed him forward in the direction of the first door and Fenwick turned to face him.

'You'll not get me in there,' he said, shaking his head, but Blunt just grinned wickedly and indicated to the pistol in his hand.

'Up to you, Fenwick. I'm quite willing to shoot you now if that's what you want. Take your choice.'

Fenwick stared at him. 'Hard man with a gun in your hand, aren't you? Did you need it when you murdered Ellie's brother?'

Blunt merely continued to smile at him. Then he suddenly swung up the gun and cracked it into Fenwick's face.

Fenwick stumbled back with the blow, his cheek on fire. When he took his hand away it was smeared with blood.

'I'll ask you one more time,' said Blunt, still smiling.

Fenwick, still holding his face, turned and moved slowly towards the door, standing by it under the eye of the revolver as Blunt opened it with a key that hung on a ring on his belt.

'Inside,' he said roughly, and Fenwick did as he was told, hearing the door clang shut and lock behind him.

He heard Blunt walk away and then there was no other sound except the sound of condensation, the small dripping noises very loud in the enveloping silence. Even the torrential rain from the storm was unheard down here. The only illumination came from the grill set in the door, and Fenwick was thankful that Blunt had left the light on. But his thanks were dashed when he heard the killer say, 'Goodnight, Fenwick,' from the bottom of the stairs. A moment later he heard a flick of a switch and he was alone in the darkness.

'Bastard!' he shouted savagely and banged with futile intensity on the door. It didn't even shake.

After a few seconds he gave up on this and started to feel his way around the small room but found no light switch. There was only one piece of furniture: a wooden chair in the centre of the room. He had seen that in the time he'd had before the light was turned out and, after a bit of fumbling, he found it and sat down.

What the fuck was going on? What did that mad bastard Ross have planned? Fenwick thought back to his conversation with the doctor. He absolutely believed what he had said. That he was able to converse with these so-called "Visitors". That, to help them, he had to kill all of humanity. In the blackness, Fenwick shook his head. It was impossible, of course. Ross and the people who followed him had extraordinary powers, there was no doubt about that. They had the ability to turn people to ashes in the blink of an eye. But Ross had seemed to think that he could get rid of *all* the people on the planet. No one could do that. Could they? In that small, black prison, Fenwick found that he could almost believe what the man had said.

And why was he still alive? What did Ross have planned for him? Why hadn't he just burned him to nothing, like he had done with so many people? Like he had done to Rachel.

The thought of his wife made Fenwick slump forward. But within seconds Rachel's face was replaced by Goddard's. God, he hoped she had got to safety.

The thought of the DS caused a slice of hope to rise in him. She would get help; he was sure of it. Whatever reason Ross had for keeping him alive, whatever he thought he was going to do tonight it, would not happen. Laura would be back with help. She would stop Ross.

He also worried about Ellie. He knew the sort of men Blunt would have sent to Goddard's house. His only hope was that Ellie could deal with them. Sitting in that black hole, he remembered what he had made her promise. He hoped she would forget this. He hoped she would kill the bastards.

A strange, disquieting groaning noise came from beyond the door and Fenwick looked up sharply, even though he couldn't see a thing. His heart missed a beat with the sound of that weird noise, but then it came again and he realised it was the sound of thunder, the walls of the cellar turning the noise into something strange, something that sounded alien. Sounded wrong.

He sat in his chair and stared at the ceiling he couldn't see. He hoped once more that Goddard had got free.

Chapter Nineteen

Newcastle, 2018

William stood facing the fire in the drawing room. He could hear low voices in his head and he could sense the excitement in those voices. There were fifty people in the house, in the library at the moment. They would be helping William later. They were already in contact with another fifty people who were placed around the country. The UK would be the first to fall. It would all start tonight. By morning thousands, maybe even millions, would be gone. The government would be impotent to stop it. Nobody could stop it.

After that it would be easy to move onto mainland Europe, Asia, and Africa. Then the USA. They would recruit the others like them along the way and they would swell their ranks. They would become ever more powerful.

William smiled as he turned to see the Visitors with him in the room. They grimaced back at him.

And the best thing about the whole event was that the humans would help in their downfall. Once it started, once people began to burn, they would feel fear, they would feel terror, and the sight of people around them being taken in a flash would enhance every base emotion in their stupid, callous bodies. They would panic. No doubt they would fight amongst themselves, as was their want. They would become even better targets, their very fear helping William and his followers target them more easily.

He could feel the excitement in the Visitors. 'More,' they insisted, 'More.'

'Be patient,' said William. 'Your time has come. Within months you will have your legacy back. We will all live in peace.'

The Visitors crowded around him, fading and wavering. 'More. More.'

William opened his arms and the Visitors came to him, flocking around him. He felt their love. He felt their gratitude. And he felt their need for revenge, their need to wipe every filthy, redundant human from this wonderful, wonderful world. And William laughed, because he knew they would do just that.

*

Blunt closed the cellar door behind him and strolled the length of the corridor, pausing as he approached the drawing room.

He placed his ear against the door. Ross was talking to himself again. He heard the leader say something, there was a pause and then he laughed.

Blunt shook his head. He didn't know what Ross was, but he knew he was dangerous, and he knew he had a power the likes of which he had never seen before. The others here had it as well. And they were going to use it to create a world where Blunt could carry out every little twisted dream he wanted, without the fear of any authorities stopping him. The leader had promised him. In Ross's new order, he would be a *king*.

He smiled as he thought of Fenwick alone in the darkness of the cellar, his only companions the shadows and the dripping of water.

He was also looking forward to seeing Ellie. He could not wait for his men to bring her to him. While Ross changed the world tonight, he planned to engage in his own entertainment, starting with that girl.

It was a pity the copper had got away. That would have made tonight very special. He had told Ross, but the other man had seemed unconcerned.

'It does not matter now,' he had said. 'The dogs will do their job. And even if she gets away, who is going to believe her? We're bringing the time forward. We will begin soon.'

Ross looked up as Blunt entered and the big man saw the excitement in the leader's face, his eyes seeming to have an illumination all of their own. He was alone. He smiled at Blunt and said, 'Get everyone prepared. We are starting now.'

Blunt smiled back, the other man's enthusiasm contagious. He turned to leave but Ross caught his arm.

'Stay close to me tonight,' he said. 'I will be far too busy to look out for myself. Don't leave my side.'

Blunt nodded eagerly. Because of what Ross had promised him, he would follow his lead forever. He hurried away to carry out his orders. He started to whistle as he stalked towards the library. Tonight would be the beginning of a new life for him.

*

Fenwick had no idea how long he had been in the cell. Time seemed to have stopped for him. He could still hear that strange, otherworldly thunder though, and decided it couldn't have been more than an hour. He blinked as light flooded the tiny room and the door opened. He stared at the now familiar face of Blunt standing silhouetted in the doorway.

'On your feet,' the big man ordered, and indicated with the inevitable handgun, stepping aside to let him out. Fenwick came out of the cell and was confronted with the sight of Ross standing talking to two other men. More of his "enforcers".

The leader looked up as Fenwick approached and smiled, his black eyes cat like in their intensity. Fenwick stopped a few yards short of him and glared defiantly.

'What now?' he asked.

The smile on Ross's face wavered for a second and the same look of uncertainty he had shown in the drawing room returned, marring his expression. He regarded Fenwick curiously.

'You are a dangerous man, Fenwick,' he said, his voice quiet.

'My instincts tell me to get rid of you now, before my work begins, and yet…'

He tailed off, the uncertainty plain on his face. 'I feel I want to show what will happen tonight. You will be the only one of your kind who will know the whole truth. I feel I want you to truly understand what myself and the Visitors will achieve.'

Fenwick shook his head in disbelief. He ignored Ross and turned to Blunt.

'You can't really believe any of this,' he said. 'You've seen real life. You can't really think that what he says is real can you? Think about it, for Christ's sake. It's utter madness.'

Blunt just smiled his smile at Fenwick, the belief plain on his face.

Fenwick turned to the other two men. 'What about you two? Are you both so stupid as to think that what he's saying is real?' There was a note of hysteria in Fenwick's voice, because even as he asked the question he saw the same look in their eyes as Blunt's. There was nothing they would not do for this man.

He turned back to Ross, but he was interrupted by Blunt.

'I'm telling you, we should just get rid of the bastard now,' he said to Ross. 'What's the point of keeping him alive? You don't need him, just give me five minutes with him and the problem will be solved.'

Ross glared at him, but his voice was still very quiet. 'When I want your opinion, Blunt, I will ask for it. Until then, keep quiet.'

Blunt started to speak again, but Ross bellowed, 'Quiet!'

It was then that Fenwick truly saw the madness in the doctor's eyes. This man was damaged beyond redemption. There was something inside him that was completely wrong, completely broken. In that instant he looked more like an animal than a person. He seemed like he wanted to rip Blunt apart. Fenwick could see that Blunt recognised this too, for he was immediately silent, his eyes downcast, his whole demeanour one of contrition.

Ross took a deep breath, closing his eyes for a second. He scratched his eyebrow with his thumb nail in a gesture of quiet irritation.

He looked at Fenwick again.

'It,' he paused, thinking of the right word. '*Offends* me that you still disbelieve. After everything you've seen, after everything you've been through, your animal brain still cannot accept the fact that what I have told you is true. I feel I need to prove myself to you, and *that* irritates me.' He gazed intently at Fenwick. 'Why do I feel this?'

Fenwick was frozen under that gaze. This man was so powerful, and so deranged, that he could do anything. Fenwick simply could not understand the motives in his head or be ready for anything he might do.

Ross then cocked his head to one side again in what seemed to be a customary habit.

'I still think you have no idea what you've blundered into,' he said. 'You have seen what we can do as a group, but you still have no concept of the powers that I alone possess.' He suddenly smiled, disarmingly.

'Watch your fate.'

One of the men beside him suddenly staggered sideways, a grunt of surprise coming from him. He had time to look at Ross in terrified surprise, perhaps wondering why he had been chosen. But Fenwick already knew why. He had been chosen simply because he was near and simply because he was ordinary.

At once, sweat broke out on the man's face, Fenwick could see it begin to pour from his skin and start running down his face. The sleeves of his shirt darkened under the armpits and he lifted a hand to his brow and stared at the wetness on its surface. The same hand suddenly grasped his throat tightly, his mouth opening, sucking in air; great, whooping gulps, as if he was having trouble breathing. His chest heaved with the effort. With a strangled gasp, he fell to his knees, his face now purple, veins standing out starkly in his neck. Ross closed his eyes.

And the man began to melt.

The skin on his hands and face began to boil and bubble, then the bubbles burst open softly and a pink watery substance ran from them down to the floor, forming waxy puddles as they cooled on the concrete. His scorched throat emitted a pitiful mewling noise as his nose seemed to stretch, the skin around his eyes beginning to run down his boiling face. Gaping holes appeared in his face where the flesh underneath cooked. His eyeballs roved hideously in that disintegrating face, until the skin of his forehead and upper lids ran into them, blinding him, burning into his eyes themselves.

His mouth widened into a gaping, dripping slash in the now unrecognisable face, then it slowly disappeared as the freely running flesh covered it. His eyes were no longer there, they had burst and slid down that awful visage, steam curling from them. His ears were just protuberances, meeting the flowing flesh of his neck and mating with it, forming one long, molten flap of skin. The hair on his head started to crackle and spit, curling into charred knots that gave off small wisps of smoke and then slid down the unrecognisable lump of flesh in chunks.

But even then he was still alive. The flesh continued to run, flowing over his clothes, thick, blackened pieces of skin peeling off and landing with a soft hissing noise in the puddles on the floor. What had been a man only moments before, was now nothing more than a flesh-coloured lump, writhing on the floor, smoking and steaming. Patches of skin were gone completely now, and the bones gleamed underneath. His jawbone, devoid of tongue or cheeks, rattled as he eventually, mercifully, died.

Fenwick stood, horrified. His brain refused to accept what he had just beheld. He was unable to believe his own eyes. He was like a statue. He was powerless to move against the dreadful scene he had witnessed.

As if sensing his work was done, Ross snapped open his eyes, gazing at the horrific results of his work. He nodded, as if satisfied. He glanced at Blunt and the big man managed to tear his gaze from the still steaming corpse on the floor, his eyes terrified that he might be next. He pleaded silently with Ross.

Fenwick still stared at the inert form of what had been a man as it lay there, cooling now on the concrete floor. He then stared at Blunt, who just looked back at him, his eyes slowly returning to their pig-like state. Then he finally turned his gaze to Ross, who stood with a totally expressionless face now. Fenwick shook his head in a daze, the man's horrific death still imprinted in his mind, unable to comprehend or understand what had just happened.

Vaguely, he heard Ross speak to Blunt. 'Question me again, and that's what will happen.'

Fenwick didn't hear Blunt's answer, but he could imagine what it would be.

An anger suddenly overcame Fenwick then, an anger such as he had never felt before. It was even stronger than he had felt in the drawing room. This bastard had just killed one of his own to make a point. This was the man who had helped kill all those innocents over the last few weeks as nothing more than target practice. And this was the man who had killed Rachel. The man who had burned her to death.

The anger was so sudden and so overwhelming, that Fenwick actually saw a red mist descend over his vision. He was completely beyond control. With a roar he tore free of Blunt's arm and leapt upon Ross, grabbing him by the throat with his left hand, his right forming into a fist that he drove again and again into Ross's face. He felt the other man's lips burst under the onslaught and he revelled in it. He punched him again, feeling small bones breaking in Ross's nose and he screamed in his pleasure and his anger.

He knocked aside Ross's arms as the man tried to fend him off and made to hit him again. He wanted to kill him, to beat him into the ground, but strong hands suddenly grabbed him and he was thrown to the floor. Then Blunt and the other man were upon him, and he felt his own lips bursting, felt his own nose break as one of then punched him hard in the face. And still they wouldn't let up. They kicked him again and again. In the body, in the face. One of them caught him in his scar laced thigh and the pain was scarlet.

Suddenly they stopped and, slowly, Fenwick looked out from

behind the arm he had brought up to protect himself. He was panting hard. Blood from his broken nose covered half his face and it dripped onto the floor beneath him. He stared up at Ross who was holding a handkerchief to his own bleeding nose.

Ross waved away Blunt who had moved to help him. Incredibly he seemed to be smiling. He stared down at Fenwick.

'You see now why I am doing this,' he said, his voice muffled by the handkerchief. 'I'm the only one strong enough to carry it through. Without me, the followers can accomplish nothing. That anger you just felt, that is within all of your kind. I knew this,' he indicated to the grizzly mess of the melted man on the floor, 'would trigger that anger. What would happen to this planet if the president of America felt that rage? Or the leader of China. Or Russia? Or any of the other countries that have nuclear weapons at their disposal? What would happen then, Fenwick? What would happen then?'

Fenwick finally realised what Ross was saying. Why he thought he had to do what he was planning to do. He believed himself to be a new messiah. He had said that the Visitors and the "higher beings" would inherit the Earth. This was why he could justify what he was about to do tonight. He really thought he was saving the planet.

Fenwick was going to speak, to try and argue with Ross, to beg him to reconsider, but a kick from Blunt's boot sent him spinning swiftly into unconsciousness. He succumbed to it with relief.

Chapter Twenty

'I don't care where he is. I want him here. Now!'

Goddard glared up at the man she had just yelled at, her eyes full of challenge. The man held her gaze steadfastly and repeated, 'I've told you; the assistant chief constable is away. He's in a conference in London. He can't be disturbed.'

Goddard stared incredulously at the other man, and then yelped as the bandage on her arm was pulled tighter.

They were at the Royal Victoria Infirmary in Newcastle, and had been at the hospital for over an hour. The doctors had patched her up the best she would allow, which wasn't much.

'Just give me something for the pain,' she had cried when the patrolman had brought her into the casualty ward, the DS leaning heavily on the man's shoulder.

The patrolman had left Goddard with a doctor and then phoned through to his superiors. And they had sent Ratcliffe.

Goddard groaned aloud when she spotted the waspish man approach the curtained-off room in casualty. She knew Ratcliffe. He was nicknamed 'Ratty' and this was not just to simplify his name. The DCI was well known throughout the force for his methods of "police procedure", and his reputation for going by the book was universally hated by many coppers who'd had cases dismissed simply because of his plodding methods.

Goddard had started off by carefully retelling him the events of the last few hours, but Ratty's constant interruptions and faintly disbelieving manner had finally boiled the DS's blood and she had ended up accusing him of wilfully disbelieving her and that if anything happened to Fenwick then it would be his fault. Ratty hadn't taken too kindly to that and his stubbornness took an even firmer grip.

'Tell me again what happened,' he said, his notebook in his hand and a sharpened pencil at the ready.

Goddard took a deep breath and tried to control her anger. The doctor she had first seen had given her an injection for the pain and it was making her nervous system twitch and jerk. She felt tired yet alert, active yet lethargic. Goddard felt cheated by her own body. She wished it would make up its mind about what it wanted. On top of this was a gnawing worry for Fenwick and what might be happening at that house. This is what made Ratty's inane questioning even more annoying.

'Look,' she said to the DCI, waving away a nurse who had come in to check her over again. 'I've been shot at, I've been attacked by dogs, and my face is a bloody mess. I have no time for this anymore. Ian Fenwick was taken away at gunpoint. God knows what's happened to him, or whether or not he's even still alive. Now are you going to do something about it or not?'

They both looked up as another doctor entered the room, holding up some x-rays.

'How is she?' asked Ratcliffe. The doctor looked at him for a second and then consulted the x-rays again, before turning to Goddard.

'There are no broken bones,' he said. 'The wound to the back of your neck has been stitched, as well as your arm. You were lucky. Usually, animal attacks leave much more damage. It must have been over fairly quickly.'

'It was. I shot the dog that bit me.' Goddard didn't know what was in the various injections she had been given but the concoction was making her very loose tongued.

The doctor stared at her again. 'Quite,' he said finally. 'Thankfully, the wound to your head just needed a couple of SteriStrips. It wasn't as bad as it looked. We've given you a tetanus injection, but you may be suffering from mild shock. We'd like to keep you in overnight, and then I'm sure you can get off home tomorrow at some point.' He smiled as if this would be what the DS wanted to hear. Her face didn't match his expectations.

Ratty turned to Goddard who sat, fuming on the bed. 'You heard the doctor,' he said. 'Why don't you get some sleep, and we'll check this house out.'

'No way. I'm coming with you.'

Ratty scratched his chin with his pencil. 'Look, the doctor says you're suffering from shock, otherwise you wouldn't be rambling on about psychic powers. And this man, Ross, what did you say he was? The lender?'

Goddard answered through gritted teeth. 'Leader,' she muttered.

'Ah!' exclaimed Ratty, as if that explained everything. He firmly crossed out *"lender"* several times in his notebook, then wrote *"leader"* in its place. He snapped the notebook shut.

'Obviously, there's something strange going on at that house,' he said. 'The fact you've been shot at and had dogs attack you is proof of that. Stay here. We'll check it out.'

'We will check it out,' said a voice behind him. 'But she's going with you.'

Ratty turned to find Parker standing there. His head was bandaged, but he was dressed and looked well rested and determined.

'And so am I,' he finished. He winked at Goddard.

*

Ellie woke with a start. She was soaked in sweat and she ran a hand across her face. She noticed it was shaking.

Sleep had eventually claimed her. She had been reaching out her thoughts, trying to protect Fenwick and Goddard from what they might encounter at Thrushton, but it was as if something was blocking her, causing the Gift to fade in and out like a poor internet connection. It had drained her. She had felt lethargy creep up on her and although she knew she had to stay awake, and despite the crashing of the storm outside, she was soon asleep on the couch.

She dreamed as she slept, and the dream showed a man screaming in agony, his face a melted mess, watery blood pouring everywhere. When she woke she knew something had happened. Something very bad had happened.

She picked up Goddard's house phone and called Fenwick's number, but got nothing. It didn't even try to connect her. She wondered what to do. It was as if her mind was not working properly. The Gift she was so used to now seemed to have deserted her, and it left her feeling lost and frightened. She simply had no idea where Fenwick and Goddard were, or what was happening to them.

She got up and walked on unsteady legs to the kitchen, where she poured herself a glass of water. She drank it down, closing her eyes as the coldness of the liquid chased away the heat of her dream.

She refilled the glass and took it back to the sitting room, setting it down on a side table, still unsure what she should do.

There was a knock on the door.

Ellie stood very still, hardly daring to breathe. She tried to stretch out her incredible mind, but it was as if her power had never existed. Something had stopped the Gift. She took a tentative step towards the door, intending to have a listen, to see if she could hear people talking.

She had just reached the door and was lowering her head to do just that, when it suddenly crashed inwards, the wooden surround splintering. Strong hands grabbed her by the throat. Two men entered the room quickly and professionally, the second one closing the inside door behind him, the raging storm outside still forking lightning across the sky. In that stuttering staccato flash, Ellie looked into the eyes of the man who had her by the throat. She saw that they were smiling.

*

The three police vehicles sped along the city streets. Although it was barely 8pm, hardly anyone was out. The storm seemed to be at its height and the police drivers had their hands full, aware of the standing water on the roads, unable to go as fast as they were trained for.

In the front car, Goddard sat beside the driver, giving him instructions that aided the Sat Nav. In the back was Ratty and Parker. The other car was full of police and a van full of armed response officers made up the trio of vehicles, called in by Parker.

Goddard squirmed in her seat. She still didn't know what was in the injections the doctor had given her, but by God, they were working. She was sweating profusely, and her heart was beating loudly in her ears, but it was as if she had become disconnected from her exhausted body. There was a shivering aura of pain around her, but she didn't care about the fresh gauze covering the wound to her neck or the throbbing of her torn arm. The only thing she could think about was getting back to that house and getting Fenwick out.

They had radioed for the local Durham police to get out there, but again they could not get through. It seemed the whole area was cut off. Email, telephone and radio did not work, and Parker reckoned it must have been the storm. Goddard believed it was something more than that, but kept quiet.

They drove in silence, each person lost in their own thoughts and the driver far too busy concentrating against the lashing rain to want to engage in idle chitchat. It wasn't until they passed Goddard's house that she noticed something was wrong. The front door was open.

That they went past her house was just coincidence, it was merely on a road that the driver took as a short cut to get onto the motorway, but when Goddard glanced habitually out of the window and saw the open door, fear suddenly leapt at her.

'Stop!' she shouted at the driver, 'Pull in here.'

The Astra pulled over smoothly and Goddard got out, once more being hammered by the driving rain. Parker joined her.

'What's up?' he asked, what's wrong?' He had to raise his voice above the sound of the lashing rain and the almost continuous thunder.

Goddard pointed at her door.

'Ellie is in there,' she said.

Parker wasted no more time with questions, but indicated to the vanload of armed response coppers, who jumped out immediately. They made their way towards Goddard's house.

Ratty had stayed in the back of the car where it was dry.

'She's off her fucking rocker, that one,' he muttered to the driver, who just smiled vaguely into the rear-view mirror. He didn't like Ratty either.

'What's the crack then?' asked the leader of the assault group when they gathered at the open door.

Goddard pointed to the door.

'Just enter that building and act on what you find.'

The leader nodded. He was a hard, professional looking individual who seemed very much in control of himself and his men. He started giving out whispered directions, but Goddard grabbed his arm.

'There's a girl in there. She's seventeen. Your number one priority is getting her out safe.'

The group leader nodded again, and the men entered the house.

Goddard and Parker stayed where they were, standing in the pouring rain. They didn't want to get in the way.

*

Ellie screamed again, managing to knock the man's hands from her throat, in her terror finding a strength she had not been aware she possessed. She stepped back, but fell over the sofa in her haste. By the time she recovered her balance the man was upon her again and once more had his hand around her throat, squeezing as hard as he could. The girl's tongue began to protrude, her breathing cut off completely.

Her hand scrabbled around desperately and closed on the glass of water she had brought into the room. She grabbed it and smashed it down as hard as she could into the side of the man's face.

The glass broke and water sprayed everywhere. The man screamed and released her, bringing his hands to his face.

The glass had shattered and carved a long, vicious-looking wound to his face, from his temple to his cheekbone. The blood began to flow immediately. Ellie sank to the carpet as the hands around her neck were released and knelt on all fours, gasping for breath.

But she didn't have long. The other man, who had so far kept back, blocking the door, now stepped forward. He swung his boot and kicked Ellie in the stomach, the force of the blow actually lifting her from the floor and throwing her onto her back.

Ellie screamed at the pain, but immediately began scrabbling backwards, trying to get away from the man, who stepped over his fallen comrade. He bent down and threw the coffee table out of his way, his hands reaching for her.

Ellie was in a total panic. The man was smiling, as his partner had been smiling moments earlier, as if he were enjoying himself. They were no longer just trying to kidnap her, if that had been their original plan. This man wanted to kill her. She could see it in his eyes. He reached into his pocket and pulled something out. The knife flicked open with a click that made Ellie's blood freeze.

But suddenly, a strange calmness came over Ellie. Here she was, lying helpless on the floor. A killer was above her with a knife in his hand and a look in his eye that said he was very much enjoying the anticipation of using it. But Ellie suddenly felt calm. So calm that she actually smiled up at the man.

'No use smiling now,' he said. 'It's too late for that. Just lie still and I'll make this as quick as I can.'

Ellie smiled because she had felt the Gift soar within in her again. It had returned, and it was every emotion. Happiness and sadness, joy and fear, guilt and euphoria. But it was back. That was the main thing. It was back.

Ellie gathered it within her, her face taking on that vacant expression, sweat beginning to bead on her upper lip. Fenwick had made her promise never to do this again, but she was in no position to take heed of that now. She stared at the man, seeing his partner rise from the floor too, one hand holding his face, blood running out from between his fingers. She looked deep into the eyes of the man with the knife.

The man started to shake, to tremble, as if he were carrying a heavy object. His eyes, so spiteful and full of malice and anticipation only a moment ago, started to widen as fear and shock came into them. They turned to his arm, as if trying to stop it from doing what it was doing. But he was powerless. He was in the grip of something he could not understand. Something he could not fight.

He straightened and turned to the other man.

His partner stared at him. 'What are you waiting for?' he hissed in his pain. 'Kill the bitch and let's get out of here.'

It was the last words he ever said. The man with the weapon simply stuck out his arm and the knife sliced into the other man's throat. It cut through his windpipe with a faint popping sound, on an upwards trajectory, piercing the thin base of the skull and entering his brain. The dying man had just enough time to give his killer an offended look, then his eyes rolled up into his head and he collapsed in a heap at the knife man's feet.

The room suddenly erupted into shouting as the armed police crowded into the room, taking in the scene immediately.

'Armed police, put down the weapon!' the group leader shouted. The knifeman had time to glance at Ellie as he felt her making him do what he did not want to do.

He managed to whine out one word. 'Please.' Ellie shook her head. The man lifted the knife with the blade facing downwards and ran at the police. There were three shots in quick succession and he was thrown backwards, smashed to the floor by the high velocity rounds. His heart gave a couple of pumps that sprayed blood from the wounds before it gave the job up as pointless. He lay as still as his comrade.

*

Goddard and Parker stood in the rain watching the door. The DS was anxious to enter her house, but she knew it was best to leave the professionals to get on with their job. She glanced at her watch. Almost 8:30. She was desperate to get to Thrushton and believed that if they didn't get there soon, something terrible might happen. She worried again about Fenwick.

When she heard the shots she jerked her head around so quickly she cricked her neck, then she was off and running, slamming into the door frame as she did so, her balance hampered by the sling on her arm. She tore her arm free of it and ran into the living room, skidding to a halt at the scene that confronted her.

Ellie was lying on the floor and, for a heart-stopping minute, Goddard thought she was dead. Then she saw her eyes move as the girl looked at her mutely and relief washed over her. She stepped over the smashed coffee table and knelt beside her, one hand gently stroking hair out of her face.

Ellie stared back at her. 'You look awful,' she said.

Goddard grinned. 'Thank you.' She stood up.

'We have to get going,' she said to Parker, who simply nodded too. But Ellie stood up on shaking legs. 'Me too,' she said.

There was a moment's indecision on the faces of the two police officers, then Parker spoke.

'Just as safe with us as anywhere else tonight,' he said. He turned to the armed officers. 'Let's go,'

'Hang on,' said the officer in charge. 'What about these two?' He indicated at the corpses on the floor.

'Don't think they're going anywhere, do you?' answered the DI. 'I'll ring someone in. We can take care of this later. For now, we need to get going.'

They left the dead men in Goddard's ruined living room.

Minutes later they were back in their vehicles and speeding once more towards Thrushton.

Chapter Twenty-One

Fenwick awoke with a jolt. Pain was coursing through his head and his body was stiff and cold. He was shaking and yet sweat had broken out all over his body. He could barely move for the agony that seemed to press into his entire body.

It was black, pitch black, and for one awful second he thought he was blind, that the beating had caused some sort of brain damage, until he realised where he was. Back in the cell. Back in the dripping darkness.

He rubbed a hand across his brow, wincing as he felt the new contours of his beaten face. He found he couldn't breathe through his nose and coughed when he sniffed a clot of blood into his throat, gagging and choking until he managed to dislodge it.

He ran his tongue around the inside of his mouth, feeling the sharp edges of a broken tooth and the coppery lumps of swollen gums. In the darkness, one eye moved slowly, but the other eye remained shut, closed from the beating as effectively as if someone had sneaked up on him and glued his eyelids together.

He had been dreaming of Rachel again. She had been standing beside Ross in the cellar, their arms around each other. She had accused him again and again for her death.

Fenwick shook his head, trying to get rid of the vivid memories, but a sharp pain slammed into his temple for his trouble. He lay still for a few seconds, waiting for the pain to subside, then in one swift movement he rolled onto his side and sat up, leaning against one of the damp walls in the small cellar. A groan escaped him. On all fours, he scrabbled around for the chair and heaved himself into it, the pain in his body, especially his leg, immense.

As he waited for that pain to subside a little more, he began to think about escape. This was now his only focus. He wanted to get away from this house of pain and fire and horror, this hideous lair where fear and madness seemed to live side by side.

The question was, of course, how? He had no idea how long he had been unconscious. He glanced at the illuminated dial of his watch but slowly realised that the second hand was not moving. His fingers ran over the glass face. Broken. The beating he had received felt like it had happened weeks ago, but he knew it was still the same night, because that weird, groaning rumbling told him that the storm still raged outside.

He stood up and, holding his left thigh, he limped unsteadily to the cell door, squinting out into the black, pit like vastness of the cellar. He couldn't see a thing. If that awful body was still lying out there, it lay in darkness and was unseen. For that, at least, he was glad.

He turned back to the chair and sat down heavily once more, an impotent rage building within him again, borne from the knowledge that he was stuck there until someone came to get him. *When* they came to kill him, like they had killed that man.

The death of the man kept coming to his mind, standing out starkly against the fading memories of the events that had brought him to the North East all those weeks ago. The memory made him shake with fear. He despised himself for his terror but he couldn't help it. What if they decided to kill him like that? He shook his head in the darkness. He wouldn't give them the chance. He would find some other way to die if it came to it. Something quicker.

With nothing else to occupy his mind he returned to the idea of escape, going over the items on his person that might have been any use to him. It didn't take long. He was an ordinary bloke, not a fictional secret agent. There was no miniature grenade in the heel of his shoe, no walkie talkie hooked into his belt. If he had been wearing his sturdy work shoes they might have been useful, but he wasn't. If he'd had his tie he could have used it to knot it around someone's throat, but he didn't. And anyway, both of those things were useless unless he had something to surprise his enemies with.

Then suddenly, a thought came to him. He had read a book once where the hero had been in much the same predicament as himself. He had used the loose coins in his pocket to throw at his attackers, surprising them enough to jump them. It was a long shot, but he really didn't have any other ideas.

Fenwick quickly went through his pockets, pulling out the loose change and laying it on the floor in a line. In that blackness, with the groaning thunder as background music, his fingers stumbled over the coins, trying to make out what they were. There wasn't very much. He had a one-pound coin, one fifty and a couple of tens. Not the best of weapons, but painful enough to throw someone off balance if he managed to hit them.

He wondered for a second if he should remove a sock and put the coins inside as a sort of improvised cosh, like Garfield's *Death Wish*, but he immediately dismissed this idea. There wasn't enough of the coins to make a really effective weapon and besides, a handful of them flying through the unsure light would be much harder to see.

There was also the chair itself, the only furniture in the tiny cell. Standing up, he fumbled around until he held it properly and lifted it, his bruised and battered body protesting at this exercise. But he smiled grimly as he did so, thankful it was an old chair, solidly put together and quite heavy. He set the chair down and sat on it. He scooped up the coins and held them in his hand. Now all he needed was for someone to come and get him. All he needed was a target.

He didn't have long to wait. About fifteen minutes passed before the light in the cellar clicked on and he heard footsteps clacking on the concrete floor. He quickly lay down behind the chair, the coins clenched in his right hand, his one good eye cracked to a mere slit, staring through his eyelashes at the door.

It opened and Fenwick noted with satisfaction that it was the other man who had been there when Ross had murdered his henchman. One of the men who had beaten him unconscious.

The man stood in the door frame, his body seeming to fill the gap and barked; 'Fenwick, get up. You've got a meeting upstairs.'

Fenwick had a good idea what this "meeting" would be. They had come to kill him. Would it be Blunt with a quick bullet through the head? Or a fate like that other man? Fenwick groaned softly for his guard's benefit.

'Help me up, will you?' he muttered.

The man sighed and his gun hand dropped to his side, obviously thinking the weapon would not be needed. He stepped towards him.

Quick as a flash, Fenwick sat bolt upright and threw the coins as hard as he could at his target. He reckoned some of them missed, but at least a couple of them caught the man full in the face. He yelped and his gun hand came up, but by then Fenwick had already stood up. Ignoring his pain, he swept up the chair and, in one fluid moment, aided by fear and adrenalin, he brought it crashing down on the other man's head, the solid wood cracking into his skull with a very satisfying thwack.

The guard stumbled backwards, and Fenwick moved again. He brought the chair up once more and smashed it down, again hitting the man on the head. The guard fell to the floor and lay still. He emitted a sudden single snore before becoming silent. Remembering his beating, Fenwick decided that one more whack couldn't hurt. He brought the chair down again. Hard.

He stood looking down at the inert form, shaking from the exertion, then he bent and took the automatic from the man's fingers. He peeked around the corner of the cell into the cellar, thankful no one else was there. He glanced once more at the figure on the floor, not absolutely sure whether he still lived or not, but absolutely not caring. He closed the door, hiding the man from sight. He limped across to the bottom of the cellar stairs and walked up slowly, the gun held in front of him. He paused at the door at the top and peered fearfully into the corridor, making sure it was empty.

No one there.

He quickly ducked back inside when one of the doors along the corridor opened and a youngish girl with long dark hair walked out. She glanced at her watch and then hurried past the cellar door he had pulled towards him. Through the gap he left, he watched her turn and head up the stairs.

Fenwick wondered what he should do. He was totally out of his depth. He quickly calculated his possible plan of action. Ross had people around the country. He had to, if what Ellie had said about the point of contact was true. It made sense that their partners, those with whom their minds would join, were right there in the house, with their leader on hand to orchestrate the whole event. He didn't know how many there were though, but it must have been a few. Say a hundred people including Ross himself and his enforcers.

What could he do? One man against all of them? He worried briefly that Ross might somehow pick up on his presence, that even now he would be sending out others to kill him, or that he was waiting for him to be brought to him, but then dismissed that thought. No point in worrying when he could do nothing about it.

He crept down the corridor towards the main door. Escape. That's what he needed to do. Just get out of this bloody house and get away. He could worry about Ross and his mad plan later.

As he moved carefully along that corridor, he wondered again about the strange powers these people held. How could it be that they had kept something this huge such a secret? How could these people exist without the world finding out about it? But then he realised that there were always stories about this sort of thing. The internet was full of them. YouTube had countless thousands of videos showing strange phenomena, but everyone just looked upon them as entertainment. No one actually believed any of it. And that's how they had succeeded. The very fact nobody would believe it, had served to hide their work.

Maybe Ross was right to want to get rid of humanity. At that point they seemed very stupid to Fenwick.

By this time he had made it to the front door. He glanced around him, and then up the stairs. Nothing. His hand had just about reached the doorknob when the door was pushed violently inwards and a dripping, scowling man stepped into the hallway.

The surprise on the man's face gave way to an almost unholy smile as he saw Fenwick standing there, open mouthed in shock.

Blunt smiled that evil smile at Fenwick.

'Well, well, well,' he said.

*

Ellie sat in the back of the police car, crammed in between Parker and Ratcliffe. Her eyes had that faraway look again, and the sweat was beading once more on her upper lip. They were close now, only about five miles from Thrushton. She closed her eyes and thrust out her mind, searching towards the house. It was no use; she still could not pick up what was happening there. Something seemed to be emanating from that house that stopped her Gift and polluted the entire area. Something she could not get past. And it seemed to be getting stronger.

Her eyes opened and she looked at the bruised and scratched face of Goddard as she turned towards her from the front seat. She shook her head at the unasked question. But her eyes betrayed her worry.

*

Ross stood alone in the huge master bedroom. It had been cleared of the bed and wardrobes and he stood in the centre of the room, his mind melded with the others in the house. Around him stood the Visitors. Their grotesque, bulbous eyes were closed as was Ross's. They helped him in his work.

This was it, thought Ross. The night he had been waiting for. The night he had been *born* for. Dimly—for his mind was almost entirely focused on his task—he exulted. Tomorrow would be the start of a new life. A new beginning. A whole new era in the world's sordid history would begin. For the first time since Cain murdered Abel, for the first time since humanity had existed, there would be no more war, no more pollution. No more *noise*. History would begin afresh.

He would lead the worthy people of this planet up to a higher plane. He and his followers from every continent would help the Visitors rebuild the Earth. To take it back to what it had once been. They would revel in their new world. They would live with it, not take from it.

It was time. His mind glided outwards, touching the others scattered around the house. Scattered around the country. A smile touched his sweat bathed face as he felt their strength add to his, his strength add to theirs. Their powers began to combine, to grow into a force that would be unstoppable.

The Visitors pressed against him, surrounding him.

'More,' they whispered in their raw, rasping voices. 'More, more, more.'

Ross smiled and gave them what they wanted.

Chapter Twenty-Two

Blunt turned and closed the door against the raging storm outside, apparently oblivious to the gun in Fenwick's hand. He stared at Fenwick and the smile slowly faded, replaced by his usual look of thuggish anticipation.

'We did a good job on you,' he said, taking in the sight of Fenwick's battered face. 'I think it's time to finish the job.' He took a step towards Fenwick but the investigator raised the automatic, pointing it straight at his chest. He stopped.

'Move out of the way, Blunt,' said Fenwick. 'Just step aside and let me go. No one else needs to get hurt.'

Blunt scoffed. 'You haven't got the balls to shoot me, Fenwick,' he said.

Fenwick stared back at him. 'Want to take that chance?'

Blunt took a deep breath. 'Looks like we're at a bit of a stalemate,' he said eventually. ''Cos you're not going to shoot an unarmed man, and I'm not letting you through this door.'

Fenwick shook his head. 'How stupid are you?' he asked. 'What do you think is going to happen to the likes of you in Ross's "new world"? He told me, you idiot. He said that once your usefulness was over he was going to get rid of you. Can't you see that you have no place in this twisted future of his?'

Blunt took another small step towards him, ignoring his words, but stopped when Fenwick shook his head.

'Blunt. Try to understand what I'm saying. He will kill you. He's already done it to your mate tonight. You mean nothing to him. In fact, he hates you because you're not like him. But all of this doesn't matter anyway, because he can't do what he says he's going to do. How far does this have to go before you finally understand that what he's talking about doing, this apocalypse of his, that it's just fantasy? It's the ravings of a madman.'

Fenwick stared hard at Blunt, willing the man to think about what he was saying, to try and get through his skull how Ross was feeding him a story that was impossible.

'Do you know how many people are on this planet?' he continued. 'Ross and his followers have some sort of power, we both know that, but have you ever even attempted to do the maths? It takes two of them to carry out their attacks, right? How many followers does he have? A hundred? Two hundred? It really doesn't matter, because there are over seven billion people on this planet.' He stared into Blunts dull eyes. 'Seven billion, Blunt. Does he have fourteen billion followers?'

'Some of those people will be like him,' said Blunt. 'They'll have the Gift too.'

Fenwick shook his head in disbelief at the man's stupidity.

'What percentage?' he asked, but Blunt simply continued to stare at him. He managed to take another small step forward. Fenwick, still trying to impress on him what he was saying, missed it.

'Let's be generous and say twenty percent,' said Fenwick. 'And let's say they're all willing to help him in his plans for mass genocide, even when they've watched their friends and family die. That means that he'll have about one and a half billion followers. That leaves five and a half *billion* people who need to die.' Fenwick shook his head again. 'It can't be done. He's a con man, Blunt, and you've been stupid enough to fall for his bullshit.'

'The Visitors will help him,' said Blunt. 'They get stronger with every death.' He shuffled another inch forward.

'When was the last time you saw these "Visitors"?' asked Fenwick. 'Where do they live?'

'In the cellar,' replied the killer, his mad eyes glittering. 'That's why we enlarged it.'

Fenwick's mouth actually dropped open at this. He couldn't talk any sort of sense to this man. He was as crazy as Ross.

Blunt suddenly lunged and Fenwick, in sudden panic, pulled the trigger. Nothing happened. Blunt punched him hard in the face, the pain intense in his already battered visage. He staggered backwards and Blunt stepped forward again and wrestled the gun from his hand, turning it to point at him.

'It's always best to take the safety off if you're serious about using a gun,' he said.

Fenwick looked into those mad eyes again as Blunt raised the pistol.

And he knew, with a sudden certainty that they would be the last thing he would ever see.

*

The girl beside Ratcliffe suddenly cried out, and he recoiled at the look of pain on her face. He was stuck in a car full of lunatics. They talked about psychic powers like it was the most natural thing in the world and they had also allowed this young girl, a *civilian*, into a police vehicle on an emergency call. Ratty smiled grimly. He was already compiling his report in his head.

Ellie, meanwhile, had noticed that she was beginning to sense things around that house again. It was as if whatever had been blocking her was getting weaker. As if it were focused on something else.

She was concentrating everything on locating Fenwick. The laconic stranger, who had come to mean so much to her was in terrible danger. She knew that much. She just couldn't work out what that danger was.

And then suddenly, an image unfolded in her mind. She saw Fenwick, holding his face, a face battered almost beyond recognition, and she saw a man standing in front of him, holding a gun. Bringing the gun up. Pointing it at Fenwick. She saw his finger beginning to squeeze the trigger.

Ellie screamed as she focused like she had never done before.

*

Blunt was smiling once more. This was something he had looked forward to for a long time. Even though he had promised Ross he would stay close to him this night, he had gone out to retrieve his car and to check in with the men he had sent out to kidnap Ellie. But he'd discovered that the car was not where he had left it. What he did find though, was the squashed remains of one of the dogs that patrolled the woods and two deep tyre tracks showing where the car had disappeared.

The bitch had got away. That meant that the police were on their way. Ross had seemed unperturbed about this eventuality, but Blunt thought he should know. He may have been needed to slow down the police until it was too late. As he tramped back through the now lessening storm, he had daydreamed again about what his new life was going to be like. He would have women and power and wealth beyond his wildest dreams. He would be able to do as he wanted and no one would be able to stop him. Whilst Ross would have his golden future with his chosen few, Blunt would have god like powers, his every whim or twisted fantasy carried out for him.

Then he had entered the house and had seen Fenwick standing there with the gun pointed at him.

He had been frightened at first. He knew Fenwick hated him, had every right to for what he'd done to him, but his instincts had soon taken over. He'd noticed the safety was still on, and he slowly formulated his plan in his limited brain. This consisted mainly of grabbing the gun and killing Fenwick. That was about as far as his intellect could take him.

And now here he was. King again. Fenwick was slowly straightening up, a look of fear in his eyes and Blunt revelled in it. He smiled in triumph at the investigator and slowly started squeezing the trigger.

Suddenly, the smile on his face faded and his eyes took on a look of terror themselves. He shook his head in desperation at what his arm started to do. The pistol slowly turned toward his own face. His head trembled as he tried to move it from the barrel, but he was caught. His body was once again not obeying his thoughts. He was merely a puppet, his strings being pulled by another.

The pistol turned fully in his hand and in a sudden, violent action, his mouth opened. It opened so far and so fast that Blunt actually heard the tendons of his jaw twang and snap, and a terrible pain filled his mouth. It was as if someone had grabbed his jaw and wrenched it open, and he cried out. The pain was intensified when his hand savagely jammed the automatic into his gaping, salivating mouth, the sight on the barrel snapping a tooth. He rammed it further into his mouth, the barrel cutting into the upper palette and making him gag. It pointed upwards.

His eyes, his desperate, terrified eyes cut to Fenwick for the last time. The investigator saw that there was only fear for himself in them. They held no remorse for the life he had led.

Fenwick stared at Blunt. He felt as much for the man in front of him as he would for a troublesome fly. The world would indeed be better off without him. He knew who was controlling his actions and he wasn't talking to Blunt when he said, 'Do it.'

With a last, despairing scream, Blunt's finger pulled the trigger.

There was an explosion, just as a last, crashing rumble of thunder rolled across the house, and the top of Blunt's head disintegrated. Blood and brains shot three feet into the air like a fountain and then, as the echo of the thunder died, they fell around him in a series of pattering drops on the varnished floorboards of the hall. His body slowly crumpled and fell to the floor. It twitched several times and then finally lay still.

Fenwick stared at the terrible tableau of Blunt's body for a second, feeling nothing but relief that the man was gone, then he bent down and took the gun from his dead hand. He looked around the hallway.

He couldn't just leave. He had to stop Ross. He still did not believe in what the man was planning, but he knew what he and his followers could do. If he didn't stop him then hundreds, perhaps thousands, of people would die tonight.

He'd thought that the cellar had been prepared for the followers to gather in, where they would begin their grizzly work, but this was obviously not to be. Blunt had said that Ross had opened up the cellar for these "Visitors" to live in, not for the inhabitants of this house.

So that was not the answer. But why would people with such powers need to be in close proximity to each other anyway? The answer, of course, was that they wouldn't. To fit ten or twenty people into each room of a house the size of Thrushton would be no trouble. That's why the girl he had seen was going upstairs. That's where they were gathered. In the bedrooms.

But what could he do? He could go upstairs and find Ross. If he had to, he would kill him. After all he had been through, after the deaths he had witnessed at the hands of the pathologist and to save the lives of the future victims of tonight, he knew he could do that, coldly and without remorse. But he didn't know which room Ross was in and he may have had some more of his enforcers with him. No, that would take too long. What he needed was some kind of diversion. Something that would force Ross and his followers from carrying out their task.

He looked around in desperation, feeling helpless. His eyes eventually settled once more on the body of Blunt. Something metallic was half hanging from the dead man's pocket. He stepped forward to get a closer look and then he bent and picked the object up.

Suddenly, he knew exactly what to do.

*

Ross was alone now. The Visitors had descended to the cellar, there to wait as their ranks swelled. From the ashes of the hated human race they would rise, one by one, then by their thousands, like a phoenix rising from the flames. They would then, each one, help in his mission. Their Gift would combine with his, magnifying it a thousand times, a million times more than it currently was. Enough to kill hundreds of people at the same time, thousands. And eventually, millions.

His brow was pouring with sweat. His Gift emanated from him in a shimmering blue-white haze; an aura that shone with an eerie silver white light. The colour of life. The colour of death. The colour of everything.

The aura, enhanced by the Visitors in the cellar, grew from his body, encasing it in that sparkling, bright silver white light. He guided it to the followers, the smile growing on his face until it became a grin. A huge, fixed, plastic looking grin.

It was cut off suddenly, and he was left with nothing. In his head he felt rather than heard the Visitors scream in anguish. His conscious mind had become aware of something, and its danger had brought him back to the real world. What was it? What had caused this to happen? He sniffed and turned around. It was then that he saw the smoke seeping under the bedroom door.

*

Fenwick limped silently along the hallway and peeked around the staircase. When he saw it was clear he sprinted up the stairs as fast as he could. The pain in his thigh was unbelievable and he believed some of the metal plates in there had been dislodged or damaged by his beating, but he tried to ignore it. His body and face were a sea of agony too, but he kept going. He had to.

He reached the landing and delved into his jeans pocket where the lighter he had taken from Blunt had been placed. He flicked it on and gazed at the dancing flame for a second. He was not unaware of the irony. He had turned from a firefighter into a fire starter. Then he stooped down and held the lighter to the thick carpet, watching as the flames quickly began to eat away at the material and started to lick at the shining woodwork.

He went down a few more steps and repeated the process, the growing fire at the top of the landing reflecting in his one good eye. Once more he bent down and lit the stair carpet, and again, until his feet were back in the hallway.

Looking up at his work, he saw with satisfaction that the flames were beginning to burn quite fiercely now, and he was surprised that no one as yet seemed to have noticed. Possibly they were too involved in their activities.

Suddenly, a cry went up from the landing. A door opened and a figure ran out, throwing up an arm as the flames threatened to consume him. He was another big man and Fenwick guessed he was another of Ross's enforcers. Before he could do anything, the man on the landing had pulled out a gun and fired down at Fenwick.

It was a reflex shot, but a lucky one. Fenwick felt something punch into his stomach, but he grimly stood his ground and fired two shots, surprised by the recoil of the handgun. The man gave a cry and slumped to the landing floor, his body quickly being consumed by the now raging fire.

By now the stairs were well alight, and screams could be heard coming from the upper rooms. Fenwick pulled up his sweater and saw a neat round hole in his abdomen, to the left of his navel. The hole was pouring blood, and the pain suddenly hit him. He hissed at the intensity of it. Then he let the sweater drop back and took a final look at the burning stairway. He turned towards the front door.

He turned back once more when he heard renewed screaming and watched as doors all along the landing were flung open, people pouring from them, panicking, their powers just a dim memory at their fear of that raging fire.

One of them, a man who may or may not have been Fox, spun and screamed, his body engulfed in flames. The others ran past him, ignoring his plight. He finally slumped to the floor and was lost to sight in the fire. Another man picked up a side table and smashed a landing window. He jumped through it and others started following him, making their escape to the soft, soaked earth under the window.

Fenwick nodded to himself. He was shaking and felt dizzy and sick. He feared the bullet may have damaged him more than he had originally thought, because he seemed to be weakening with every second. He managed to reach the door and pulled it inwards, heaving in great lungfuls of damp, wonderfully clean air, only then noticing how acrid the smoke inside the house was becoming.

Straight in front of him was his crumpled Audi, still parked where he had left it what seemed like days before. He made his way towards it. People who had escaped the burning building ran around him through the now only light rain, ignoring him in their panic. He hoped the keys were still in the centre console pocket where he had left them.

Suddenly, only about five feet away from the car he stopped, his feet skidding on the gravel driveway. Blood dripped from the gunshot wound onto his shoes. He turned and looked up at the fiercely burning house. Flames were licking at the top floor now and curling around the eaves of the roof and he could see the orange glow beyond the front door. He knew from experience that if anyone was left on the top floors, they were not going to get out alive.

His eyes roved the crackling frontage of the house, searching for something. Some instinct was telling him that he was still in danger and he scanned the burning house rapidly. He looked at the twin dormer bedroom windows, the burning, crackling ivy on the walls curling and floating away in incandescent wisps. Then he looked at the large window in the centre of the first floor. And he stared straight into the face of Ross.

Chapter Twenty-Three

The three police vehicles were now almost at the house, turning from the main road onto the single track that led to Thrushton.

Ellie sat with her head on Parker's shoulder. She was sleeping, a sleep so deep that even the motion of the speeding car and the noise of the sirens could not wake her.

She had screamed when she had thrown the Gift from her to save Fenwick. She had felt something tear inside her. She had damaged something with the intensity of making Blunt do her bidding. She had thought it was because of that shield around the house, an energy that tried to stop her from getting through. The effort of tearing through that energy had done something to her. She had succeeded in saving Fenwick, but it had cost her. The scream had been one of pain as well as effort.

After that, her head had slumped. She had tried to keep her eyes open but they would not obey her. She had been staring at Goddard's frantic, bruised face, trying to concentrate on what the DS was saying, but it was no use. Her head slumped and she passed out.

Parker put two fingers to her neck for a pulse and felt it beating in strong steady throbs, but she was out to the world.

'She's okay,' he said to Goddard. 'Just sleeping, I think.' Then he looked past the DS at the orange glow in the distance. 'Christ,' he muttered.

Goddard turned her head to the front and saw Thrushton burning. She heard Parker behind her radioing for the fire service and seemingly getting through straight away, the lines now re-open, giving weight to his theory about the passing storm.

She could only stare at the house. And pray.

*

This could not be happening! Not now! Not after so many years, so much work. Not when he was on the very brink of success!

Ross wrenched open the bedroom door, stepping back quickly and slamming it shut again against the intense heat and flames in the passageway outside it. He turned back to the window and howled his fury.

He could hear the Visitors in his head. They screeched and raged. At him! They blamed *him* for this failure.

'It's not my fault,' he screamed aloud. 'It's him. It's Fenwick's fault!'

But the Visitors would not listen. They screamed back at him in his head and he feared the noise would kill him. The diabolical sound of their anger grew louder and louder and Ross clasped his hands over his ears as it grew into a screeching cacophony he could not bear.

And then it suddenly stopped. And Ross knew they had gone. The realisation left a desolate, vacant hole in him. He had never been alone. He had never been without them. For a second he just stood, staring at nothing. He felt lost and adrift. He felt *lonely* and that feeling made him clutch at himself, tears of self-pity springing into his eyes.

But then that feeling was replaced by something else. Anger. That man! That man had ruined everything! He knew it was Fenwick. He should have listened to his senses. He should have killed him when he had first set foot in Newcastle. Should have kept trying until he had rid himself of his nemesis. He should have listened to that brute, Blunt! Those flashes he'd had when in the man's presence, they had been warning him, telling him to just get rid of the investigator. But he hadn't listened. He had wanted

Fenwick to see what was happening. In his arrogance he'd wanted him to know that what he had said was real. Wanted to make him believe everything. About the Gift. About the Visitors.

The Visitors! Where were they?

He stretched out his mind, trying to locate them. But he got nothing except a blankness, a terrible, terrible blankness, the likes of which he had never known.

All his life they had been with him. Every second of every day they had surrounded him. When he worked they stood beside him, staring down at the corpses in his charge and he had explained the workings of the human body. They sat with him as he listened to music on warm evenings and he had told them about the various composers, about their history, about their lives. They had watched over him as he slept, guarding him, nurturing him, and readying him for his task. And now that task was ruined. And they had deserted him. For the first time in his life, Ross, *William*, was alone.

And it was all down to Fenwick.

He walked slowly towards the window and stared down. He saw his followers running, also deserting him, their ingratitude to what he had shown them making his blood boil. He saw the black Audi. And he saw Fenwick, limping and bleeding, moving towards the car, making his escape as Ross's future burned.

And Ross forgot about his followers, he forgot about the burning house he stood in. He even forgot about the Visitors. He forgot about everything except his need for revenge. Fenwick had to pay for ruining his life. For ruining the planet's life.

Ross closed his eyes. He leaned on the windowsill and concentrated.

*

Fenwick gazed up at Ross. The fire raged around him, his body silhouetted by the fiery orange glow. His hair seemed to blow around his face in the heat eddies.

Fenwick suddenly remembered his dream. He knew now who that man had been laughing at him. A man silhouetted by fire, his hair tossed by the heat. He remembered what the man had shown him in the dream. His naked, dead wife and his best friend, locked in an ecstatic embrace, and he suddenly remembered what the man's words had been that he had forgotten until now.

'She was the first, she won't be the last. She was the first, she won't be the last.'

Fenwick suddenly knew what he had to do. If Ross escaped, it would start again. If he managed to get away from this night alive, then more people would die. Fenwick could not have that.

Knowing he had no choice Fenwick lifted the gun. He took careful aim, and fired.

*

This would be his finest kill. Not only because he was doing it alone, without the help of his so-called followers or the Visitors who had deserted him, but because it would mean the end of Fenwick. The man who had thwarted his plans for a future of gold, who had stopped the world's new beginning. The man who had taken away his only companions, who had caused the Visitors to leave him. Ross's beaten face smiled and took on that lost, vacant expression. He summoned up everything inside of him. Every thought, every emotion. The Gift was strongest in him, always had been. He did not need his followers. He didn't even need the Visitors, for they did not deserve the world he had so nearly created for them. For the first time in William's life, he was doing something for himself. He deserved it. And it would be wonderful.

He pulled the Gift inside of himself, tensing his body for the huge effort. He was not just going to kill Fenwick, he was going to erase him. To wipe him from the face of this filthy, germ laden rock the humans called *their* planet.

The Gift tumbled from his mind, becoming a physical force. It was a mini sun, an incandescent energy, and it broiled around him. It was brought forth solely for destruction. Ross would make Fenwick burn!

Ross opened his eyes in time to see Fenwick move. Then the bullets smashed through the window and cracked open his head like an egg.

He fell to the floor, his blood spurting from the huge wound, and he stared upwards with eyes that were wide with shock. As he lay there, as his brain started to shut down, as he died, he thought he saw shapes moving: dark figures seen vaguely in the dimming seconds of his life. They were reaching towards him, bending over him, and he saw, for the first and last time, the dreadful reality of the Visitors. He saw what they really were. He screamed in stupefying terror as they scrabbled towards him. Their gnarled, hook-clawed hands groped at him. They grabbed his soul and dragged him, kicking and screaming to his death.

The Gift arced from his dead body, whirling and soaring in a maelstrom of silver white energy: a rainbow of kaleidoscopic power, unleashed, yet untargeted. It flailed about the bedroom, rebounding, growing bigger and bigger with every millisecond. It was terrible in its potency, useless without an order. It melted everything it touched. The broken windows turned into glowing, red, molten glass that dripped in huge gobbets of fire, the wallpaper erupted into flame, the mirror on the wall silvered in a flash. The Gift whirled and soared and destroyed. Finally, having no other direction to go, it smashed back into the mind whence it had come.

Ross's body didn't just explode. It disintegrated; vaporised instantly into a billion fragments, these fragments ripped into a billion more. The Gift billowed outwards with these particles and smashed through the front of the house, tumbling outwards. It was mindless in its fury; a huge, thundering frenzy of pure energy that ignited into a fireball, consuming everything in its path.

*

Fenwick saw Ross's body fall, knew he had hit him, but he didn't even have time to lower his weapon before the entire front of the house disintegrated and a massive, glowing fireball rushed towards him. He turned to run, but he was far too slow. It caught him as he turned and lifted him from the ground, throwing him into the air. Something, perhaps debris from the house, smashed into him and he felt ribs crack. Something else clattered into his face, breaking his jaw.

As Fenwick soared through the air, his body engulfed in pain, he caught sight of the raging house and the now clearing sky, both of these things seen through a curtain of scorching fire. He felt his clothes ignite with the heat, felt the skin on his face tighten, his hair crackling and burning, then he was smashed into the roof of his car, his broken ribs screaming again.

He somersaulted over the roof and slammed violently down onto the driveway, tumbling and sliding like a leaf on the wind, the gravel tearing wickedly into his face and his hands as he put them out to try and stop himself.

He rolled over one last time and lay on his back, his shocked mind taking in the sight of the Audi rocking on its springs as the Gift consumed it. He winced when the tank gave way and the petrol within it was ignited, and he weakly tried to cover his head as pieces of the burning car rained down around him.

When he opened his eyes again there was nothing left of the car except a blackened chassis, flames curling around the wheels and melted tyres. But it had done him more service that he could have imagined when he'd picked it up only a few weeks ago. It had saved him from certain death, its solid body sheltering him and taking the brunt of the consuming fireball that disappeared now as fast as it had appeared. Fenwick realised his lungs were working again, that fireball having had a vacuum effect, and he sucked in a huge lungful of smoke-laden air, grimacing at the pain all over his body. He strained to lift his head and looked at the house.

It was nothing more than jagged, blackened timbers now. The power of the explosion had literally snuffed the flames out, and it stood in silence, only the hissing of the now light drizzle on its scorched innards making any noise.

Survivors were milling about, too shocked to try and make their escape, even as sirens and blue lights flooded the night. They just stood around, their faces blank, lost without their leader, their futures destroyed along with the house.

Fenwick let his head thump softly back to the gravel, every inch of his body in agony. He heard the sounds of car doors opening and slamming shut, and he heard running footsteps, crunching through the wet gravel of the driveway. Then warm hands were cradling his face, lifting his aching head onto soft knees.

'What have they done to you?' asked Goddard softly, tears sliding down her own bruised and beaten face.

Fenwick's own face was almost beyond recognition. It was swollen from the beating, scorched by the fire and blackened all down one side. Dark lumps that she recognised as gravel were embedded under his skin and his eyebrows had been seared away. Blood trickled from hundreds of small wounds.

Fenwick tried to talk, but he couldn't. His broken jaw wouldn't allow it. Instead, he just stared at her face, loving what he saw. Then slowly, his eyes closed, and he slipped into the waiting arms of oblivion.

Goddard sat with his head on her lap, stroking his face. Her gaze wandered to the ravaged house, and then back to Fenwick. In a second she would be a police officer again. She would be calm and efficient. But just for this moment, she could do nothing except cradle him. She would hold him. Just for a while.

Chapter Twenty-Four

The three figures strolled around Jesmond Dene slowly, wrapped up against the cold. A black Labrador puppy named Maisie ran around their feet, looking up at them eagerly, before running off again, delighting in the snow she snuffled through.

Seven months had passed. Fenwick had nearly died. The bullet had nicked an artery and it was only the quick reactions of the paramedics called to the scene and a blood transfusion that had saved his life.

He'd spent many weeks in hospital, with Goddard and Ellie constantly by his side. The DS's wounds had healed quicker than his, although she still bore the scars from the dog bite on her arm. They were fading though.

Fenwick was less lucky. His jaw had been set, the gravel had been picked from his skin, and his cuts had been stitched. But he still bore the scars on his face and body from that night, and they would be there until the day he died. Laura said she liked the scars and that they made him look mean and moody. He pretended to believe her.

They both laughed as Ellie sank to her knees in the snow and Maisie leapt upon her, both of them rolling over and over. Ellie's laughter was light and carefree.

The Gift was no longer within her. Something had broken when she had forced Blunt to kill himself. She had slept for over twenty hours after that night and, when she woke, she had known she was not the same as she'd been before. She was free of her powers. Fenwick was pleased about that. He wanted the girl he had come to think of as a daughter to have an ordinary life. He believed the Gift was a burden she could well do without. They had located her extended family but, as she was now eighteen, she could really do as she wanted. And what she wanted, for now, was to stay with Fenwick and Goddard. And they were more than happy for that to happen.

The inquest into what had happened at Thrushton, and the events that had led up to that night were indecisive. The investigation into the mysterious deaths that had occurred around the city were recorded as "inconclusive" and the time given to them had been wound down. The investigation was still technically open, but no one was actively looking into it.

It was decided that Thrushton had been struck by lightning in that huge storm. That was what caused the destruction of the house and the deaths of twenty-seven people inside. The followers who had got out were still somewhere "safe". Mysterious individuals from the government had descended soon after the fire and had taken them away for questioning. Parker had argued against that, but after a brief meeting with them, he'd emerged from his office and simply shook his head at Goddard. There was nothing they could do about it.

The other followers, the ones who had been placed around the country, were still being hunted. Most of them had been rounded up quickly and quietly with the help of some of the survivors from the house; it seemed they were suddenly very keen to help. But some were still missing. Those mysterious men from the government with their dark suits and impassive, unsmiling faces had not disclosed what shape that particular investigation was taking, only that it was now out of the hands of the police. Fenwick didn't know what they were doing with the followers they had collected, but he could guess.

For now, however, he was just happy to be spending time with his new family. He had sold his part of the company to Bill, who was busy making it even bigger and better. With some of the money from the sale he had bought a nice Edwardian terraced house in Gosforth. Goddard had officially moved in three weeks ago and Ellie had her own room for however long she wanted it. They had just finished decorating and were taking a walk on that cold January morning to celebrate. For the moment, Fenwick classed himself as retired. He believed he'd earned it.

Ellie came pelting past them, with Maisie barking excitedly in her wake. Fenwick indicated to a nearby bench, his leg tiring, and he and Goddard sat down, wiping snow from the bench first. They watched the girl and the dog as they played.

Fenwick turned and smiled at Goddard, who smiled back at him, regarding his newly crooked nose and the fading scars on his face.

'Time to be happy again,' she said, taking his gloved hand in hers. And as he looked into those incredible green eyes he loved so much, he knew what she meant.

He nodded, his mind free of guilt at last.

Time to be happy again.

London, 2019

They walked along the uniform grey and green corridors slowly, for the young woman could barely move now. They shuffled past armed guards on every corner, but ignored them. They were used to them by now. They made their way past the TV room where some of their number were watching "Deal or No Deal". They always chose the correct box.

The couple then turned another corner, past the room where the "tests" were carried out, past another guard and moved through the communal eating area. Its walls were decorated with artwork, and soothing classical music played softly from a CD player in the corner. It was designed to be a calm environment.

Eventually, they found themselves in the medical area. The two young women approached Doctor Soames.

'I think it's time,' said one of the two women.

Soames nodded and took the other girl by the hand, lying her down on a hospital bed just inside one of the rooms. As she lay down a small groan escaped the girl's lips, and her hand cupped her swollen stomach.

Soames smiled at her reassuringly.

'Don't worry,' he said. 'This won't take long.'

Two midwives came into the room and they closed the door on the young girl who had escorted the pregnant woman. She suddenly felt redundant. She had been chosen to look after her friend when they had found out William had impregnated her, and she had done so every day since that terrible night months ago. Now that Sarah was about to give birth, she guessed she would just re-join the rest of the followers, her special position gone now. She peeked through the small, round *window in the door and gave Sarah a wave. It was as much a wave goodbye as a wave of good luck.*

Inside the room, hundreds of feet below the streets of the capital, the midwives went about their business. At six minutes past seven, the baby was born. It was a girl.

Once everything was sorted and they had both been checked over to make sure they were comfortable, the mother and baby were left to rest alone. Or as alone as one could be in that place; cameras lined every room.

As the mother slept, the new-born baby squirmed and moved, staring up at the world she had been born into.

And, unseen to her at the moment, for her eyes were new and did not focus properly yet, the Visitors crowded around her.

Their clawed hands gripped the sides of the crib. And they smiled their terrible smiles down upon her. They waited.

THE END

Did You Enjoy This Book?

If so, you can make a HUGE difference.

For any author, the single most important way we have of getting our books noticed is a really simple one—and one which you can help with.

Yes, you.

Us indie authors and publishers don't have the financial muscle of the big guys to take out full-page ads in the newspaper or put posters on the subway.

But we do have something much more powerful and effective than that, and it's something that those big publishers would kill to get their hands on.

A committed and loyal bunch of readers.

Honest reviews of our books help bring them to the attention of other readers.

If you've enjoyed this book, I would be really grateful if you could spend just a couple of minutes leaving a review (it can be as short as you like) on this book's page on your favourite store and website.

Acknowledgements

This book is dedicated to everyone who has enjoyed any of my strange witterings on paper. I thank you all.

To my family, my friends and the fantastic people I work with. You all mean the world to me.

Finally, a special thanks to the late, great James Herbert. Without his amazing books, I would have never have put pen to paper all those years ago.

About the Author

Richard Ayre was born in Northumberland, too many years ago now to remember. He has had a variety of jobs including roofer, milkman and factory worker. Tiring of this, Richard studied for a degree with the Open University and now teaches History for a living.

At an impressionable age he fell in love with new wave Heavy Metal and rock music and at about the same time read his first James Herbert novel. The combination of these two magnificent things led him to write his first novel, Minstrel's Bargain, a tale of music and horror. He now lives in Newcastle upon Tyne where he continues to write whenever he can. When not writing, or putting children on detention, he can be found pottering around the Northumberland landscape on his motorcycle, Tanya.

You can contact Richard via FaceBook, Twitter, or through his website: https://richardayre1.wixsite.com/richard-ayre-author

About Burning Chair

Burning Chair is an independent publishing company based in the UK, but covering readers and authors around the globe. We are passionate about both writing and reading books and, at our core, we just want to get great books out to the world.

Our aim is to offer something exciting; something innovative; something that puts the author and their book first. From first class editing to cutting edge marketing and promotion, we provide the care and attention that makes sure every book fulfils its potential.

We are:

Different

Passionate

Nimble and cutting edge

Invested in our authors' success

If you're an author and would like to know more about our submissions requirements and receive our free guide to book publishing, visit:

www.burningchairpublishing.com

If you're a reader and are interested in hearing more about our books, being the first to hear about our new releases or great offers, or becoming a beta reader for us, again please visit:

www.burningchairpublishing.com

Other Books by Burning Chair Publishing

Spy Game, by John Fullerton

The Curse of Becton Manor, by Patricia Ayling

Near Death, by Richard Wall

Blue Bird, by Trish Finnegan

The Tom Novak series, by Neil Lancaster
Going Dark
Going Rogue
Going Back

10:59, by N R Baker

Love Is Dead(ly), by Gene Kendall

A Life Eternal, by Richard Ayre

Haven Wakes, by Fi Phillips

Beyond, by Georgia Springate

Burning, An Anthology of Short Thrillers, edited by Simon Finnie and Peter Oxley

The Infernal Aether series, by Peter Oxley
The Infernal Aether
A Christmas Aether
The Demon Inside
Beyond the Aether
The Old Lady of the Skies: 1: Plague

The Wedding Speech Manual: The Complete Guide to Preparing, Writing and Performing Your Wedding Speech, by Peter Oxley

www.burningchairpublishing.com

POINT OF CONTACT

258